MW00608524

1/22

DANGEROUS DOCTOR

A Dr. Annabel Tilson Novel

DANGEROUS DOCTOR

by Barbara Ebel, M.D.

A Dr. Annabel Tilson Novel

Book One: Dead Still
Book Two: Deadly Delusions
Book Three: Desperate to Die
Book Four: Death Grip
Book Five: Downright Dead
Book Six: Dangerous Doctor

Copyright © 2019 by Barbara Ebel, M.D.

All rights reserved. No part of this book may be reproduced, stored, or transmitted by any means – whether auditory, graphic, mechanical, or electronic – without written permission of both publisher and author, except in the case of brief excerpts used in critical articles and reviews. Unauthorized reproduction of any part of this work is illegal and is punishable by law.

Paperback ISBN-13: 978-1-7324466-4-9
eBook ISBN-13: 978-1-7324466-3-2

This book is a work of fiction. Names, characters, places and events are the product of the author's imagination or are used fictitiously. Any resemblance to actual events, persons, or locations is coincidental.

Acknowledgements

A very special thank you to Sheriff Patrick Ray in middle Tennessee for his input on particular police matters in my novel.

CHAPTER 1

The thickset man stood with a girth as solid as a tree trunk, his eyes peering at a patient's chart from underneath bushy eyebrows. He stood barely at five-foot-six inches and his firm abdomen protruded from the middle of his white coat, enough to mimic a woman's early pregnancy. His name was George Gillespie, or more formerly noted on his desk placard as "Dr. George Gillespie, Pediatrician."

Medical student Annabel Tilson had no clue what the attending doctor was reading from inside the folder he held in his stubby fingers. It was not yet noon and she had tailgated him all morning in his private practice, which he shared with one other physician. Now, as well as earlier, the man's facial expression was full of prim self-restraint.

He wore a thin black mustache; one so inconspicuous that she wondered why he bothered to let it grow at all. Below it, his lips failed to crack a smile. Nor did he verbally share an observation with her about what he surmised from the preliminary information noted in the chart about the patient's visit. He closed the file, gave a knuckle tap on the door, and turned the doorknob. With a slight nod of his head, he motioned for her to follow him into the room.

Sitting in a chair, a woman straightened her shoulders and squared her glasses on her nose. Her son, Toby, swung his legs from the examination table and flinched as Dr. Gillespie took two steps forward. The eleven-year-old extended his arms behind him and leaned back like he was giving himself space to evaluate George's approach.

Annabel remembered being the young boy's age and a pediatrician's office was the last place the red-headed youngster would want to be. In the height of the summer, before school started back, there were plenty of activities he could be engaged

1

in outside.

"Hi, Dr. Gillespie," the woman said. "You previously told me that Toby is old enough to be seen without me, but I want to address two issues with one visit." She stayed put, appearing comfortable in shorts and a loose white blouse, and darted her eyes to Annabel.

"Mrs. Owens," Dr. Gillespie said, "Annabel is the newest medical student shadowing me on her pediatric rotation."

"No problem." She shrugged while reaching down to a single folded piece of paper lying on top of her pocketbook. Toby and Annabel cracked a smile at each other.

Dr. Gillespie took the form she handed him: *"Ohio Department of Health • School and Adolescent Health • Physical Examination."* He rotated his arm to the side and handed it off to Annabel. "A back-to-school form for the nurse's office."

Annabel scanned the sheet, which included boxes for a physical exam, health history, screening for vision, hearing, and posture, as well as questions related to speech and ability to participate in academics and sports.

"Let's get going, then," George said. He asked Toby to lean forward while he peered into his ears with an otoscope.

"Dr. Gillespie always says not to wait until the last minute to bring your kid in before school starts," Anne explained to Annabel. "Otherwise, the waiting room is so jam-packed, you'd think he and his partner were giving away free tickets to a Reds baseball game."

Dr. Gillespie tapped his finger on Toby's chest. The youth grasped the Florida tourist T-shirt he was wearing and swiped it over his head as if on cue. The pediatrician listened to his heart and lungs and soon asked Toby to walk back and forth in the room. He paid strict attention to his patient and then sat on a stool with the entire medical folder. Annabel handed him back the sheet.

"Does Toby wear glasses that I'm not aware of?"

"No," Anne said.

George checked off multiple boxes for "yes" or "no" responses and collaborated with Mrs. Owens that Toby had no new physical or academic limitations.

"Tell Dr. Gillespie what you've been complaining about," Mrs. Owens said to her son as she handed him back his shirt.

George glanced over at her and grinned. He hated twofers; when a patient's office visit ended up with two chief complaints and diagnostic problems because he could only bill for one. A robust yearly salary was not what he was in the specialty for, however, it was becoming more difficult these days to make a reasonable living despite all the hours he put in.

Toby popped his head through his top and grimaced. "Mom, it's not a problem and I've hardly been complaining."

"I know you better. You don't want to miss swimming or soccer when school starts, but you did complain twice since we came back from our Florida vacation."

Toby rolled his eyes with emphasis. "I guess my legs are getting some muscle pain. And yesterday, it started in my back and arms."

"On physical exam," George said, "you're a healthy young eleven-year-old and you're walking fine. If you have that symptom tonight, one aspirin may chase it away." He closed Toby's record and stood. "I'm giving the school form to the front desk so they can make a copy. You two can pick it up on the way out."

Annabel, Anne, and Toby followed Dr. Gillespie out the door. At the front desk, he added with a sour face, "You know where to find us, but chances are, Toby's muscles are starting to go through a growth spurt. Before you know it, he'll be too old to visit a pediatrician anymore."

"Thanks, Dr. Gillespie," Anne said, taking the original school form.

"Bye," Annabel said. "Enjoy the remaining time you have off, Toby, before school starts."

"Thanks. Nice meeting you."

Mother and son disappeared out the door. For Annabel's benefit, Dr. Gillespie muttered out loud as he wrote cursive at the bottom of Toby's office note. "Last-minute comment after school physical: myalgias for several days."

Annabel sighed. For her, gone were the summers spent with her family enjoying the great outdoors in Tennessee. Amazingly enough, however, this was her last real summer in medical school because this time next year, she'd be starting residency. Pediatrics was her last major subject specialty rotation and maybe it was going to be easier than she thought. She would appreciate a more relaxed atmosphere after her experiences so far.

Another medical student friend, Stuart Schneider, was shadowing the other doctor practicing in the pediatrician's two-physician practice. She would be glad for Stuart's comradery, she thought. Then, after the next two weeks with Dr. Gillespie, she and Stuart would finish pediatrics with a team at the University Hospital's children's ward.

Annabel realized the two pediatricians were very accommodating to allow medical students to learn, yet clutter up, their office, and also knew that doctors affiliated with teaching through the medical school or residency were skilled physicians on top of their specialties. In her educational experience, most of them had big hearts to pass on their knowledge and instruct the upcoming new generation of physicians, and the ones not working full time for the University did so for little pay or secondary gain.

She eyed George Gillespie. Annabel had no opinion yet; she couldn't discern what to make of the little sturdy physician who didn't talk a lot.

Behind the spacious front desk area, a thin wall separated one room into two. An economical kitchenette was to the right. The room adjacent to it functioned as a supply room with a compact old-fashioned Xerox machine, a stuffed bookshelf, and a card table. Stuart dawdled in there, his hands jammed in his student white jacket. The pediatrician he was following, Heather Clark, had her head posed over a pediatric manual.

Annabel and Stuart nodded at each other like some secret code to express their feeling of ineptness. At least on the internal medicine rotation they had shared, they felt needed, if not abused with "busy" work when more significant events were not keeping them occupied. They recently did OB/GYN at the same time too, but they were on opposite daily time slots.

"Annabel," Dr. Gillespie said, "come see one more patient with me and then you two can go to lunch."

She marched after him and he pulled another folder from the inbox outside an exam room. Inside, a young girl stood next to her mother, who sat on the chair. The six-year-old first exchanged a weary glance at Dr. Gillespie and then rested her hand on her mother's shoulder.

"Good morning," Dr. Gillespie said. "Jump up on the exam table, Kellie."

"She's not jumping anywhere lately," Mrs. Hill said. "She gets tuckered out quicker these days compared to her friends. We need a refill of her albuterol inhaler."

Kellie withdrew her hand and did as she was asked. The paper on the exam table rustled as she shimmied up and got comfortable. She had thin, dry hair neatly pulled back in a ponytail and her fingernails were painted a bold pink.

George licked his finger and flipped a few pages to check the patient's medication and prescription history. "Appears like you're going through your inhaler quickly. Tell me in your own words, Kellie, what's going on with your asthma."

Dr. Gillespie slid the chart on the counter and rubbed his right thumb along the tips of his fingers. Annabel kept a low profile behind him, especially since no one had mentioned her presence.

Kellie shrugged her shoulders. "I use the inhaler almost every other day because I'm coughing. Sometimes I wake up in the middle of the night too."

"I heard her coughing last night and made her use it," her mother interjected.

"I bet you're a pro at this," the pediatrician said, standing squarely in front of Kellie, "but are you using it correctly?"

The young girl nodded. "I breathe deep and spray with my mouth around it tight. I count to ten holding my breath, take it away, and breathe out slowly."

"She is a pro," Mrs. Hill added and George bobbed his head in agreement.

Annabel shifted her weight from one foot to another as an overwhelming sense of déjà vu came over her. The discomfort continued as Dr. Gillespie asked his patient more questions and then examined her. When he was almost finished, Kellie had a coughing spell and took the almost-empty inhaler from her mother. She held it steady in her hand, ready to use it.

Annabel pursed her lips. She closed her eyes for a moment as a wave of emotion crept over her. She fought back tearing up. This little girl's chief complaint, her sitting there with symptoms of asthma, affected her personally.

Annabel's older sister, Melissa, had battled with asthma, and now the memory and what happened to her came to the forefront of her thoughts. She had not zeroed in thinking about her sister's death for a long time, the way she died, the travesty of it. Like Kellie, her sister lived with asthma as she grew up. She was fragile, pale, and sweet and was the "trailblazer" for her and her other sister. It was Melissa that first started calling their grandfather "Pop-Pop" and the granddaughter that adored biology based on his love of the natural world.

It was impossible to not consider what her sister would have become and where she'd be right now. No doubt a physician, a veterinarian, or a biologist. She was sure the both of them would have been thick as thieves, as opposed to her younger sister, Nancy, whom she hadn't talked to in months.

Annabel wished she could go off and privately sob the held-back tears that she was harboring, but it wasn't the time or the place. Dr. Gillespie had put all his examining tools away and was standing to the side of the black table.

"It appears Kellie's mild asthma has become more persistent," he said. "What she needs to be on now is a daily controller medication. I'm going to prescribe another inhaler for chronic therapy, but this one is an inhaled corticosteroid. It will reduce Kellie's hyperresponsive airway and it works differently than the short-acting beta-adrenergic agonist, or albuterol, which rapidly reverses bronchoconstriction."

"Whatever you say, Doctor," Mrs. Hill said.

"My nurse will come back in to answer any questions you two may have about using it. Make a follow-up appointment if she doesn't improve. In any case, I can see how she's doing when you schedule her school physical."

Behind the front desk, Stuart waited for Annabel.

"By the way," Dr. Gillespie said to both of them, "corticosteroids are super anti-inflammatory drugs and can be given by different routes. In Annabel's last patient's case, the inhaler will deliver a decent dosage to her lungs and not deliver as many side effects as the oral route. We want to prevent adverse effects on our young patient's bone mineral density, immune function, and growth."

"Thanks," Annabel said without much enthusiasm. "I didn't know steroids could be inhaled."

A stout middle-aged woman handed paperwork to a parent

through the window and faced the students. "By the way, I'm Becky. Despite what the doctors or their two nurses think, I keep this place afloat."

"That means you have to listen to her," Dr. Gillespie said and walked away.

"Since you're going to lunch, there are basically two selections within a short distance: one trendy with great coffee and the other with melt-in-your mouth pizza and pasta. Usually, we tell students to be back within forty-five minutes."

Stuart nodded for the both of them. They took off their jackets, went through the waiting room, and out the front door. But Annabel's heart felt heavy. She was fifteen when her sister Melissa died at seventeen years old and now, years later, she realized that she never adequately mourned the passing of her older sister and best friend.

CHAPTER 2

Annabel was grateful she walked the few short urban blocks with Stuart, who was dependably introverted, quiet, and yet extremely bright. He was quite thin, his weight not budging up or down during medical school, and his head usually hung down as if he absorbed his smartness from something emanating up from the floor. They waited for a utility vehicle to pass and then crossed a street.

It was early summer, Annabel remembered, one of the days that were always special to each member of the family. Their grandfather and parents would break away from their suburban Nashville homes and bring the girls to middle Tennessee. Their destination was the Caney Fork River.

The three sisters were playing, poking sticks between the rocks along the riverbed, around the first bend below the massive Center Hill Dam. Clad in flip-flops, their feet and hands were wet, and occasionally, they'd stare forward at their Pop-Pop. He waded in the river with his fishing pole dangling in front of him. Behind them, both of their parents sat in folding chairs flanked by coolers. A bit of flirting occurred between them and then her father, Danny, leaned over and gave her mother, Sara, a quick kiss.

That summer, Annabel began transitioning to the eventual tomboy she became during her teenage years. She wore a baseball cap while her sisters wore sunhats with wide brims. One of her front teeth had also grown crooked; it would be several more years before braces would become fixtures during her formative teenage years.

The river they played at changed its height, shape, and course depending on the rainfall and the Tennessee Valley Authority's manipulation of the dam's gates. That day, a few vultures soared over the forested area, a barely perceptible current passed, and time and again, a rainbow trout splashed at the surface. There was no minimum length to catch and keep those trout, only a maximum daily limit to catch seven. Their Pop-Pop had three in his bucket near the girls and smiled every time another fish jumped up, letting him know its whereabouts.

Melissa, Annabel, and Nancy all squatted around a snail, which made no attempt to move except for its tentacles perched on the top of its head, which quivered back and forth. From the corner of her eye, Annabel noticed a turtle lumbering out of the water. She jumped up and rushed straight over. How she loved turtles and frogs, and most living things, for that matter. The large aquatic reptile had a rough, dark shell mostly covered with mud and algae, but that didn't hinder her in the least. She reached down to pick him up.

A hand gave her a shove and she almost landed on her butt, but she swung her hands in midair and righted herself before she toppled over.

"Melissa, what did you do that for?" she yelled.

"No, what are you doing?" Melissa's voice was lower than her sister's, with a control and authority mature for her age.

"Picking up this turtle. Look how big he is! I want to show him to you and Nancy, Pop-Pop when he stops fishing, and Mom and Dad too."

Melissa sighed and took a step back, moving her toes further away from the specimen with an ancient history. "I wouldn't if I were you. That's a snapping turtle."

Annabel reeled back with surprise and replied with skepticism, "How do you know?"

"See? It has a large pointed head and a long ridged tail. Pop-Pop explained them to me and he's the expert."

Annabel listened but nevertheless picked up a stick the length of her forearm. She poked it in front of the turtle's mouth, enticing him like the stick was alive. Suddenly, the reptile lurched with a defensive quick and powerful snap.

Both girls jumped. "I told you," Melissa said.

"Good thing that wasn't my finger," Annabel said, peering back at her parents, who weren't watching. "Otherwise, Daddy would have to sew it back on this afternoon."

Melissa grimaced. "But Dad said doctors aren't supposed to treat their own family."

"I bet you're going to be like him when you grow up."

"Not as smart or successful as you, though."

"What's that supposed to mean?"

"You may do more stupid stuff than me, but that makes you learn more lessons. You take riskier chances, are more curious, and solve more problems than me."

Annabel let that sink in. Maybe there was some merit to what she said. Her older sister also doubled as a guardian angel when it came to her and Nancy.

The turtle finally decided to amble off and Melissa and Annabel told Nancy what they saw. Their younger sister stopped playing with the snail and ran back to her parents. No way would she stay in the vicinity of a snapping turtle.

The two girls ignored Nancy as she left and checked out their grandfather's bucket of fish. The same three trout flip-flopped inside, so they glanced out at him, hoping he was ready to reel in another. At their feet, however, water began seeping on their flip-flops and their toes began disappearing under river water.

"Look," Melissa said with alarm. The serenity of the water had quickly changed; it was gaining speed, especially in the center of the river. As bad, or worse, the water level was rising rapidly.

Annabel's eyes grew wide, she grabbed the bucket, and both girls sprang back.

"Pop-Pop," Melissa yelled.

The heartrates of both girls sped up as they stood helpless, their Pop-Pop struggling to stand and fight from being pulled away with the sweeping current. Failing to maintain a strong hold on his fishing pole, it was yanked out of his grip, and drowned in the mayhem of water racing past him.

The girls ran towards Danny and Sara. "Pop-Pop needs help," Annabel yelled as Melissa lingered behind. A shortness of breath took hold of Melissa and she began to cough.

Danny and Sara bolted up from their chairs. "Oh my God," Danny said. "The TVA started the generators."

Because of previous instruction from their parents, the girls understood. Once the dam's generators came on, they would force a large volume of water into the river.

"Sara, grab me two ropes from the car trunk. The extra ones."

Putting on a life vest, Danny raced to the shore and scouted the trees close by. When Sara handed him the marine-grade ropes, he knotted one around a small trunk. The other end he circled and tied around himself. Holding the other one, he headed out into the water. Barely in time, since his father could no longer fight the power of the water and his feet left the bottom of the river.

Danny was further down from where his father had fished and the bend worked out in their favor. His father, Greg Tilson, was robust enough to keep his head up and Danny shouted as loud as he could as he threw out the other end of the second rope.

Although Annabel wanted to shut her eyes in fear that her Pop-Pop would soon be gone forever, she watched as he fought with all his might against the current and wrapped his strong hands around the thick rope. Danny held and pulled his end with all his might. His father was a big man and a river in the midst of a man-made onslaught of water would be a challenge for men even stronger and more able-bodied than Danny.

Greg clasped his son's upper arm as they united in knee-high water. They both ambled out of the water while Annabel's eyes stayed glued on the situation.

"Pop-Pop," she yelled, running to him. He leaned over to

catch his breath while Danny rolled up the free rope and then untied himself from the tree.

"Annabel!"

Annabel turned quickly. Her mother shouted her name again, so she ran over. Her sister coughed excessively and could only look down at the ground.

"Her coughing won't stop," Sara said. "Run quickly. Her inhaler is in the back seat of the car."

Annabel sped away. Her legs couldn't have worked any faster. Now it was her turn to come to the rescue. When she returned, she placed the prescription inhaler in Melissa's hand and waited as the amazing medicine for asthma worked enough magic to bring her sister's breathing back to normal.

Annabel and Stuart crossed another street. Her colleague voiced one or two pleasantries while she went back to pondering that eventful day at the Caney Fork River when she was nine years old. She realized what an iconic day that had been and wondered why she had never realized it before. Of course, the patient's asthma attack in the office had stirred up her memories.

As the family scrambled to pack up their things to prematurely leave the river that morning, Melissa made progress with the dissipation of her asthma attack and the panic she'd felt due to her grandfather's mishap. Her breathing slowed down and the little bit of wheezing she had experienced also stopped. Six years later, her luck ran out; she died on the upstairs landing of their grandparents' house. Yet that day on the river, it was as if she'd read a crystal ball into the future and foresaw Annabel's ability to become someone extraordinary and have a meaningful purpose. It was as if she took herself out of the equation.

There was also the situation with her grandfather, who had forgotten the day before to visit the Tennessee Valley Authority website and consult the generation schedule for the next day. Danny had reminded his father to do so, and yet perhaps his failure to check was a forerunner of what eventually happened. Her Pop-Pop, in the end, had dementia. Maybe it was not all related to the stroke he'd had. There may have been more "forgetful" incidents those preceding years so as to not lump all his forgetfulness into a "vascular dementia" etiology. Sadly enough, she thought, her grandmother had already passed years before from cancer.

Annabel and Stuart stopped in the front of the small restaurant that the office manager, Becky, had mentioned.

"Let's go to this one," he said. Not waiting for a response, he opened the door.

Inside, the tables were all round with two or four chairs. The colorful place mats matched the paint colors on the walls; it was a cheery atmosphere. When a waitress seated them, both students studied the menu and soon gave their order.

For once, Stuart spoke before Annabel. "At least they'll be springing us from that small office for lunch every day. It will give us a break from kids with runny noses and sore throats."

"It is a bit claustrophobic in there, isn't it?"

"I agree, but I am glad to be paired with Dr. Clark. She's energetic, the kids seem to like her, and she's quick to teach."

"Good for you, Stuart, especially since you disliked OB."

"I'm not saying peds is my thing, however."

Annabel unwrapped her utensils from a paper napkin and stared out the window.

"You're awfully pensive since we left the office," Stuart commented, "and you look sad."

"Hmm. I didn't know it showed."

Stuart focused on her and raised his eyebrows.

"Dr. Gillespie and I just saw a young girl with asthma. She

hit too close to home. A half-buried memory of my older sister's death from asthma has blasted itself into my thoughts. I can't shake it, but I will."

Stuart kept his arms on his lap but leaned in closer. "Annabel, I bet that's the worst thing to do. I heard you mention your sister once during our internal medicine rotation. Don't block her out. I bet you two were close."

"We were inseparable. Close as twins, or at least that's my perception of our relationship now. She would have gone into biology or medicine or something like that. Along with my parents and grandfather, she probably steered me to where I am now." Annabel fidgeted with her spoon as the waitress placed down two glasses of water and left. A pool of moisture gathered in her eyes again, and she swiped at both of them.

"If she was diagnosed with asthma, how did she die?"

"She had an attack at my grandfather's house while no one else was there. Her inhaler had run out and she was getting a new one that day. She called for help. My Uncle Casey, who's a paramedic, raced with his colleague to the house, but they wasted time. Melissa hadn't mentioned that she wasn't at our house. When they finally arrived at our grandfather's home, the front door was locked. Anyway, long story short, she didn't survive; they found her dead inside." Annabel swallowed hard and focused on the place mat in front of her. "And to make matters worse, for some time, my dad was angry at Casey because he initially went to the wrong house. But it wasn't his fault."

"Especially being a young girl, that was a lot to process. No wonder a similar patient brought all the memories back. I can understand why you're feeling the void of your sister."

Annabel wiped away a tear. "And my parents. How on earth did they get through the following days, or month, or years? I hear that losing a child is the worst thing imaginable."

"They suffered in silence. They still had two girls to look

after. I bet they still grieve and think about her just like you're doing today. You should have a talk with them about it someday. Not a decade from now, but in the near future. I bet your mom would especially like that."

"You're right." She managed a chuckle. "I sure didn't mean to lay my family drama on you."

The waitress placed down their sandwiches and, noting their subdued conversation, left right away.

"Thanks, Stuart. I guess I needed to talk about what was bothering me."

"Don't mention it. You know, crying is therapeutic. It looks like you've been storing tears for your sister in a hidden closet."

She nodded. "You still are planning on a psychiatry residency, aren't you?"

"Absolutely."

"You are going to be the best."

"Maybe. Or close to it," he said and grinned.

Annabel continued to feel better as she polished off a burger and then smiled at her classmate. "Stuart, did you ever attempt to play with a snapping turtle when you were a kid?"

CHAPTER 3

A few weeks before eleven-year-old Toby Owens' medical appointment with Dr. Gillespie, he and his friend, Jonathon Harmon, rode a wave onto shore and scrambled out of the crystal-clear water. They hated to leave the sugary white Destin, Florida beach for the time being, but the day was early and there was plenty more fun on their agenda. Besides, they would be back later. The two youths were not finished swimming for the day.

The boys had spread a blanket down on the sand on which to place their things. They picked up their towels and dried themselves off. "I'll race you to the room," Toby said.

Without hesitation, Jonathon slipped into his sandals, jammed his towel under his arm, and followed. When the boys made it off the beach, they ran around a fenced-in-pool and several zigzag-edy paths around gardens and arrived at the ground-floor rooms of the hotel their mothers had booked.

Toby wore a proud smile. "Beat you again."

"You always do."

"You can't help it that you're as pigeon-toed as a pigeon."

Toby's red hair stood on end and his face was flushed, partly from the sun and partly from running. His upper cheeks were dusted with tiny freckles that still peeked out of his slight sunburn. "Change into shorts and I'll meet you out here in a few minutes."

Jonathon skulked his way into his room, and Toby hurried into his. They soon materialized in dry summer clothes.

"Come on," Jonathon said. "We only have fifteen minutes to meet our moms."

Although it was their first visit to the Panhandle, they had a strong familiarity of the touristy area around where they were staying. The boys had picked other kids' brains about the area … especially the "rich" kids who often took such vacations.

Plus, this trip was the highlight of Toby and Jonathon's whole summer, as well as their mothers'. Anne Owens and her friend had flown down to Ft. Walton Beach with their sons, rented a car, and driven the short distance east. Both boys' dads had given their blessing. For a change, the women were having a trip free of their husbands to shop, sunbathe, and drink margaritas.

The boys decided to avoid the main east-west thoroughfare of 98 and walked instead along the Destin Harbor Boardwalk. They came to a deck and an overhanging restaurant sign where a big palm tree grew out of the sand next to the steps going inside. Both boys scanned the open-air inside seating where they were supposed to meet their mothers for lunch, but didn't spot them anywhere.

"They must still be shopping at the mall across the street," Toby said.

"I don't understand. There's shopping in Ohio. Why buy stuff here when you can be chilling at the beach?"

Toby shrugged his shoulders. "My mom loves to shop. This is her vacation too. I guess they can do what they want."

Two boys from inside the restaurant stepped down and sat on the same step as Toby and Jonathon. The two groups of boys still had space between them on the wide staircase.

"Hey," one of the older boys said. He wore a pair of shorts that doubled as a bathing suit and had a scar on his forehead. He looked close to fourteen years old; his buddy seemed older too, and chewed a mint he swiped from a bowl back at the cashier's counter.

"Have you been inside yet?" the same boy asked them.

"No," Jonathon answered. "We're waiting on our moms. We're going to the go-kart track after lunch. Have you been there?"

"Of course. You two must be tourists."

"We're from Ohio. Isn't everybody a tourist?"

"Not exactly. We live an hour away. The Gulf Coast is a regular trip for us."

"Yeah," the other boy spoke up. "As long as a family member is heading this way."

"I'm hungry." Jonathon turned back to look at the restaurant. "What's to chow down on in there?"

"The best hush puppies and mudbugs anywhere," the first boy said.

"Mudbugs?!" Jonathon exclaimed. "Eew. What are they?"

"Are you kidding me? You two are stupid out-of-towners. They're crawfish." He glanced at his friend for a better explanation.

"They're freshwater crustaceans," his buddy responded. "Like miniature lobsters. Chefs fry 'em up along the coast in Creole seasoning."

"They truly come out of the Louisiana mud," the first boy emphasized.

"Yukk, they sound disgusting," Jonathon said.

"Not any worse than that slug crawling along the bottom of the staircase," he replied. "You two really are wimps. My buddy and I would eat that slug in a heartbeat if someone would bet us on it."

Toby had had enough of listening to their ridicule. Just because he and Jonathon were from the north didn't make them less adventurous. If the two boys from Florida could ingest mudbugs and slugs, so could the two of them.

"Why do you need a bet?" Toby asked. "Can't you guzzle that thing down whether or not there's money riding on it?"

"I dare you," the first boy said. "And because you're probably poor, my buddy and I will both chip in three dollars to watch you eat it."

"In which case," his friend said, "we'll still have that money later to spend at the go-kart track next door."

Toby was seething mad. He glanced at Jonathon, who

Barbara Ebel

acknowledged him with a nod. He studied the brown, slimy slug on the bottom board. It was almost an inch long. The thought of sliding it down his throat was disgusting, but not taking the dare would be worse to his ego. He wouldn't even taste it if he put it in his mouth and swallowed. He would show them and he'd walk away with six bucks.

He moved his feet and slid his buttocks down to the next step. With a straight face, he picked up the shell-less mollusk. It recoiled slightly and Toby closed his eyes for a second. Opening them back up, he popped the thing in his mouth, worked it to the back of his throat, and swallowed with as much saliva as he could generate.

With a bemused smile, he patted his hands back and forth. "There. Hand it over. Six bucks."

Jonathan scrunched up his face with disbelief and the two other boys shrugged like there was nothing to the dare.

"We've eaten worse," the boy with the scar said. "But a bet's a bet." He dug his hand in his pocket. "Hey," he motioned to his friend, "pay him and I'll owe you. I don't have any money."

With a sigh of relief, Toby watched as the other boy pulled out the cash and forked it over to him. They made small talk for a while, their feud-like talk subsiding, until Anne Owens and Lucy Harmon showed up at the top of the steps and told the boys it was time for lunch.

Jonathon rose and said "bye" to the older youths. When he and Toby followed their mothers to a table, he whispered, "I can't believe you did that, but I'm glad you did. Did it taste gross?"

"Not as bad as the thought of it."

When they all sat down for lunch, neither boy mentioned to their mother the appetizer that Toby had already ingested.

20

Mrs. Owens and her son left the pediatrician's office after Toby's appointment with Dr. Gillespie and drove straight home. It proved to be a gorgeous sunny day, perfect for the basketball game that Toby and his friends agreed on for that afternoon. Without much enthusiasm for his favorite peanut butter and jelly sandwich, he ate lunch and went to the solitude of his room.

Toby kicked off his shoes and plopped onto his bed. He had actually made his bed that morning, but there wasn't much else in the room that looked that neat. Dirty clothes hung on the back of his chair, sneakers and socks were strewn on the floor, and two sets of earbuds were tangled up on his nightstand. A thumbtack had fallen out of his bulletin board and a poster was dangling in midair. And although he had emptied his clothes to be washed from his Florida vacation two weeks ago, his suitcase was open and empty on the floor.

The youth yanked the pillow out of the covers and propped it behind him. The thought of going to the nearby park to shoot some baskets became less and less inviting to him. His bed felt too damn comfortable.

He crossed his ankles and heard the landline phone ring out in the hallway. His mother answered, rapped on his door, and stuck her head in. "Jonathon's on the phone."

Toby padded to the door with a grimace. Half the kids his age were walking around with their own cell phones, but his parents were not springing for his until he turned thirteen. "Thanks, Mom." He turned back with the portable.

"What's up?" Toby said.

"I thought you'd be here by now."

Toby glanced over at his digital clock. "If you're at the park, you're fifteen minutes early."

"So? What else is there to do? We can warm up before the other guys get here."

"I only just got home."

"Where've you been?"

"I got my school physical out of the way. I hate going to the doctor's office."

"I don't mind it. My mother takes me to Dr. Clark. She's really cool and funny sometimes."

"I know her. She's in the office with my pediatrician, Dr. Gillespie. Maybe I could change doctors."

"I bet your mother won't do that. What don't you like about him?"

Back on his bed, Toby put one knee over the other and rubbed his calf with his free hand. "I don't know. He's too quiet and seems odd. At least my mother was with me in the exam room today."

"You're the one who's odd. So how'd your physical go? Did you manage to get out of going back to school?" Jonathon laughed. "Maybe I can come up with some lame excuse on my doctor's visit to stall sixth grade!"

"That's a lame idea. I already passed my school physical."

A lull surfaced in the conversation. Toby switched the phone into his left hand, switched legs, and massaged his left calf with his right hand.

"So what's taking you so long?"

Their other friend, Robby, sprinted into their local sports building and pointed his thumbs up at Jonathon.

"All right already, I'm on my way." Toby placed the phone back in the cradle outside his room and weaved his way through the neighborhood to the county office buildings and community center. After signing in, he stepped into the basketball court.

Without a hello, Robby pitched him the ball. "It's not like you to be the last one here."

Toby dribbled the ball to warm up, and then Jonathon put his hands on his hips after waiting too long for his buddy to throw or toss the ball.

"Doesn't walking over here count as a warm-up?" Jonathan

asked.

Toby scowled and ran to the basket, but his shooting hand wasn't in line with the rim and he made a lousy shot. For the next ten minutes, Jonathon and Robby had complete control of the ball. They sprang up like their sneakers were light-footed appendages and they were mustering up as much fun as possible, pushing away the thought of school starting soon.

Toby continued, giving the sport and his friends his best attempt. But he wasn't sure if his heart wasn't in the game or if it was his body. He went to the wall and slid down to the floor.

"What are you doing?" Jonathon asked, bouncing the ball in front of him.

Toby flexed his knees and wrapped his arms around them. "Watching your sneakers toe in. I swear you do it even when you're in the air in the middle of a shot!"

Jonathon brushed off his remark and kept working the ball. "Time's up."

"I gotta rest my legs. I must be tired."

Robby wiped some sweat off his forehead. "Why don't you go buy a banana from the snack bar inside? My mom says they help when you're playing sports and your potassium gets low."

"Come on," Jonathon said. "We'll go with you."

A little after 5 p.m., Dr. Gillespie hung his white coat on a hook behind the front desk and noticed the students. "Unless Dr. Clark needs you two, you're finished for the day. Be back bright and early at 8 a.m." He nodded at his employees to do the same. He was the first to leave work behind, his small-scale steps like a pigmy's as he went out the door.

"If I remember correctly," Heather Clark said to the students, "the first day of a new rotation can be overwhelming. Not that either of you had a difficult day today. I'm referring to the volume and scope of material you need to ingest over the next few weeks. These two weeks will be your easier part before you do your pediatric stint, with overnight call, in the hospital. So, I suggest taking as much time in the beginning to read."

Annabel and Stuart followed her into the kitchenette. Heather was slightly overweight and had full robust cheeks and a warm smile. Annabel already assumed that her young patients opened up to her quite easily.

"Dr. Clark," Annabel said, "do you have any words of advice about pediatrics for Stuart and me?"

"Sure. Sit down. The best thing to do in peds is to segregate your patients in your mind. In internal medicine, you can categorize patients into adult, middle-aged folks, and the distinct elderly geriatric patients. But a child is way more compartmentalized because they are growing and developing. We deal with infancy, preschoolers, middle childhood years, and adolescence. And each of those periods can be categorized into their own developmental milestones. In pediatrics, we must know what's normal for the age in question because that then allows us to spot what's abnormal. Which in turn allows us to diagnose and potentially correct or thwart a medical problem that could become worse."

Stuart nodded and Annabel leaned back in her chair.

"As far as growth, there is a basic pattern that is normal. A surprising fact is that after an infant is born, they will initially lose weight, a whole five to ten percent of their birth weight. Then by about two weeks old, that infant should start gaining weight and grow quickly, so that by four to six months old, the infant's weight should have doubled. I always find it amusing when parents come in with their baby, exclaiming how big he or she grew during that time, as if theirs is unique like a superhero character.

"Ha." Heather chuckled. "Once, a father came in holding his infant on his shoulders and proclaimed he was raising the next

Superman. His wife told him to quit bragging or other parents would put kryptonite in the waiting room.

"However, the second half of the first year, growth is not as dramatic, and then, at the toddler age of one to two, and up to age five, they'll gain about five pounds per year. The child's development should remain steady, but then a final growth spurt should take off."

"Puberty?" Stuart guessed.

"Sure thing. Between nine and fifteen. Imagine, also, the nutrient needs during these ages. That small infant growing like a weed needs a lot of calories in relation to its size and, later, the same thing happens with the adolescent.

"A healthy child will fall into a normal growth curve and yet follow his or her own individual pattern. In my opinion, never in a human being's life are healthy diet habits more important than in the pediatric population. Parents play a significant role to prevent problems for their children, especially obesity.

"If kids aren't eating a proper diet, they'll be tired at school, be slow to learn, or get sick. I try to encourage parents to send their kids to school after a decent breakfast."

Dr. Clark scooted her iPhone close and picked it up. "Even though this information is well known to me, I carry the data with me. I will, however, give both of you a paper copy separate from what you can find in your textbook." She tapped on an app and handed it to Annabel.

Annabel scrolled the list of developmental milestones, each one specific for each age. Four, nine, twelve, and eighteen months were listed as well as two to five, and then a preschooler, school-age, and a puberty and adolescent developmental list. She handed Heather's phone to Stuart. "I never gave this information much thought. Like you alluded to, you are taking care of a glut of patients with these age-specific growth periods and developmental milestones. What if you miss something?"

"Exactly," Heather said.

"I had a patient on OB," Annabel said, "who delivered a girl who was soon diagnosed with osteogenesis imperfecta. The pediatrician caught that abnormality right away with DNA testing."

"Which is the way it should be. That baby's brittle bones will probably change her progression on her growth curve, but the doctors will know about it."

Stuart finished scrolling the list and handed it back to Dr. Clark. She grinned at the students. "I hope I didn't keep you two too long."

"On the contrary," Annabel said. "Time spent with you was more fruitful than that time buried in a book."

Heather rose. "Tomorrow then." But before they left, she handed them the paper she promised them.

CHAPTER 4

Annabel stood on the porch of the pediatrician's office, leaning against one of the stately white vertical columns. She scrolled to the car service app on her phone to schedule a ride home.

Stuart looked back from the bottom step. "You want a ride home?"

"I wouldn't want you to go out of your way."

"Come on," he said as he waved.

Never invited to ride in Stuart's vintage car before, Annabel bounded down the steps. The black 1984 Jaguar coupe was parked in the back of the building in the corner and Stuart ran his eyes over all four sides.

"Do you check her over every time?" Annabel asked.

"Routinely. Somehow, she's still ding-free and squeaky clean."

Annabel got in on the opposite side and settled into the tan interior leather. "How many miles does it have?"

"Eighty thousand."

"Nice."

"Your car will record a low odometer reading too if you keep calling Uber to ride you back and forth on your rotations."

"Yeah, but my car is just transportation. My SUV is not a Jaguar."

Stuart smiled and started the ignition while Annabel took out her iPhone. He peered over at her. "Which one are you calling?"

Annabel made a face at him and Stuart raised his eyebrows.

"It's a legitimate question," he said. "Are you calling our medical student friend or your boyfriend; or vice versa whichever."

"Stuart! More and more, people are giving me grief about

who's who. For once and for all, Bob is my medical school friend. And yours too. And Dustin is my boyfriend."

"Whatever you say."

"Let's compare notes with Bob. He can tell us about the first day of hospital pediatrics and we can fill him in on Gillespie and Clark's private practice." She tapped his number and he answered right away.

"Hey, Stuart and I are finished for the day. How about you?"

"Just leaving. I never expected to be out before six. Can't complain."

"I have an idea. How about I walk Oliver and we all meet at Pete's Café?" She glanced at Stuart.

"Good idea," Bob said. "See you soon."

Stuart nodded when she got off the phone. "I'll eat with you two."

"I'm glad. I did store some decent leftovers for the week at home, but I can save them."

"Me too."

"Do you cook when you're home or do you mostly grab food from outside?"

Stuart waited for a light at an intersection. "I sautéed chicken with vegetables yesterday and made brown rice. I parceled out four more dinner containers for the week after I ate."

She gave him a side-glance.

"I do more than study, you know."

"Sorry. You never mentioned your cooking talents before."

"No different. You never talked about your sister before, not like today."

"Cooking and a death in the family are two different things. It's just that you earned a reputation among the medical school students as being brainy and quiet. During internal medicine, our team grew to know you more than before. We all enjoyed your company; you sure are easy to work with."

"Because I blend into the wall and don't cause any trouble."

Annabel flinched. Had she and Bob and some of the others made him feel uncomfortable on some of the rotations?

"Don't give me a second thought. I'm probably going into psychiatry because of my own awkward self, which allows me to understand those in need better."

She wondered where he was coming from and realized how little she knew about him after three years of medical school and all the months of sharing the wards with him. "You don't hog a conversation, Stuart, but I wouldn't call that awkward. I bet your parents don't think you're awkward or timid or whatever you want to call it."

"My parents …." He left the words dangling in the air after a note of cynicism in his voice.

"What about them, Stuart?"

"I was adopted. I grew up in a children's home. My parents who took me in did so when I was ten years old. They had one of their own, a boy, who was three years older. They suffered with a few miscarriages after him, so I was their attempt to bring an unfulfilled second child into their home. But their idea of an instant child was different from the reality of me and I don't think I measured up to what they wanted."

"Wow. Do you wish you had stayed in the children's home, although that must not have been much fun?"

"Both experiences had their drawbacks." He shrugged his right shoulder.

"Your background makes you more exceptional. Heck, your class rank has been unbeatable. You're super smart despite the precarious home life you've dealt with."

Stuart sighed and allowed himself a small smile. "I read books to escape. In my teen years, I started reading more and more advanced material while my parents were ogling over my older brother's sports accomplishments."

Annabel shook her head. "Aren't you glad you did?"

"You're probably thinking I wouldn't be where I am now if

my situation had been different. I realize that and try to justify what happened. Don't get me wrong, my parents aren't really bad people. Underneath their narrow focus, they meant well."

"I can understand. What about medical school? Are they helping you out financially?"

"They pay my rent, which is something. Otherwise, by the end of next year, I'll be strapped with a six-figure loan debt for med school." He glanced over. "You're lucky."

"I'm grateful for my situation, Stuart. My parents work hard, and my grandparents did too. Actually, their work ethic, which resulted in success, has spilled down to me and made things easier for me, at least financially. As you know, I don't take it for granted, and I'm working hard to become a doctor just like the rest of our classmates."

Stuart came to the intersection of Pete's Café and Annabel pointed. "My apartment is down this street. Park anywhere you find a spot."

After circling the block and parking, the two students jumped out of the Jaguar.

"Bob may be at Pete's already," Annabel said. "I'll go fetch Oliver and walk him. You two sit outside and I'll bring him with me. After all, he's Bob's dog too."

"You two made an unusual arrangement to share a dog," he said, shaking his head.

Annabel slung her backpack on her shoulder. "It's about time you meet him as well. Oliver, that is."

Annabel ran up the two flights of stairs to her apartment. During all of medical school, she had been the tenant of the third story of the residential house and now, more than ever, she absolutely looked forward to opening her door when she arrived home. That was because of her new dog, Oliver, whom she shared with Bob Palmer. The two medical students' schedules were hectic, but between the two of them, they could usually avoid Oliver staying by himself for extremely long days.

She inserted her key and flung open the door to an eager face with big brown eyes. Oliver's long billowy tail swung back and forth with glee to see her.

"Oliver, look at you!" Annabel ditched all her things on the kitchen counter and leaned down. While she wrapped her arms around his head and torso, he obliged and leaned against her. She rustled his soft, long coat and planted a kiss on his forehead, smack between his eyes.

She rose and scanned the kitchen floor and her bedroom. "You are a marvelous dog to hold your bladder since seven thirty this morning. Come on, let's spring you out of here. Get your leash."

Oliver went halfway to the dangling red and white striped leash draped on the stool but rethought her command.

"Yes, go fetch you leash."

Oliver swung around and gripped the leash in his mouth, jimmied it off, and brought it over.

"Good boy!" She hooked him up, grabbed a pet clean-up bag, and they scurried down the steps side-by-side. The dog wasted no time raising his leg to the tree out front and they hustled up the block. She remembered her past walks up to the Cafe and acknowledged to herself that it was much more fun when Oliver accompanied her. Even her running with him through the neighborhood and down to the Ohio River had become much better too.

"Hey, guys," Annabel said over the black fence at Pete's Café where she tethered Oliver. Bob came around, squatted in front of the dog, and massaged his neck.

"He's a beauty," Stuart said. "What kind of dog is he?" He put his hand through the fence and Oliver sniffed and continued wagging his tail.

"We did his DNA to find out," Bob answered, "because we adopted him from the shelter and we wanted to understand him better."

"Bob was the first to examine the results," Annabel said. "He's fifty percent Australian Shepherd and his other half, inherited from his mom or dad, is a conglomerate of breeds, so much so that they couldn't even make a guess."

"Yes," Bob said, "his gene pool mix made him a stunner. And his results confirmed to us something Annabel and I both noticed. That he likes to push against you, especially while you're walking. He possesses a herding instinct like an Aussie."

"I worked with him a little bit," Annabel chuckled, "to prevent him from bumping into me as much."

Oliver made himself comfortable on the cement and Annabel and Bob walked around to the wrought-iron table.

"How old is he?" Stuart asked.

"We took him in during our OB/GYN rotation at about nine-months old. He's around a year old now. Ha! He's pretty much finished growing into the size of his paws. He's a big dog, yet he's lean and wiry, so his weight and strength is not an issue."

"His admixture of coat colors is remarkable." Oliver glanced back intermittently at Annabel and Bob. Picking up his iced tea, Stuart held it in mid-air. In a low voice, he added, "Now that's an adoption story that's working out for everybody." He stared at Annabel and she frowned. She wished the same would have happened for him.

Stuart downed a barbecue sandwich much quicker than Annabel and Bob and stood up after paying his bill. "I'm off to start some serious studying tonight. See you in the morning, Annabel, and good luck on the wards tomorrow, Bob." He gave Oliver a pat on the head and another one on his back. The dog's fur was extra soft.

"Thanks for the classy ride home," Annabel called after him.

Stuart gave her a wave and headed towards his car.

Annabel dunked a French fry into ketchup. "Stuart made a comment about Oliver's adoption. I hope he doesn't mind me repeating it, but are you aware that he was adopted?"

"No. He's not exactly liberal in sharing his personal information with us."

"My thoughts exactly. Maybe we are partly to blame. Some of us hung out together the last few years; maybe we should have been more forthcoming with him to join our conversations, study groups, and socials."

"He's on our rotation again and I sure have nothing against him. In the end, it's his choice whether to spend more time with us or not."

"Well, I'm glad he offered me a ride home. That and the fact that he was a good listener today when I got down about my sister's death."

"Melissa?"

Annabel nodded.

"Next time you're in Nashville, set a bouquet of flowers on her grave. That may provide some solace."

"I like that. I will. A mixture of flowers and colors, the way she liked them. Now what about Oliver? When would you like your turn with him?"

"Can't take him tomorrow because it will be my team's first night on call."

"So then I can drop him at your place the day after when you're post-call and before you get home. I'll let him in with my key on my way to the pediatric practice."

Bob grinned at Oliver. "He'd like that, but I'll enjoy his visit even more."

Annabel polished off the rest of her barbecue sandwich and listened while Bob discussed the pediatric patients he acquired on the service. She listened intently; his inpatients were a lot more ill than the outpatient children she was seeing in Dr. Gillespie's office.

"By the way," she added when he finished. "As opposed to your hospital rotation, when we flip-flop in two weeks and you're in Dr. Gillespie's office, you will appreciate the absence of med student scut work. The office works well without us, and Stuart and I aren't doing busy work. We're there solely to watch and learn. And so far, Stuart's attending is a bit more open-ended about teaching us."

"I'll look forward to that." Bob fixated on her one more time with his rich blue eyes and pushed away from the table. At six foot, he stood tall. He searched his wallet for a bill and went inside.

Annabel put some money on the table and untied Oliver.

"Put this back," Bob said when he came back out. He handed Annabel her money. "I paid Pete inside. You can grab the bill next time."

She shook her head. "There'd better be a next time soon."

"Let's stop at my car. I bought something for Oliver because of the thunderstorm phobia he has."

"The night he and I were in my apartment at the end of OB/GYN was the worst. He shuddered with fear from all the lightning and thunder, and he wanted to hide in the recesses of a cave, which obviously wasn't available."

Bob waved her to his car and took a package out from the front seat.

"A thunder shirt?" she asked.

Bob wore a cheerful expression and pushed back his tapered blonde hair from the front of his head. "It is also called a calming coat or an anxiety wrap. This medium one should fit Oliver. The theory is that the shirt applies constant gentle pressure against a dog's torso, similar to us swaddling an infant, and makes him or her feel more secure. So we can put it on him, hopefully before a storm gets too bad."

"Thanks for buying this and learning about it. I bet Oliver will appreciate it too."

"We'll keep it with his things that go back and forth."

"Ha, like divorced kids going from one parent to the next."

"Yeah, like that."

"I didn't tell you, but Stuart was in a children's home before he was adopted."

"That must have been rough. I bet he's going to make a super psychiatrist because he'll be empathetic to what people go through."

Annabel nodded. "Time to study. Oliver will give you a kiss and away we go."

"There's nothing holding us back from studying together now for an hour or two."

"Except the fact that I'm going to get clad in skimpy pajamas and curl on my bed."

"Like I said, there's …"

"Bob Palmer!" She smiled, stuck the thunder shirt under her arm, and tugged at Oliver's leash.

CHAPTER 5

Dustin Lowe took his police officer duties seriously. In his late twenties, he liked all aspects of his job except being confined to a desk at the station for hours on end. Luckily, that rarely happened. He followed legalities down to the letter of the law and treated people with respect and without bias as much as he could. Not all policemen were like him, but he had learned already that he possessed no jurisdiction over his colleagues' actions. Luckily, Sean, the officer that was his partner, had grown to be a close friend and confidant.

Dustin worked the day shift on Monday and now used the fading sunlight to help him put a second, overdue coat of paint on the side of his house facing his car port. The dark navy paint he stroked on the siding matched the color of his blue jeans, so he didn't mind the spots he'd splashed on his legs. They would eventually blend in or be washed out, he thought as he stood straight and examined the last panel on the bottom.

He always preferred to do the work himself and stood back to admire the color and the job he'd done. Something about painting relaxed him and, in the end, he had something to show for it and a feeling of accomplishment. But more than that, he could think deeply about issues going on in his life while the paintbrush stroked new color across a drab surface.

Placing the moist brush on the tray, he started packing up. His mother was staying with him after showing up the day before for a surprise visit, so the timing of his completed project was perfect. Plus, he needed to get his girlfriend, Annabel Tilson, out of his head for a little while. Well, just a little bit, because she could flood his thoughts despite what he didn't like about her. What he didn't like was in her past, but not being a hundred percent certain of that and questioning himself whether he could live with her previous "loose" behavior with men gave his thoughts much turmoil. After all, he had almost proposed to her and then backed out without her suspecting his intentions.

He washed the paintbrush under the outside faucet and put away all the supplies in his laundry room when he entered the back door. His receding thick black hair sprang from his scalp in coiled ringlets ... more than usual because of the humidity.

Inside, his mother, Vicky, sat at the kitchen table. Dustin couldn't blame her for coming. Although she only lived forty miles away, he didn't see her as much as he should. His father had died; she had downsized to an apartment, and at fifty-eight years old, she still worked as a bank cashier.

Vicky had a slight stooped posture, which Dustin wondered about since it had materialized in the last few months since their last visit. She wore big brown-rimmed glasses, which sat on the bumpy bridge of her nose, and shot her son a warm smile when he stepped in.

"Sorry, Mom," Dustin said. "Nothing like you visiting to find me gone at the station or working on the house. But I'm glad that project is finished."

"I know how it goes. You have a small house and a small lot, but there is still upkeep to owning a home. I'm happy to use a few days off to visit you in Cincinnati but still hope I'm not an imposition."

"My goodness, Mom, don't even think that." Dustin rubbed his jaw, which included resting his finger in the dimple on his chin. "Is Solar behaving with you?"

His yellow-naped Amazon parrot was on the counter in the kitchen, the room modern yet compact. Dustin wondered what the bird was doing; his beak bobbed inside a mug.

Solar clicked his tongue in approval of whatever he was drinking. "Mmm," he said.

"What the...?" Dustin strolled over.

"My cold coffee is sitting over there," Vicki said. "Solar's taken a liking to it."

Dustin took a peek inside the mug. Sure enough … black French roast. He rolled his eyes. "Don't go bouncing off the walls with that caffeine."

"If it's any consolation," Vicki said, "I made caffeine-free."

Dustin shook his head and came back to the table with crackers and cheese and set them down. He snapped open a beer can and took a scant sip.

"I'm taking you out to dinner tomorrow night, Mom. To the nicest place around here."

"Are you going to invite the young lady you're dating? I'd like to meet her."

"I may have mentioned she's a medical student. She started a new rotation this week, so breaking away from studying may be difficult. I'll ask her, however."

Vicki topped a cracker with a dollop of Brie cheese. She chewed for a while and then rubbed her hand on her forehead.

"I wasn't snooping. I would never do such a thing. Since I'm in your spare bedroom, I put a few clothing articles in the top dresser. There's a velvet case in there with an engagement ring."

The words hung flat in the air. It would be all right if Dustin offered an explanation, but if not, Vicki was fine if he kept his love life to himself; at least for the time being.

"Annabel stays here sometimes. I put the ring in the spare bedroom to make sure I didn't accidentally leave it in my room where she'd see it. I was ready to ask her to marry me, but then I had second thoughts. There is no reason to rush a lifetime commitment. I'm waiting, that's all."

Vicki scrunched up her forehead. "Waiting for what?"

"I don't know."

Vicki nodded and thought it best to change the subject. "Solar's become bored with the drink. It's about time."

"What's your problem?" the bird asked.

"Sorry, Mom. He says that a lot."

"So I found out. He practiced on me while you were outside painting."

Annabel opened the bathroom door, a towel wrapped around her after showering. Oliver gazed up from the floor, his eyes never leaving her. He clung close by as she rummaged through the drawer looking for lightweight pajamas.

She grabbed a pediatric paperback and settled on the bed while Oliver sat, intent on gathering her attention. He popped up and wagged his tail, reluctant to sit again.

"Don't tell me you want to go out again?"

Excited, the dog went in the kitchen and wagged his tail. He didn't stand near the door. Annabel realized what was churning around in his clever mind as she followed him and stuck her hand into the biscuit box on the counter. "You're training *me*, not the other way around. So give me your paw."

Oliver obliged and lowered himself to the floor with the biscuit dangling from his mouth.

She went back to her bed with a pediatric paperback. Although she saw a case or two during her surgery rotation, she figured appendicitis would show up during her new rotation – either clinically or on a test. It was time to review the clinician's approach to the problem, diagnosis, and definitive treatment.

After an hour, with an adequate review behind her, she thought it best to call it a night. Her iPhone rang as she was about to close the chapter.

"Hey, Dustin," she said.

"I'm taking a chance calling this late. You're not in bed yet, are you?"

She laughed. "Dustin Lowe, you're cutting it close. I suppose it's my fault. I should have called you, and earlier, especially since you're dying to know how my first day went on pediatrics."

"Not really," he joked. "Nevertheless, what's your initial opinion of looking in children's ears and throats all day?"

"Ha! Is that what lay people, or officers of the law, think about that specialty? Rather narrow-minded, isn't it?"

"Eww. Feisty tonight, are we?"

"Try me. Do you know how nonspecific the first symptoms are of a budding case of appendicitis? An appendix, that GI appendage that can rupture in a kid's abdomen and put them in the hospital with a myriad of problems. It takes an astute physician to recognize appendicitis early on, not one just thinking about a bellyache after a corn dog at the county fair."

"Double feisty, but remind me not to eat a corn dog when I take you to the yearly fair."

"Is that a date?"

"Sure is. A girl from Tennessee must know about state and county fairs."

"Sure do. Especially the memories with my family: my grandparents, my mom and dad, and sisters." Her tone changed and she became quiet.

"Some of those memories weren't pleasant?"

"They were all wonderful. Today I'm missing my older sister, that's all."

"I bet you were close."

"Very true. These days, I would be sharing girl talk with her about the guy I'm dating."

"You can tell me."

"No chance. Anyway, how was your day?"

"Fine, and I have a surprise, an overdue guest visiting me since yesterday ... my mom."

"Aren't you lucky. She's staying with you?"

"Yup. For a few days. How about dinner tomorrow night and you can meet her?"

"I would love to make her acquaintance. Will you be

understanding that I can't kill my whole night, however?"

"Absolutely. How about we pick you up at 7 p.m.?"

"That'll be tight. I can do it without getting totally dolled up."

"You always look dolled up without dolling up, so be yourself. We'll pop over to the Cajun place and I'll ask the waiter not to dilly dally."

"See you then."

Annabel hung up and stared at Oliver. She left the paperback in the space between her crisscrossed legs and thought about their conversation. A woman meeting the mother of the man she's dating? This was a big deal. This was a step up in their relationship.

So far, Annabel was totally happy dating Dustin and she liked him a lot. Things had been perking along fine. He was a fine man, admirable, good-looking, pleasant, and fun to be with, and well, she could not really find any negatives about him. Of course, their fields were totally different, yet stressful and demanding. There was, however, only so much she could share with him that he understood or was interested in.

Another point, she thought, was that in her stage of training, getting super serious with any man would pose a problem. Or would it? Perhaps she should give their relationship more substantial thought. Maybe he was doing that, especially if tomorrow night she was meeting the special lady who had brought him into the world.

Annabel slipped in the front door of the office and hustled to the back room of Gillespie's practice.

Stuart stored his backpack and frowned at her. "You're cutting our start time close too. How come when we're given more time in the morning before beginning our day, we tend to come in later?"

"Makes no sense. In my defense, however, I didn't have Oliver to walk during the other rotations. But you're correct. Do you think we've become slackers?"

"More like lazy slouchers."

Annabel also donned her jacket. "Darn, I dressed, walked the dog, and called for a ride. I never made coffee. My Keurig machine was a gift from Bob, so my first burst of coffee is more than a hot beverage. It's a send-off to my day from our thoughtful colleague."

"He didn't give me one." Stuart threw her a glance. "Come on, before we get in trouble, if that's possible. There are patients' medical folders in the hallway chart holders."

Annabel smoothed a handful of silky hair to both sides of her collar. She followed Stuart to the hallway, where Dr. Gillespie and Dr. Clark were both bent over charts.

"Good morning," Heather said, acknowledging them. "Welcome back. Follow me, Dr. Schneider."

"Miss Tilson," Dr. Gillespie said, "come on." He knocked and, inside, a little girl sat on her father's lap. She turned to him and buried her head into his chest.

George introduced Annabel and handed her the record. While her attending made small talk to them, she read the notes. The patient, Stephanie Miller, was a three-year-old. Mr. Miller told the nurse he brought her in for a "lump below her belly button" and that "she wasn't very hungry."

Dr. Gillespie coaxed the girl to the examining table and continued gaining a history of the patient's chief complaint. As Annabel now saw the girl in full, the area around her eyes stood out. It was as if the skin had been stained darker than the rest of her pale face.

"Tell me about the lump," Dr. Gillespie said. "When did it start?"

"It may have been there before, but my wife and I noticed it about two weeks ago. We thought it would go away. Instead, the bump is getting bigger. We realized Stephie is also picking at her food, not even eating macaroni and cheese, which she usually loves."

"Any fever, night sweats, or changes in her behavior like lack of energy?"

"Seems like she's less peppy. Yeah, she's been avoiding playing in the backyard. More or less, she has been sticking to lying on the couch in the afternoons. That's what my wife notices the days she has off from work."

Annabel scanned the office folder again to find Stephanie's vital signs to be normal. When she checked her prior history, it was negative for surgeries or medical illnesses. She was even born a full-term, healthy infant.

Mr. Miller turned from the table and sat back in the corner. The attending looked in the girl's ears and nose and checked her eyes. He lingered at the sight of her periorbital discoloration. Stephie flinched when he put his cold stethoscope to her chest and listened.

Annabel stepped to the bottom of the table. George pulled her pair of shorts down and her underwear. "Just going to see that bump your daddy is telling me about," he said.

For sure, Annabel noticed, there was a distinct mass in Stephie's left lower quadrant, which extended somewhat to the right; a bump like a big pebble underneath the skin of a small girl.

Dr. Gillespie didn't touch it when he pointed and asked, "Does it hurt?"

Stephie remained stoic. George palpated her abdomen and her mass. He turned his head slightly to glimpse at Mr. Miller, who was watching intently. Stephie squirmed very little with his examination.

The pediatrician examined her lower abdomen so slowly that Annabel switched her weight from one foot to the other. The pace in a private office surely was slow compared to the wards, she thought, but then admonished herself for thinking such a thing. *Good medicine takes place out of the hospital,* she reminded herself, *and is the backbone to the diagnoses of many cases that get admitted.*

After another minute elapsed, George began pulling up Stephie's underwear. Mr. Miller shot up and helped.

"Stephie, dear," Dr. Gillespie said, "we need to take a few tests to find out why you don't feel so well." He looked at Mr. Miller. "We'll need to take some blood. Also, for some of the testing, we'll need a twenty-four-hour urine sample from her. My nurse will come back in to give you the supplies to use at home and explain it to you. Please bring the sample back in when you have it, and my office will schedule a return visit after the results are back."

Mr. Miller raised his eyebrows. His thick arms picked up his daughter and he rocked her like an infant. "What are you thinking, doc?"

With a shake of his head, the pediatrician said, "Can't say. It would be like giving a test score before you took the exam. Let's wait and see, because we're only talking a few days at the most." He nodded and stepped out.

Annabel patted Stephanie on the back. "I hope you feel better, Stephie. Nice to meet you, sir. Lots of luck with her. She's a sweetheart."

Stephie shyly turned her head and returned a tiny smile.

CHAPTER 6

Annabel poured coffee into a cup in the kitchenette and then inched one over to Stuart. She dumped two flavored creamers into her own.

"You're the one who needs these calories, not me," she said.

"Can't help it. The background I told you about … orphanages aren't known for their food. Not eating much those early years simply stuck with me, even after I was adopted."

"A gust of wind will sweep you away one of these days. I, on the other hand, wish we were back with Dr. Schott on internal medicine, when boxes of donuts would materialize in the office."

"I heard that," Dr. Clark said, stepping behind them. "We do indulge once in a while, but with all the women in this office, we make a point to not tempt ourselves very often."

The office manager stood in the doorway. "Dr. Clark, these poor medical students are famished. I'll do something about that tomorrow."

"If you stop on the way in, I'll reimburse you. If the neon sign is blaring 'hot donuts' or 'just made,' I'll even pay you double to veer in and pick up a dozen." She laughed at her own plea.

"Sounds like a generous bribe. Also, the University department just called to remind us to spring the students this afternoon for pediatric grand rounds downtown."

"Thanks, Becky," Heather said. "You two leave later for lunch today and then go straight to the department lecture at 3 p.m."

"And then we're done for the day?" Annabel asked.

"Sure. By the time you would drive back to the office, we'll be closing up. And, Stuart, our next patient is here, but his mom went back to the car for insurance information. He's by himself in the waiting room. Feel free to make him comfortable and find out why he's here."

Heather left and Stuart placed his unfinished coffee on the counter. He walked past the front desk and out the door to the waiting area, so Annabel followed with her coffee.

Stuart crouched down to the only child in the room. "What's your name?"

A little boy with big ears grinned up from a building block set. "My name is Thomas. I am a whole six years old."

"Wow. You are big enough to make a skyscraper with those blocks."

"What's a skyscraper?"

"A tall building." Stuart inched his arms up over the boy's head and Thomas put his hand over his mouth in surprise.

"I'm going to try and fix the blocks up high. Just watch me."

"Why did your mom bring you to see the doctor today?"

"My throat hurts. Last time, the doctor gave me a shot." He contorted his face with displeasure and went on. "I'm afraid of shots and I don't want one."

Stuart eased himself onto a child-sized plastic stool and handed Thomas several blocks of different shapes. Slowly, the boy stacked them up on his growing creation.

Annabel found several Legos under her chair and handed them over for their project. She had never seen Stuart before with a child and his easy-going interaction was a surprise. Now the two males bent their heads over and the building was gaining width as well as height.

Stuart tilted his head and admired their work. "I think a boy who can build a magnificent skyscraper like this isn't too afraid of a shot of medicine to make him better. If the doctor thinks he needs it, of course."

Thomas tugged on the cartoon character T-shirt he was wearing and eyed the two medical students like he'd been awarded a trophy. "I should make buildings when I grow up ... or be a doctor!"

"Maybe. There is plenty of time to think about that."

Thomas's mother came in the main door waving her insurance cards at the front desk. "Has Thomas behaved himself?"

"Most certainly," Stuart said. "I'm one of the medical students and we'll see Thomas in the back in a little while."

Annabel warmed her coffee in the microwave while Stuart and Dr. Clark went in to see their patient. She was on her own because Dr. Gillespie had left for a lunch meeting.

"Dr. Clark invited you in back there," Becky said, popping her head in. Her short, prematurely gray hair was stunning enough for an *AARP* magazine cover and she patted the bun at the back of her head.

Annabel nodded. "Sure thing. Don't want to miss little Thomas's sore throat."

"The rooms get crowded," Becky added. "Med students rarely can double up."

Annabel opened the door quietly. Thomas was on the table fully dressed and Dr. Clark held some kind of kit. "This is our other medical student, Dr. Tilson. I also want to show her Thomas's throat."

On cue, Thomas opened his mouth wide and Annabel took a look.

"We'll do a rapid antigen test," Heather informed them, "but this appears to be classic strep throat with red tonsils and white patches in the back. Thomas's lymph nodes are swollen in his neck too." She opened the package and rubbed a swab in the back of his throat. "Please bring this to the lab, Annabel."

Annabel left with the sample, appreciative of being called

into the case. After waiting in the lab, she relayed the result to Dr. Clark.

Heather scanned the sheet. "Sure enough, Thomas has strep bacteria like he had one other time. I'm going to prescribe an oral antibiotic and, to relieve throat pain and reduce his slight fever, please give him Tylenol at home."

Thomas's mother nodded. "No shot?"

"No shot."

The little boy looked past Heather and grinned at Stuart, who gave him a thumbs-up.

Heather approached the door. "We're finished. You get better and bounce back to your normal health, Thomas, and drink lots of fluids like your mom tells you."

"Bye," Thomas responded. "And, Dr. Stuart, I wouldn't of cried if Dr. Clark gave me a shot."

"I figured that. After all, you're a master Lego builder."

Along with a broad smile, Thomas's eyes twinkled, and Annabel was sure that Stuart had made a friend.

"Since we're not coming back here," Annabel said, "I can't forget my stuff."

Stuart didn't respond and both students stuffed their paperbacks into their backpacks. The heat hit them heavy when they stepped outside. The sun was in full force and not a leaf stirred.

"I'll give you a ride downtown," Stuart waved, "but first let's eat. Same place as yesterday?"

Annabel bobbed her head. "You ever have strep throat as a kid?"

"Never. How about you?"

"Never." They walked a medium pace to avoid working up a sweat, yet fast enough to soon pop into the restaurant's air conditioning. This time, they were led to the area with a yellow-painted wall, which seemed to correlate with the sunshine outside.

"Any interesting patients this morning?" Stuart asked.

"A three-year old with an abdominal mass. Who knows what the heck that will be?"

"Hmm. I bet the differential covers a whole list of possibilities, yet I wouldn't have a clue."

"I don't believe that."

A waitress with long nails and a wrap-around wrist tattoo poured ice water into their glasses. "What'll it be?"

Annabel wasted no time. "Any specials of the day?"

"BLT on Texas toast and fries."

Annabel nodded. "Make that two," Stuart said.

"Substitute a small salad for the fries," Annabel said.

The waitress reached into her pocket and dumped ketchup packets and two straws. "Coming right up. I bet you two are the new recruits in Dr. Gillespie's office. I'm Donna."

"Thanks, Donna, we are," Annabel said.

Donna slapped an order slip at the kitchen window and Stuart leaned across the table. "Regarding the kid with an abdominal mass, I guess the patient's age has a huge bearing on the possibilities. However, I would segregate categories in my mind. Such as flank masses … whether they are renal or nonrenal. Then whether I suspect a GI mass or a hepatobiliary mass, related to only the liver or biliary system. And heck, there are always pelvic masses to think about. If it's a girl, it could stem from an ovarian problem. Could it be an abscess related to the appendix?"

"This was more to the left and midline, but it was lower abdominal. I would think the patient would have been sicker if she had appendicitis with an abscess."

"What about labs?"

"Dr. Gillespie ordered the bloodwork and electrolytes and

more than the usual. He even ordered a twenty-four-hour urine."

"What amazes me is that these doctors we work with are like detectives. Most of the time, within a few minutes of hearing the patient's history, they have a strong suspicion of the medical possibilities and order what they need to know. Do you think we'll ever get there?"

"Stuart, we're on our way. You need to acknowledge that to yourself. Especially you."

The waitress came with the food and now slipped packets of salad dressing on the table. "Bon appetite."

Annabel took a bite of the toasted sandwich. "This is tasty, but dinner tonight will surely be better."

"You're not going out on a Tuesday night, are you?"

"I'm going to meet Dustin's mother."

Stuart looked up from his hunched position over his food. "I'm not saying a word."

"Come on, Stuart, spill it out. I have my own ideas whirling around inside my head. If it were you, would you be conjuring up ideas about a more serious turn in a relationship?"

"Are you going to her house for dinner?"

"No. She lives far away, so she's visiting her son. We're going to a restaurant."

"Much better. My advice? Don't work yourself up with anticipation. It won't be as scary as you think and she will probably like you immediately. Just don't spill your wine on the tablecloth or take out your cell phone."

Annabel mulled over the first things he said as they finished eating. "I'm grabbing the tab today, Stuart. I'm being a freeloader as far as hopping car rides from you."

"Not a problem."

Stuart and Annabel went back to the office parking lot and slid into his Jaguar. "Another thing," he said. "It might be a nice gesture if you bring your future mother-in-law a tiny, tiny gift or something for her and her son to share later that night. She'll be left with a last impression … one that is positive, no matter how much she likes or dislikes you."

"Stuart?"

"What?"

"Future mother-in-law?!"

Stuart cocked his head with a bemused smile and started the ignition.

The high-wattage bulbs of the pediatric conference room blared down into the room as Annabel and Stuart stood in the back on the top step. A frantic chief resident prepared his Power Point slides on the stage with the help of a technician. The one screen behind them lit up with the topic of the talk: "Lead Poisoning."

"Interesting topic. I'm heading down front," Stuart said and peeled away. *Just like him*, Annabel thought, and admired his tenacity to learn.

"You can't sit here." Annabel turned to the side as Bob swiped the chair next to him, imitating the bus scene from *Forrest Gump*.

Annabel laughed and scooted in, brushing his hand away. To the left of him sat the other three students on his pediatric hospital team. Two female students with crossed legs and skirts sat next to him.

"Hey, Annabel." The girl next to him bobbed her head and then fumbled in a bag on the floor. She had long hair like Annabel, but it was pulled back and smartly braided. She pulled out a notebook and tapped it on Bob's knee. "This is a rare topic. I bet our chief resident will be throwing us some questions this week about his talk. Why don't I take notes for us? We may not find this information in a textbook."

Bob nodded. "Smart thinking, Nell. We might not ever see a

case of lead poisoning, but we won't forget the topic."

She shrugged her side into him. "Let me borrow your pen."

Bob grabbed a pen off his top pocket and then Nell wrote the topic in fine cursive. Annabel noted her thick bracelet and dangling ivory earrings and wondered, *Linnell may be studying to become a doctor, but where is her sensitivity to other species? Buying that type of jewelry may help out poachers, and they slaughter elephants.*

"Annabel," Nell said, "our chief resident is up there on stage. We have the best chief of all three hospital teams, don't we, Bob?"

Bob nodded. "We lucked out. Sorry you're not with us, Annabel."

Annabel knew Linnell was an in-state student, born and raised in Ohio, and the fact that her goal was to become a general surgeon. They were both around the same age, and although Annabel had a healthy complexion, Nell's shined like she massaged her face with pure cocoa butter.

The resident up front tapped the microphone a few times. "I'm going to begin, so everyone please take a seat."

"So how's it going?" Bob whispered.

"My relationship with Dustin must be ramping up. He wants me to meet his mother tonight."

Bob bobbed his head. "I meant in Dr. Gillespie's office."

Annabel swallowed hard, realizing she'd inserted a personal, off-topic remark. "Oh, fine, I suppose."

"As you know, our team is on call tonight. Nell already picked up a patient on life support in the ICU because a deer came through the front car window at her and I gained a young boy as an admission for newly diagnosed Type 1 Diabetes. These poor children. Can you imagine?"

Annabel shook her head. "There should be a law against children getting medical problems."

"Wishful thinking," Nell inserted, extending herself in front of Bob.

The microphone volume ramped up and the chief resident began. "Regulatory interventions have helped to decrease the incidence of lead poisoning in children, but this talk will make you aware of this still existent clinical problem. One takeaway point is where the major source of it now comes from ... older buildings that still contain lead paint."

Bob tried to focus, but what Annabel had said continued to stalk his mind. He had camouflaged his surprise when she said she was meeting Dustin Lowe's mother, but she'd made a point that their relationship was "ramping up." It was difficult to appear as if he was neutral or happy about her dating him, but if it escalated further, the blow to his emotions would be awful. It was challenging enough to manage medical school while being in love with Annabel Tilson.

CHAPTER 7

"Come on, Oliver." The dog's tail swished back and forth and he boomed out a gregarious bark in anticipation of a walk. Annabel startled and dropped his leash.

"No, no. No barking for that reason. Sit." She waited for his eyes to settle on her, and as he sat quietly, she praised him. "Much better; now let's go so you can pee on your favorite tree."

They bounded down the stairs and she gave Oliver ample time to sniff along the way as they headed in the direction of Pete's. She would be annoyed at herself if she didn't follow Stuart's suggestion about giving Mrs. Lowe some trinket as a gift. It couldn't hurt. However, she still needed to change for dinner; maybe Pete had something appropriate in his case of desserts.

Annabel fixed Oliver's leash to the fence outside and stepped into the Café to the tinkle of the door bells above. Tables were joined together and a group of high school students were eating and socializing. She studied the items for sale, both in the see-through cases and shelves against the back wooden wall.

Pete come out from the kitchen. "Anything in particular I can help you with, Annabel?"

"Hi, Pete. I wish. Something small to bring someone I'm meeting tonight - Dustin's mother. This is a last-minute thought. Maybe dessert for the two of them for later tonight?"

"That's the boyfriend, right?"

She rolled her eyes and nodded.

"Just making doubly sure. Triply sure. Never mind; I'll shut up. I may have the perfect treat. How about a fresh blueberry cheesecake? The chef made a dozen miniature ones today. Each is the perfect size for two servings and I can put it in an extra fancy box lined with pink paper."

"You're a lifesaver. I'll take one." She dug her credit card out while Pete boxed it up. "And add these." She grabbed a box of chocolate expresso beans and chocolate-covered blueberries, which she and Bob appreciated when they were together. "Thanks, Pete."

When Annabel ambled outside, now with a small paper bag, Oliver planted his eyes on her. Two girls from the social event inside were cross-legged on the ground, giving him their utmost attention. "He's gorgeous," one of them said. "Is he yours?"

"Yes. His name is Oliver."

Oliver's tail swiped the girl in the face. "If you ever need a dog sitter, I'll take care of him."

"Better yet," the other one said, "if you ever need to give him up for any reason, I'll take him!"

"Those are generous offers. In essence, he already has two owners, so he's spread thin. It is ironic that we saved him from living in a shelter and from being euthanized. The list of people who can or would take care of him for us keeps growing."

The two girls glanced at each other. "Wow," the first one said. "When the time comes to get a dog, I think I'll check the county shelter first."

"I can't do it right now," Annabel said, "but when my career settles down, I'm going to keep two dogs. One from a shelter and a purebred dog of my choice from a breeder."

The two girls giggled. In unison, they said good-bye to Oliver. As they scrambled back into Pete's, Annabel overheard, "Okay, you get the purebred and I'll get the shelter dog and they can be best buddies."

Annabel grinned. "Oliver, you're making people who meet you dog-crazy." As they approached her apartment house and turned in to the staircase, she mumbled, "Now what should I wear?"

In response to a knock, Annabel opened her apartment door at 7 p.m. "Police officers keep perfect time."

"So do doctors." Dustin leaned over and ruffled Oliver's coat. "Hey, boy. Sorry we can't take you with us."

Oliver nudged his leash from the other side of the door handle and it dropped to the floor. He picked it up and tried to present it to them.

"I'll see you later," Annabel said and hung the leash back. "You mind the house." She opened the refrigerator and grabbed the paper bag. Much to Oliver's disappointment, the couple slipped out the door and Annabel locked it behind her.

Dustin glanced up and down. "By the way, you look great. You said you wouldn't have time to doll up. You don't need to."

She glanced down at her outfit: a pair of sandals, a short-sleeved dress with a belt, and a touch of jewelry. Around her neck, and to the side, she wore a multi-pocketed flat bag with her personal items. With only a thin line of eyeliner and a touch of lipstick, her hair, looks, and figure spoke for itself.

"Thank you, and I'm looking forward to meeting your mom."

"I had to double park."

Downstairs, Dustin opened the car door and Annabel looked towards the back. "Hi, Vicki, I've heard all about you. Nice to meet you."

"Likewise. I'm glad you could make it tonight. Between both your jobs, it must be difficult to schedule a date."

Dustin popped in and cruised the car away from her street. "Somehow we work around our schedules. It's amazing what you can accomplish when you set your mind to it."

Annabel grasped on to what he said. He seemed to have faith

in their dating despite the complexity of their careers and her training demands. Her stomach churned with butterflies as she stole a glance. Unfortunately, from the side, she couldn't see the flattering dimple in his chin.

Twelve minutes later, Dustin parked his Acura behind the restaurant and they made small talk to the front door.

"Good evening," the maître d' said once they were inside. "Would you like to sit at a table by the bar or on this side of the restaurant?"

Dustin squirmed. He couldn't possibly sit in the bar area, where last time, they ran into a man Annabel had had a fling with. "We'll take a booth inside."

Vicki scooted into a black booth and Annabel sat across from her. She smiled at Dustin as he slid in next to her.

"Your son always takes this side," Annabel said. "Any side that faces the main entrance so he can monitor what goes on. One time when we were together, his habit helped out the restaurant because, while I was doing the Heimlich maneuver on someone, he was catching a crook stealing from the register. I also happen to know that his trick comes in handy quite often while he's working."

Vicki smiled a mischievous grin. Annabel could now see the resemblance between mother and son, a subtlety across the cheekbones and their full mouths. She had a medium build with a thin waist and wore a loose cotton top. A dangling gemstone hung off a silver necklace above her chest. She took her glasses off and placed them to the side of the tablecloth.

"Ahh. You two must be thick as thieves. He ushers me around too while he polices the environment around us whenever we're together. He only does that with people he loves."

"Mom!" Dustin said and shrugged his shoulders.

Annabel quickly rose her glass of ice water and took a sip.

"So what kind of doctor are you studying to be?"

"I have yet to make that decision, but the time is drawing near. In the coming weeks, I must put in applications to land a residency spot and then match day comes in the spring."

A female waiter stepped to the table. "Good evening. Would you like to order yet?"

"I think so," Dustin said, nodding several times at Annabel.

She nodded back, knowing he understood her need to study. "How about your catch of the day, Cajun style, and asparagus."

"And you, Ma'am?"

"The special," Vicki said. "With the understanding I'll be boxing some up for tomorrow."

Dustin handed her the three menus. "I'll take a medium ribeye and two house-favorite vegetable sides."

The waitress bowed her head. "Any bread or wine in the interim?"

"Bring them on," Dustin said. "Would you prefer white, ladies?"

"I'm skipping," Annabel said.

Vicki tapped the wine list on the table. "Chardonnay."

The woman left and Annabel began to relax much more. Dustin's mother was friendly and she didn't seem to be judging her.

Vicki spun right back into Annabel's medical journey. "What area of medicine are you doing right now?"

"Pediatrics. But please tell me about yourself. I understand you work in a bank?"

"I do. The same one for eight years. There was one take-over, but I stayed on without a problem and I enjoy meeting customers at my window."

"Sounds pleasant enough. Do you ever worry about being held up?"

"My son drove that possibility into my head. He says, 'Toss over the money and not your life.'"

Dustin laughed. "Other than that, believe me, she has the last word about everything else."

Vicki winked at Annabel, acknowledging her son's statement. When the wine was poured, Annabel still passed, but she was so at ease, it already felt like she'd drunk a whole glass.

"Feel free to drop me off at the house," Vicki said back in Dustin's car. "I'm tired enough to chill and you two can go on to Annabel's place. Besides, if I want to keep up a conversation, I'll have Solar to talk to."

"My place is close, Mom, so I'll drop you off."

Dustin soon pulled up in front of his house.

"Take care, Annabel, it was nice meeting you."

"You, too, Ma'am." She reached down and handed Vicki the bag with blueberry cheesecake through the open window. "This is a little something for dessert, especially since we didn't splurge at the restaurant. It should go in the fridge if you don't get to eat any tonight."

"How thoughtful of you, dear." Vicki turned to her son, approval written all over her face.

Dustin unlocked the front door for his mother and strutted back. The dinner went well, he thought, and he heaved a sigh of relief that no man from Annabel's past had showed up.

A few parking places were available on Annabel's street, so Dustin parked across the street.

Annabel stretched one leg out of the Acura. "I should walk Oliver one last time. Would you like to join us?"

Dustin nodded. "The trials and tribulations of pet ownership. Is he proving himself worth it?"

"Of course. No different than your cleaning out Solar's cage, which he seems to never be in."

"I'm yanking your chain. Oliver is a sweetheart. A guy could get jealous over all the bonding you've got going with him."

They stepped on the third floor landing and Annabel unlocked the door.

"Not to worry. I have a right and left heart. You know, two atriums and two ventricles. I hereby declare the right side to go to Oliver and the stronger left side is to be reserved for my male human love life."

"Wow. That's quite a proclamation."

Annabel glanced at her watch and grimaced while Oliver's feather duster of a tail greeted them.

Noticing her uncomfortableness, surely about study time, he decided to volunteer. "Why don't you start your bedtime routine and I walk Oliver?"

She crouched down and gave Oliver a hug. "Dustin is going to walk you." Springing up, she planted a kiss on Dustin. "Thanks and thanks for inviting me to dinner with your mom."

"You're welcome." He pranced Oliver out the door, the two of them with enough energy to bolt downstairs and around the street to the neighborhood garden park.

Annabel changed into summery pajama shorts and a body-clinging top. She tossed her shoes in the closet and grabbed her pediatric paperback. Bob's case he mentioned that morning had sounded interesting, so she opened up a chapter on "Type 1 Diabetes in Children." Maybe she could give him some tips if his night on call was too busy to allow him to read. The condensed reading format of the topic was useful, and she absorbed quite a bit by the time she heard a rap on the door and Oliver bounded in to greet her before Dustin.

"Look at you. Dustin gave you a police officer's top-notch training and exercise walk."

Dustin replaced the striped leash on the door handle. "That's a mouthful," he said, standing between the bedroom and kitchen. His eyes took in Annabel as she rose to greet him.

She padded over in bare feet, but even she wasn't sure if her motive was to see him to the door.

Oliver finished panting and lowered flat down. Dustin stepped over him and put his hands in her hair, behind her head. With a slight tug, they closed the gap, and his lips met hers.

He wrapped her body in his embrace and Annabel responded, circling her arms to his back and smoothing her hands along his muscles. Their mouths became hungrier and Dustin tucked his hands under the ribbed cotton top smack against her skin. Annabel felt as good as she looked and he picked her up like she was important cargo to take possession of. After lowering her on the bed, he yanked off his clothes faster than she could help him.

Swiftly, Dustin was on and in her and they drained all the passion they'd saved since last time. Even though her apartment was adequately air-conditioned, their bodies were laced with sweat.

Dustin rolled off, and he swiped his hand across his chest while Annabel slid her nearby top across her abdomen. "I think I'll be needing a different top tonight."

"Sorry about that."

She rotated to the side. "Nothing to be sorry about. It was meant to be; we made our own bed."

"Your bed. How about I do a sleep over and not disturb you? I'm three to eleven tomorrow. I can even take you to the pediatrician's office in the morning."

"If you can drive me first to Bob's so I can drop off Oliver. He gets him tomorrow, since he's post-call."

"Sure."

"Should you let your mom know you're not coming home?"

"She's probably sleeping already." He touched her hand. "If she finds me missing, she'll figure it out."

"I'm jumping into the shower. When I come out, I'll expect you to be fast asleep. Then I'll finish the chapter I was reading. Deal?"

"Deal."

CHAPTER 8

Linnell planted herself against the pole facing the ambulance bay of the ER. The pediatric team, as well as the emergency department, stayed steady with admissions. At least, she figured, they weren't tremendously swamped on their first night on call, a time when the students were the most green about what they were doing.

For the time being, Bob Palmer was the student working up the newest patient with a resident. A little kid with a pale, sickly appearance came in with overbearing, demanding parents and she was glad she missed the opportunity to "learn" about whatever ailed him. Bob was a lot more patient and sympathetic than her, but hopefully, the next pediatric patient would be a snap because she was "up" next.

After the sun slid down a few hours ago, the temperature cooled down, mostly due to a perky breeze, which made her take more, deeper breaths than normal. It was like cleaning out a carburetor, or in this case, her lungs. The end of her cigarette glowed as she inhaled and, in a moment, she tapped the growing ash on the ground. She was guilty of mostly hiding or downplaying her cigarette smoking from the medical colleagues, residents, and attendings that she worked with. After all, a doctor was supposed to set a good example, but she didn't think that entailed giving up every last thing she treasured in her life to appease the look of professionalism that was expected for someone taking the Hippocratic Oath.

Yes, she smoked, but she did try her best to keep it to a minimum. Chain smokers were the worst. Plus, taking the habit that far could cause her teeth to yellow or for people to smell tobacco on her breath. No way would she ever burn through cigarettes like a chain smoker.

She savored the last puff while peeking around; best to make sure no one on her team had stepped outside the ER to escape for a moment, especially Bob. Only since starting the rotation with him did she realize that he was potential relationship material. At present, he had no girlfriend and she hadn't dated since freshman year. He'd been a guy doing his master's in engineering, and after that failed experience, she made up her mind to eventually marry her own kind - a doctor.

Linnell's future was laid out and un-bendable for multiple reasons. Now all she needed to do was to find the right guy … much easier said than done. Fortunately, there was no ultimate hurry; she had time, but she needed to start whittling down the possibilities.

Her cigarette was down to the butt, so she flew it past the curb with a flick of the finger. She swallowed a lump in her throat and dug into an inside pocket for a peppermint. Stepping past the automatic doors to the waiting area, she hesitated next to a paper and magazine rack and popped the mint into her mouth. The prominent stack on top of the pile was a schedule for the county fair.

Nell picked up the schedule, basically a book of week-long events and what was entailed to participate or to attend. It contained little advertising from sponsors, and she remembered the past years she attended. It had been a few years back, but a true county or state fair was well worth a visit. From truck and tractor pulls, to livestock shows, to baking, agricultural, and beauty contests, it was that and so much more.

A light went on in her head as she mulled over the ice breaker she held in her hands. Their team would have off on Saturday after the next night on call and it would be the perfect day and event to try and steal Bob on a more personal level. Asking him to attend a fair would not come across as being too forward by asking him out on a date.

But what could she use as a fair "hook?" She stood off to the side so as to not block the aisle and read the index of events. A western horse show was at night, but she wanted something special during the day. And then she saw it. Eleven o'clock in the morning was registration to participate in a pet show, mostly dogs. She counted eight categories for dogs besides the exotic pets like rabbits, chickens, and birds. Her mouth curled up in a smile. For two days, she'd heard all about Bob's new dog named Oliver, from his thunderstorm phobia, to his "herding" instincts, to, more importantly, how awesome he was. Surely pet shows need handsome dogs and she was just the one to convince Bob that they should go.

Bob handed the chart to the orderly so it could accompany his patient out of the ER and to his designated hospital room. Since the team had decided to admit the young boy, Bob had written up a full H&P, or history and physical. He wrapped his stethoscope back around his neck and headed for the staircase.

"Bob, hey, wait up." Linnell hurried her steps and Bob paused. "Are you finished with your admission?"

"Just about, except for waiting on more labs. Poor kid has sickle cell disease and came in with pain in his thigh. A vaso-occlusive crisis triggered by an infection." He rubbed his right temple and grimaced. "It's unbelievable what some kids go through. Makes me grateful for growing up in good health."

They walked through the automatic doors and Nell waved the booklet. "We're both free at the moment. Want to grab something to drink? I'd like to show you this."

"Sure. Our upper levels preach to us about staying hydrated on call."

They veered down the narrow hallway to the snack area adjacent to the cafeteria, and after cascading ice and sweet tea into Styrofoam cups, they whipped out money and paid at the register.

Bob yanked a chair out from a small table while Nell put down the fair information. "The county fair started," she said, "and is going on this weekend. I haven't been in two years and would love a change of pace on Saturday after our call. It would be awesome to take in the animal and livestock exhibits and eat junk food. But better than that, there's a pet show, just like a judged dog show you watch on television. After seeing the announcement here, all I can think of is your new dog. Why don't you enter him?"

Bob scrunched up his eyes with doubt as she pointed directly to the page. "But real dog shows judge dog breed categories. Oliver is mostly an Australian Shepherd, but other breeds had a past influence in his making too."

"So he's a bastard or illegitimate?"

Bob laughed. "More like a love child from a variety of breeds." He stuck a straw through the cover of his drink and dropped his head to read a whole set of rules: "Only dogs on a leash can be accepted; pet show is only for amateurs; one handler per class; and you must be a resident of the county. First through fourth winners earn a ribbon, and first-place winners also receive cash and a trophy." He scanned the categories: sporting, working, herding, hound, terrier, and toy breeds. Oliver didn't officially fit any of those, but then he came to it … an actual class for "mixed breeds," for dogs not identified in the first seven classes.

Bob popped his head up. Nell waited in anticipation with a mischievous smile. "See, I told you," she said. "If you don't enter him for your own amusement, enter it for him. Your dog deserves the accolades if what you say about him is true."

Nell's enthusiasm was overwhelming and she had a point. Even if Oliver didn't win a fourth-place ribbon, he could mix and mingle with other dogs. Plus, what a deserved half day out for the two students after the first week of pediatrics.

"It says here registration on Saturday morning is between eleven and twelve," Bob said. "I hope we're out of the hospital bright and early after Friday night's call."

Linnell clasped her hands. "I can't wait to see this."

Annabel dragged her feet in the morning after getting up. It was a treat having Dustin stay over, one that she purposefully kept to a minimum. Besides, his house and his queen bed were much more comfortable for the two of them anyway.

"Don't go back to sleep," she said, leaning down and rubbing his bare shoulder.

"Wouldn't think of it." A text sounded on his phone and he grabbed it from the night stand. "My mom says the cheesecake last night was delicious."

"I'm glad, especially since you abandoned her last night."

"No I didn't." He tossed a pillow at her.

Oliver moved his head from one to the other, waiting to be included in whatever was coming next. Annabel stayed focused, finished dressing, and patted him on the head. "You're going to Bob's."

"Will he be there?" Dustin asked.

"Depends on what time the team does their morning rounds. If the attending shows up, it'll be a bit later. However, I have a key to his place, so Oliver gets dropped off no matter what." She pulled a key ring off a shelf and purposefully dangled it.

Dustin cringed, uneasy that she had another man's keys in her possession. Although he constantly pushed away the thought of a possible romantic tie between the two of them, he had not even given her a set of his own house keys.

During the car ride, Annabel pointed out directions to Bob's apartment complex. When they arrived, she spotted his Honda outside.

"Isn't he lucky?" Annabel commented and pointed. "He left the hospital already. But I better give Oliver a decent walk before I hand him over."

"I'll be happy to help out."

Annabel leashed Oliver and handed him over. As they passed the unoccupied pool in the common area, Dustin's instinct for directions and attention to detail was in full gear. Now he knew where his girlfriend's best male friend lived as well as what kind of car he drove.

Better yet, he was soon to come face-to-face with the guy. After a long time during which the two men came and went at different time frames in Annabel's life, as if the two of them were going round and round in a revolving door with Annabel in the middle, they were to meet in person. Surely he had the advantage; in addition, it was early in the morning, which certainly meant that he and Annabel had just spent the night together!

Annabel rapped on the door of Bob's ground-floor apartment while Oliver sat and Dustin made a mental note of the number on the door. He couldn't help it; it was what he did, he thought, justifying his thinking.

The door swung open and Bob's tired eyes grappled with what he saw. Could it be? Annabel's boyfriend and she brought him here? And at this time; on the way to pediatrics? Finally, he knew what Dustin looked like: good-looking, fit and muscular like a trained cop, not like a med student devoid of gym weight training. He stood transfixed in his crumpled sweats while Oliver slid inside between him and the door.

Dustin lingered behind Annabel's right shoulder as the door opened and he laid eyes on Bob Palmer. He did not know what to expect, but he categorized him quickly: a little younger and more "modern-looking" than himself; rich blue eyes females probably loved, tapered blonde hair, and a cheeriness underneath both the tiredness and surprise Dustin gathered from his expression.

"Wow!" Annabel said. "You're home early. My door key was poised and ready to insert, but I noticed your vehicle."

"We rounded without the attending, and my upper levels were bursting to go home." His eyes kept popping behind her as he realized why they were together at this time of the morning.

Annabel nodded. "Perfect. Now you'll have more time to spend with Oliver after you get some rest. And this is Dustin." She stepped to the side.

"Nice to meet you," Bob said. "Come in a minute."

Annabel went straight past him and put down Oliver's leash. Dustin extended his hand and the two men shook.

Bob spun around. "Annabel, I have something to show you. I can't wait to see what you think of the idea." With a grin on his face, he handed her the fair book, open to the pet show page.

She read the highlights. Dustin glanced around at Bob's apartment, grateful to not spot any pictures of him with Annabel.

"A dog show?"

"Yeah. Why don't we put Oliver in it?!"

"Really? Just like that?"

"Sure. Read the blurb for 'mixed breeds.' He qualifies for all the admission criteria."

Annabel quietly read the details. "This is hilarious. A trip to a county fair with our rescued dog. Who probably doesn't stand a chance to win anything, but it would be a riot to see him prance around a show ring." She peered over at Oliver, his head on the floor between his paws.

Bob beamed. "Then you're coming with us and Oliver?"

"Us?"

"Linnell from my team found out about this event. She needs a getaway from medicine too, so she wants to go."

"Okay," Annabel stammered. "I'll make sure to brush him

every day he's at my place to make sure his coat stays handsome."

Dustin cleared his throat. "Apparently, I'm like the two of you and have never been to a dog show."

Annabel took his hand. "Are you working on Saturday? Want to come?"

"Three to eleven all week. I wouldn't miss it for the world."

Dustin petted Oliver before they left. Perhaps there were more reasons why he wanted to go to the fair with them. Was he taking a vigilant stance in guarding Annabel from Bob? Was he intolerant of potential rivalry with the med student?

Bob thumped the fair schedule on the counter after Annabel and Dustin left and slumped into his oversized leather chair next to Oliver. How had he composed the quirky hostility he felt towards Dustin ... a "rival" who had the advantage over him with Annabel? He let out a sigh. What a mess. Now Saturday's event would be complicated. Annabel and Dustin were a "couple" and he would be in their presence when it would be difficult not to exhibit any jealousy.

CHAPTER 9

Annabel waved back at Dustin as he pulled away from the curb outside Dr. Gillespie and Dr. Clark's office. A wave of anticipation raced through her body as she thought of Saturday's plan. There did exist the potential in medical school to have some fun on the side and, with her usual due diligence, she needed to pay strict attention in the pediatric physician's office and study hard at home the next few days.

Ultimately, as with other rotations, she had to pass the rotation's written test and clinical evaluation. Dr. Gillespie proved difficult to read, however. Her impression so far was that he was a quiet, introverted man. What kind of clinical evaluations did he usually write for his students?

Annabel strode through the waiting room, where the early appointments dotted the corners of the room. Two children poked through a plastic toy box and dropped toys on the rug.

She entered the kitchenette and frowned. Everyone else beat her in and were well established eating their first donut.

"My function this morning was as the donut gofer," Becky said, "but Dr. Clark was the payee."

"Spoken like a true business manager," Dr. Clark said.

"Help yourself," Dr. Gillespie said to Annabel.

Stuart turned from the coffee pot. "Hopefully, there's a blueberry one left for Annabel."

"You've been paying attention," Annabel said. The open box proved to be half full, but she found what she wanted. "My morning was busy already, but nowhere was a blueberry donut included along the way. Thanks, Dr. Clark and Becky." She grabbed a cup of coffee like everyone else and hurried to eat and drink. Dr. Gillespie wiped his hands and wobbled towards the exam rooms.

She covered the other half of her donut and caught up to the squatty man as he thumbed through the patient's record.

"A well-baby visit," he said. "They make up a chunk of our practice. Based on recommendations by the American Academy of Pediatricians, we see babies about seven times in the first year of life following their first evaluation after they're born. We monitor an infant's growth and development, and measure the baby's length, weight, and head circumference, and record them on a growth chart. That information serves as a comparison to infants the same age and can alert us to any problems."

"How old is the baby we're going to see?"

He handed her the folder. "Four months old. Today, she's also due for a second dose of certain immunizations. Be aware the evaluation covers more than those measurements. I'll evaluate developmental milestones, do a psychosocial and behavioral assessment, and perform a physical exam." He began to raise his fist to knock on the door but paused. "What part of a physical exam is unique to this age group?"

Delighted that he was teaching her something, she unashamedly shrugged.

"The soft spots on a baby's head. In this patient, they should disappear within eight to fourteen months."

"Fontanels," Annabel said.

"Of course. I'll also make note of the baby's head shape. It should be rounding out nicely." He knocked and went straight in.

A woman stood alongside the exam table against the wall. She interacted with her daughter, Mandy, and also served as a protective barrier in case the baby slipped toward the edge.

"Hi, Dr. Gillespie." Mrs. Stanton broke out in a smile and glanced at Annabel.

"A new student is with me," he said. "Annabel Tilson."

Annabel nodded, and not sure where to stand, she sat down.

"Can you believe how big Mandy has grown since last time?!" Mrs. Stanton's eyes grew wide as a proud expression crossed her face. Without being asked, she began describing Mandy's behavior since her last visit and backed up into a chair at a right angle to Annabel. Dr. Gillespie's ears were already hooked up to his stethoscope, which rested on Mandy's chest.

Annabel saw intermittent parts of his exam as he stepped from right to left. He examined the baby's skull and then checked her eyes, ears, and mouth.

"Mandy switched over to formula without any problems," Mrs. Stanton went on, "but I miss breastfeeding her."

Dr. Gillespie palpated Mandy's abdomen and undid the plastic tab on her diaper. He pulled the diaper out from under her by holding her two legs up for a moment. He moved her hips and legs, apparently satisfied with their movement, and then held her little legs apart. After fixed on looking at her genitalia longer than a brief moment, he slipped something out of his pocket.

Annabel wondered if he noted an abnormality. He placed something over one eye. With a somewhat obstructed view, she realized it was a magnifying glass. She thought she heard low humming. It was George. It must be more of a habit of his than she thought.

The pediatrician separated Mandy's labia. That much she was sure of. Annabel wondered why she ever thought that the first significant exposure a female had to a very private exam from a doctor was as a teenager or a young woman having an OB/GYN pelvic exam. Obviously, this wasn't an internal pelvic exam, but it was as private as it gets.

Annabel diverted her eyes. At least she could focus on something else. Above the exam table hung a large print of an alphabet zoo. She stared at the "M" square with a friendly-looking picture of a monkey.

Dr. Gillespie's humming sped up and he pocketed his

magnifying glass before he fastened the baby's diaper back on. In the meantime, Mrs. Stanton used the free time for herself and rearranged and cleaned out her purse.

George turned around. "Annabel, stand here a moment."

Annabel rose and took a step to watch over the baby. Dr. Gillespie brought the growth curve chart over to Mrs. Stanton. "Mandy is coming along just fine. She's in the middle of growth and development for her age. My nurse will be back in to get a little blood so we can test Mandy's hemoglobin and she also needs her second doses of immunizations today. Schedule an appointment in two more months before leaving."

"Thanks, Dr. Gillespie."

Annabel followed George out the door and went back to the kitchenette while Dr. Gillespie finished recording the office visit. She grabbed the rest of her donut while wondering about the first year of life and what the standard of care was for well-baby visits. Opening her paperback, she checked the guidelines. The chapter said that babies should get a head-to-toe exam from the doctor at each visit — ears, eyes, mouth, skin, heart and lungs, abdomen, hips and legs, and genitalia. She closed the book and gulped down the last bite.

Toby Owens pranced up and down shoe aisles, one step behind his mother. They were there to select a new pair of sneakers for him in the nearby mall's shoe store and, after checking many price tags, she had more enthusiasm to buy him a no-name pair of sneakers than the Nike, Adidas, and Jordans on the end displays.

Mrs. Owens picked up a pair with a luster of silver and turned them over. Toby shook his head at her and grabbed the same style in a white with black accents.

"Try them on," she said.

He went to the bench and untied the laces to the pair he wore. As he took them off, he glanced at the soles. His mother had dragged him to the store with her because they were worn down. He'd worn them for almost a year; for school, for basketball, and the whole summer so far. Any kid would be ecstatic to be buying new ones; he just wished he didn't feel so achy. Not only achy, but a bit nauseous since he had eaten breakfast. No way was he was going to give up the opportunity for a new pair, however, so he went along with her shopping plan.

Toby shoved both feet into the sneakers, stood, and strode past his mother. He stopped at the mirror in the middle of the aisle and turned at forty-five degree angles. They would do fine, just fine; as a matter of fact, he liked them. No name brand, but stylish, and they hugged his feet like a baby in a blanket.

"How do they fit?" his mom asked.

"Pretty good. Can we buy them?"

"You betcha."

Relief swept over him. He wasn't fond of shopping and at least it didn't take too long to find something he liked. Sitting back down, he switched shoes and peered at the price tag. Expensive enough, but nothing like the name brand sneakers. He rose, which caused his nausea to ramp up. Stagnant food in his GI tract churned upward instead of downward.

Mrs. Owens walked away, but not in the direction he wanted. She went further to the back of the store and disappeared around the corner. In slow pursuit, he followed to find her stepping into the women's shoe section, where aisles were full of shoes of various heights, colors, and styles. His mother remained oblivious to him and intently stood in one spot looking high and low on the racks.

This would be purgatory, he thought. When she shopped, it was insane. She took forever and, plus, she could be damn picky. He glanced in the mirror as he headed past her. He had to admit that he looked pasty; even his freckles looked pale.

Toby kept walking to the bench to sit. He needed to be more comfortable to endure however long she would take. She was only two shoes further along in her quest than when he turned into the aisle, but she hesitated, holding one pair. With a nudge to a shoe she was wearing, it fell on the carpet, and she slipped on a low-heeled tan shoe.

He put his head lower towards his knees, but that didn't suppress the bile-like acid taste in his mouth. Looking around, he figured the rest rooms were located in the back corner of the store, so he went around another aisle and barely made it to the men's room. Without a soul inside, he flew to a stall and spewed forth his breakfast. His stomach felt like a washing machine spinning everything around and, after a second time, there was little left to heave up. He grabbed some toilet paper, wiped his mouth, and stood straight. Actually, now he felt a tad bit better. He headed to the sink and thought it over … whether or not to tell his mother. No sense in her making a big deal about it, he thought, so better not to say anything.

When he went back to the aisle, Mrs. Owens was at the end of the same aisle and she still didn't have a pair that she liked. He sat next to his box of sneakers and waited it out.

Annabel and Stuart peeled out of the pediatrician's office at lunch time, grateful that they didn't have to stay with their attendings for the next patients. Families had been heavy with questions during the morning visits and Dr. Gillespie and Dr. Clark were both behind.

"So how'd it go last night?" Stuart asked.

Annabel laughed to herself. He couldn't be referring to her sex with Dustin, but that was what she thought of first.

"Dustin's mom was really nice. I think we hit it off with no problems. And thanks to you, she enjoyed the blueberry cheesecake I bought her. Nice touch." They stepped off a curb and she added, "You're already a practiced psychologist, soon-to-be future psychiatrist."

Stuart glanced up and nodded. "Glad to help."

"So Bob survived his first night on pediatric call last night. They were pretty busy."

"Is he getting any studying done?"

"Less than we are."

"Did you have any interesting cases this morning?"

"Mostly well-baby checks," she said, frowning. "But later today, a three-year-old and her father who came in yesterday should return with a twenty-four-hour urine sample. I don't know what tree Dr. Gillespie is barking up with that one."

"Our attendings both seem knowledgeable and dedicated."

"I would have preferred working with Dr. Clark if I had a choice."

"Why?"

"I don't know. Maybe being in a room with a same sex doctor makes more sense for doing physical exams in such a private setting."

"But all exams are 'quote' private, and that shouldn't make a difference. Didn't mean anything, even when we did our OB hospital rotation, and think how intimate that was."

"Yeah, you're right."

They stopped in front of the restaurant and Stuart peered at the chalkboard on the sidewalk listing their lunch special. "What are you getting today?"

"Beats me. Let's get back quick, though. I'd like to study."

At 4 p.m., the buzz of sick children coughing and sneezing and the clatter of toys from the kids in for school physicals was down to a quiet calm. Annabel was bent over a book while Dr.

Gillespie was in his office talking to a family.

Becky came and hung out in the doorway. The bun in the back of her head was starting to unravel, so she un-speared a bobby pin and pierced it back through a clump of hair. "Mr. Miller is here from yesterday," she said, "and Dr. Gillespie asked if you could go get the urine sample he should've brought in. It goes to the lab."

"I'd be happy to." Annabel left her study materials and went to the front desk, where Stuart was leaning against the exit counter. "Let's go check out the toys," she said and laughed.

The students entered the kids' space. Legos were strewn on the carpet, a brown bear was face down, and a plastic doll was stuck in a dollhouse chimney. The children's books in a wire rack were mostly stacked neatly in a row. Next to them, little Stephanie sat on a yellow plastic chair and her legs swung back and forth.

"Hi, Mr. Miller," Annabel said and glanced at Stephie. "How are you today?"

"I'm okay. Daddy said I have to sit like a nice girl because we won't be here long."

"You are doing a fine job. This is my friend Stuart."

"Hi, Stephie," Stuart said. "You are wearing the prettiest shoes in here all day."

Annabel turned to Mr. Miller. "Were you successful obtaining Stephanie's urine for twenty-four hours?"

"My wife and I managed. Stephie's cooperation was easier to get than getting her to clean up her toys every night. We told her it was for the doctor. He would test her pee, which might help him understand the bump in her belly." He rolled his eyes at the mention of "pee."

Mr. Miller's muscular arms reached under his chair and he handed Annabel a bag with the container in it.

"Dr. Gillespie said we'll see you and Stephie on Friday after all the test results are back."

Mr. Miller rose. "Thanks, doc; see you then."

Stephie and Stuart had a "Chester the Chesapeake" paperback from the book stand; she pointed to a picture of the dog wearing sun glasses and giggled.

"Do you have a dog at home?" Stuart asked.

"Our dog is old, but we love him."

"He's young at heart, I'm sure."

"Bye," Mr. Miller said as they left. Stephie looked back and waved.

Stuart held the door while Annabel carried the urine sample. "I was close to her," Stuart said, "I couldn't help but notice the pallor of her conjunctivae. Does that have anything to do with her sickness?"

"I don't know. That and the lump in her belly. How do you tie those two signs and symptoms into one entity?"

"Or maybe they are two separate issues."

"Precisely. Medicine is like an investigative police work field."

"That explains it. There's so much in common with that field of work, that's why you get along with, and you're dating, a police officer."

CHAPTER 10

Toby sat on the front step of his house waiting for his friend Jonathon to show up with his mother. He admired the new sneakers his own mother had bought him earlier in the day. The urge to wear them had been too great and he had sprung them out of the box. That shopping excursion had cost him dearly, however, because his mother took no less than another hour to decide on not one pair of shoes for herself, but two. Then she dragged him to a coffee shop, where she lingered over a strong cup of caffeine. The smell of it practically made him puke again.

He didn't want to do much, but when Jonathon called after dinner wanting him to go to the movies, and didn't ask him to go play basketball, he decided it was better than hanging out in his room. His mother, however, had warned, "You're still having those muscle aches, so head home right after the show."

Two SUVs went down his narrow dead-end street. Next, Jonathon's mother came to a halt in a sedan wearing minor door damage. Toby pranced down the path past two Crepe Myrtles on either side and made sure to go around the back of the vehicle so he didn't sit on the side of the previous accident. He didn't trust the driving of his friend's mother anyway.

Lucy Harmon and Jonathon greeted Toby as he settled in the back seat. She turned around in the cul-de-sac and focused again on the public radio discussion about a local political race.

"Nice sneakers," Jonathon said. "When did you get them?"

"Today." Toby rolled his eyes. "A shopping excursion," he said softly.

"Still, you got something to show for it."

Toby nodded. "I don't feel like going this week, but I'll have to try them out on the basketball court."

"What do you mean? You don't want to play this whole week?"

"Don't tell my mom, but I threw up today. And my mom and

dad didn't see it before, but I scraped most of my dinner into the trash. After all, it'd be better to sit through a superhero movie tonight than have them confine me to my room."

"I hear ya. I won't say anything. I'll eat popcorn for both of us."

Toby stuck out his tongue with disgust and Jonathon giggled.

Lucy Harmon pulled into the multi-screen cinema complex and followed a line of cars with drivers looking for the best parking spaces. She glanced into the back mirror as she headed towards the front doors to let the boys out. "I'll be back outside here at nine thirty sharp to pick you both up …"

The sound of loud pop music grew louder and drowned out Mrs. Harmon's words as a four-by-four vehicle raced from the side street into the front lane of the entrance to the theatre. A loud metallic sound ensued as the Harmon's sedan careened from the impact of the high-set vehicle. As movie-goers jumped out of the way, their vehicle pitched and vibrated until it came to a stop halfway up the curb.

As the side of her car still seemed to moan, Lucy Harmon caught her breath and recovered from the surprise and shock of what happened. She realized she was probably not injured and immediately turned around to the boys.

Toby still had his right foot up on the console, where he'd been showing off his sneakers to Jonathon. But the crush to the right side of the car had shoved the front passenger seat. Toby held his leg, his face grimacing with pain. Her own son held his eyes wide open, and with a squeaky voice, said, "Mom?"

"You okay?" she asked.

"I think."

They both looked at Toby, knowing his leg was not unscathed.

The entrance of the movie theatre became an accident scene as two officers wrote up a report. Two EMS personnel deposited Toby on a stretcher and loaded him in the back of their ambulance.

"The cause of the accident is a twofer," one cop said to the other while putting his pen back on the clipboard. "Between that driver's reckless speeding in a crawl zone and that lady's lack of attention, we got ourselves real live action outside the theatre instead of on the broad screen."

They silenced as Mrs. Harmon walked over to say one last thing. "I called Toby's parents and they'll go straight to the ER, and a tow truck driver said it'll be twenty minutes before someone gets here."

"Another one is on the way for the other vehicle," the clipboard officer said. "Do either of you want to hop into that ambulance and get checked out in the ER?"

"We're good." Lucy walked over to the ambulance with Jonathon and said good-bye to Toby.

Toby had never been in an ambulance or an accident before, nor had he ever broken a bone. He guessed he was lucky to make it to eleven years without any significant medical problems. All these years, all his mother or father did was to bring him to Dr. Gillespie's for physicals and stupid stuff like a sore throat or spring allergies. Now it seemed like bad luck was crushing on top of his whole life. In one day, some kind of GI bug was making him sick and his leg just took the brunt of an accident and it screamed out in pain.

With the beginning of sixth grade imminent, he couldn't bear to consider what this all meant. He stared with a blank expression while a paramedic took his vital signs and the other one started the vehicle and pulled away from the scene. He disliked the bright lights inside, which spotlighted the medic as he began putting an IV in his forearm. After a substantial gulp, he held his breath as the catheter slid in.

The paramedic asked him more questions about his health history and made a big deal whether he was allergic to any medications. Soon the ambulance stopped and the two men wheeled him out and into more bright lights. Faces peered down at him as the stretcher stopped in a curtained cubicle.

The drapes flung open and Anne Owens burst in. She ripped her glasses off, rubbed tears away, and then stuck her glasses back on. "Oh my God!" she exclaimed. Toby's father, Jack Owens, ended up at the end of the stretcher while personnel hooked Toby up to monitors.

Toby's heart pounded in his chest with all the commotion. He heard the paramedics tell the doctors what happened and then his mother echoed his health history all over again. Someone stuck a needle into the IV port, and a few seconds later, the pain in his leg eased away like a calm after a storm. Next thing he knew, he was in a different, dark room, where an X-ray tech manipulated him on a table to snap the leg images that a doctor ordered.

Toby dozed off and woke in another quiet room near a large machine. "Toby, go back to sleep," a young woman said. "We're going to give you a ride into the CT scanner."

An orderly wheeled Toby back into his cubicle and Mr. and Mrs. Owens jumped out of their seats. A middle-aged man wearing a surgical hat and white coat followed close behind. "In all the commotion before, I'm not sure if I properly introduced myself. I'm Dr. Castle, the orthopedic surgeon on call tonight."

With enthusiasm for his job, he pushed the X-ray he carried

up on the view box. "With Toby's accident, and pain, tenderness, and bruising in that right leg," he said, "you both have probably assumed correctly that your son has suffered a broken leg." He pointed to the film. "His fibula, which is the outer, smaller bone of the lower leg, has a shaft fracture - a break right in the middle of the leg."

As her pupils dilated, Anne Owens rushed her hand up to her mouth. Toby vaguely listened but grasped the important points and formulated questions. No more basketball and would he be able to walk? What about school?

"Your son is very lucky that the larger bone next to it, the tibia, is not broken and that he does not have an open fracture." He glanced at both adults.

Jack Owens grimaced at the film. "Can you fix his break?"

"Yes, with a closed reduction. I can set the bone without surgery so that it will grow back together. However, the procedure is painful and I don't want to expose him to that, especially at his age. Better for all concerned if we take him to the OR for IV sedation or a general anesthetic. The anesthesiologists are experts at taking care of airways and sedation while I do my job."

Anne and Jack glanced at each other and nodded. "Whatever's best for our son," Anne said.

"Then I'll put him on the OR schedule. After a bone breaks, it is best to realign the ends as soon as possible, which will also lower the risk of infection in the bone." He nodded with encouragement. "We're admitting him to a room. It may be a few hours, so you all may be more comfortable waiting upstairs. After surgery, he'll go back to the same room until I decide about discharging him."

Thursday morning, Bob Palmer strolled into his pediatric

hospital team's office in fine spirits. After a day of rest after call, more studying under his belt, and time with Oliver, he was energized for a new day.

Linnell and his chief resident, Rick Mares, were slipping into their white jackets. Rick was an effective team leader and teacher and overly zealous about tackling his last year in residency. He had a pinched nose and a small chin and his long strides in the pediatric hallways were difficult to keep up with. He put his index finger on a piece of paper on the table and glanced at both students.

"We've been asked to do a consult this morning. Why don't one of you get started with it and report back to me while I start rounds with the other students?"

Bob guessed Nell would deliberately pretend to be thinking about it; she was skilled at deflecting work when she wanted.

"I'll do it," he said.

Rick handed him the piece of paper. "Patient's name is Toby Owens and he's eleven years old. Consult says he was in a car accident last evening and suffered a broken fibula. Dr. Castle did a closed reduction under anesthesia in the middle of the night and the kid just got back to his room an hour or two ago."

"So why does the ortho team want pediatrics involved?"

"Apparently, the kid already had a fever in the OR. Dr. Castle is being cautious and not sending him home today. There's always a chance for infection in a bone break and he would rather have us overseeing any medical concerns."

Bob stuck the paper in his pocket. "I'll go see him and talk to the family if they're there."

"The basics, Bob. An H&P and anything pertinent."

Bob slipped through the office door while Nell pretended to be studying the team's list of patients on the board. He left the pediatric floor and headed to the orthopedic wing, where there were no cartoon character pictures hanging in the hallways and no rooms designated for play therapy.

At the nurses' station, he stood aside and went through Toby's chart, which was up-to-date with his admission information and the surgeon's operative procedure note. He strolled into Room 532 where the youth was semi-inclined in the bed and focused on the drip, drip, drip of the IV fluids hanging from the nearby pole.

"Hi, Toby, I'm Dr. Palmer, a medical student in training. Sorry to see you laid up like this, but I'm glad you are not more injured from the car accident. Hopefully, Dr. Castle will have you back on your feet in no time."

Toby curled his lips with displeasure. "I don't ever want to be in an accident again. Totally scary. Anyway, a physical therapist is supposed to come by later today to show me how to walk with a cast and crutches."

"You'll do fine, especially since you're at the age when you're playing sports and are fit and growing. Are your parents around?"

"They went to eat. They stayed all night long."

"Can I ask you some questions? The orthopedic doctor asked my team to look over your medical care during your short stay in the hospital and I'll report back to my chief resident. We cover pediatric patients in the hospital."

Toby nodded and looked back up at the IV bag.

"I suspect they'll shut that off soon," Bob said. "Especially since you're probably famished and will be eating soon. Breakfast should be on the way."

"The nurse and I talked about that. I don't really want to eat because I feel nauseous."

"Maybe that's because of the anesthesia you had and it's still wearing off. They can give you a medication to alleviate that sensation."

"She did. Anyway, they don't want to ditch the fluids until my stomach settles down and I eat something."

"Maybe by lunch time, then. So, looking at your chart, it

appears like you've been healthy growing up. Do you have a regular pediatrician?"

"Yeah. Dr. Gillespie's my doctor. I just saw him this week for my school physical. Do you know him?"

"No. But my medical school friend is with him in his office for two weeks and I will be soon. I guess you're up to date with all your shots."

"Besides Dr. Gillespie, my mom makes sure of it."

"Super." Bob pulled his stethoscope off from around his neck and stepped up to the bed. "Mind if I examine you?"

"You don't need to stick your finger up my butt, do you?"

A woman's and man's voice approached the door, and Anne and Jack Owens entered. "Another doctor?" Anne asked.

Bob finished raising his eyebrows at Toby's remark and turned around. "I'm one of the medical students on the pediatric service. We're going to offer assistance to the orthopedic service in taking care of Toby."

"Good," Anne said. "Obviously, we're his parents."

"Toby was just telling me of his nausea after his surgery."

Mrs. Owens moved to the head of the bed beside her son. "Too bad because he's missing out on the hospital's scrambled eggs. He's not one to complain or look downtrodden; despite the broken leg, I assumed he would be better natured and well this morning."

"But I was already queasy yesterday before the doctor set my leg and I had anesthesia."

"What are you talking about? You mean after the accident, don't you?"

Toby avoided her eyes. "Kind of before."

"When before?"

"Like when we went shoe shopping."

Mrs. Owens right arm showed no restraint and she clunked him on the head. "Why didn't you tell me?"

"Anne," Jack said, "leave him alone. He's at that age where

he can't tell his mother everything."

Bob stayed out of the family squabble and pressed on with his short but diligent physical exam.

CHAPTER 11

Bob raced downstairs to catch up with rounds and found Rick Mares at the head of the team hurrying down the hallway. "We're finished, slow poke," Dr. Mares said. "We're going to the office to talk about all our patients and you can tell me about our consult."

Rick nodded for the last medical student in to close the door.

Nell squeezed into the couch, making a contiguous line of medical students as Rick pulled up a chair. "If I didn't know any better, you four look like green first-day medical students."

Bob wiggled in the upholstery. Nell was so close, their thighs and hips bumped alongside each other.

"We are still green to pediatrics," Nell offered. "We need your supervision and leadership." Her dark almond-shaped eyes darted to Bob as if she was buttering up their chief resident for all of them.

"Take your pediatrics rotation very seriously," Rick said. "Think of pediatricians as the gatekeepers to springing kids into healthy lifestyles for the rest of their adult lives. There is no other specialty that can impact the future of patients like peds. During their formative years, children are open to the suggestions of their doctor. Often the parents are the ones who steer kids the wrong way by setting bad examples. Also, a friendly, skilled, and nonjudgmental doctor is important, as is the way he or she performs a physical exam. Children are developing self-worth and are coming to grips with wanting privacy over their own bodies. The physical exam must be executed with sincerity and respect."

Rick wiped his brow and leaned forward. "So, Dr. Palmer, we'll start with you. I want you to follow Dr. Castle's patient now that you've seen him. Fill us in, please."

Wishing Nell would afford him more space, Bob wiggled his hand into his pocket and took out the index card on his new patient. "Toby Owens is an eleven-year-old male, status post an MVA late yesterday. He suffered a fractured fibula and Dr. Castle did a closed reduction in the OR early this morning. He has no allergies to medicines and no prior medical or surgical history. To the surprise of his mother in the room, he mentioned a bout of nausea and vomiting yesterday before the accident.

"On physical exam, he is a well-nourished young male who was a bit groggy from his night of events and anesthesia, and is wearing a cast on his right leg. His vital signs were normal except for a temperature that has been creeping up. A tech just took one while I was leaving and it was 101.2. His lungs and chest sounded fine and abdomen felt normal, as well as his ears and nose."

He checked the index card to make sure he had Toby's temperature correct and flipped it over.

"Dr. Crystal confirmed that he set the bone in the right position with an X-ray after the procedure. The little lab work ordered on his admission was normal."

"Thank you," Dr. Castle said. "Nice job and I'll jump in here. Obviously, the cast was put on to keep the bone in the correct position and to protect it while it heals. So, I want to say a word about post-operative fevers in children. A surprising fact is that they are a common occurrence after surgery. Testing for infectious sources of fever is not usually required, it can be costly, and most of the time not diagnostic.

"In addition, according to a recent large study, patients undergoing orthopedic surgeries have one of the highest incidences of postoperative fevers, but they were no more likely to have an infection. Even children who stayed in the intensive care unit or who suffered high fevers were more likely to undergo testing. And lo and behold, they were no more likely to have an identified infection. The vast majority of kids with an infectious source of fever had an identifiable risk factor, such as a urinary catheter or central venous catheter in place.

"All of this has told us that a post-op fever may be part of the body's expected inflammatory response after surgery. It is rarely due to an infection!"

Bob scrunched his eyebrows. "But my patient didn't undergo a real surgery."

"Exactly. Yet he had a bone break, which is still an insult to his body; there is always a risk of an infection in the bone. So it's confusing, and a good doctor must weigh the clinical picture. Toby's fever may be from an infectious etiology or a normal response. To compound the issue, he didn't feel well yesterday. But heck, he may have been swimming in a pool all morning and became dehydrated and nauseous."

Dr. Mares rose and wrote Toby's name to the team's list of patients on the wall board as Bob slightly moved his upper body to stick the index card back in his white jacket. Nell plucked it from his hand and slid her hand into his pocket and left the card. Her gesture surprised him, but he kept his expression neutral.

Rick turned around. "For sure, Dr. Castle is aware of literature surrounding post-orthopedic surgical fevers, yet he knows that we are the bible when it comes to children's medical care and the most recent information such as the study I just cited. He is being diligent in asking us to oversee Toby's hospitalization. I'll write a note on the chart to recommend a 'watch and wait' plan."

Annabel woke before her alarm clock startled her out of bed. She decided to get up, get ready, and use the time to study. It was Friday and she was headed into an entire weekend off when attending a county fair would be like stepping back in time and enjoying the sights and sounds she'd experienced as a kid. *Tomorrow's excursion*, she thought, *may prove to be the best ever*. Bringing Oliver and showing him off in a ring was going to be an absolute adventure. Whenever she took him on walks, everyone commented about how gorgeous he was. Would those remarks be substantiated by the judges of a dog show? Highly unlikely, but it was going to be fun anyway.

Since Bob was back on call for the night, she also had to retrieve Oliver later from his apartment so he could be walked. They were fortunate they didn't live on opposite ends of Cincinnati. She finished in the bathroom, opened the blinds to the front street, and poured a one-cup French vanilla brew. Before she sat down to read, she schemed about her travel arrangements for the day. She needed to use her own car; later, she would be transporting a dog and, other than service dogs, car transport services probably didn't allow them. She blocked out all extraneous thoughts other than Type 1 Diabetes for almost two hours and then scurried out the door with one more cup of coffee.

The techs and nursing staff were still preliminarily checking in patients and putting them in exam rooms. Dr. Clark cluttered up the kitchen doorway, so Annabel stopped and waited there for Dr. Gillespie's arrival.

"Don't be shy to tell me what you really think," Heather said. "How do you like pediatrics?"

"It's fine," Annabel answered truthfully. "Too early to tell if I will consider it as my specialty. At least Stuart and I are with seasoned pediatricians good at their jobs. Dr. Gillespie seems thorough with his history and physicals, succinct with shorter exams for patients with specific chief complaints."

Heather brought her hands up to her mouth. Her fingers were extended in thought. More like a prayer-like hand gesture, Annabel thought.

Dr. Clark turned, stepped inside, and poured a cup of coffee.

"Would you like one?"

"No thank you. I had two at home. I woke early and studied. It was marvelous." Anabel leaned against the counter. "What percentage of your patients are Type 1 diabetics?"

"You bring up a good question. Not as many as you would think. Yes, Type 1 is the juvenile diabetes that develops in childhood, but the peak age of diagnosis is more often made around fourteen years of age."

"Hmm. I didn't realize that."

"It's a terrible disease, one that I consider to take over a patient's lifestyle ... both Type 1 and Type 2. Of course, the prevalence of Type 2 is way higher at around nine percent of the adult population. The obesity epidemic in America doesn't help."

"Too many of the patients I helped take care of on internal medicine had diabetes. I ended up considering it a disease process, because it rarely presents in a patient just by itself."

"Yes. Hypertension, heart disease, eye problems, cognitive dysfunction," Dr. Clark added. "Ha, that's one reason I stayed out of internal medicine. Trying to take care of those diagnoses wore me down. There is something about children that makes my heart bleed a lot more, so I reach down into my gut to try and help them over and above what I would do for the adult population."

"Makes sense."

Stuart walked in, followed by Dr. Gillespie.

"I'm finishing the coffee before you two get here," Heather said. "They're still putting my patients in the back rooms, so I'll be happy to put on another pot."

Stuart stayed quiet and Dr. Gillespie was in his own world and not listening.

"Stuart never asks for a thing," Annabel said.

"Then I'll make a pot and hope that he'll sample some."

Becky poked her head in. "Feel free to wander back and start seeing patients," she prodded. "Mr. Miller is here with his daughter, Stephanie, in Room One."

"We're on, Dr. Tilson." Dr. Gillespie pointed a stubby finger towards the door and they left Dr. Clark brewing coffee. He went straight to his office and thumbed through the neat pile of lab work on his desk. Annabel waited by the door.

"Here we have it," he said, waving some papers. "Do you remember three-year old Stephie?"

"Yes. With raccoon eyes and a lump in her belly." Annabel took a deep breath. Maybe Dr. Gillespie had an answer to the little girl's symptoms; she could only hope that it was something minor or easily remedied.

At home, Annabel had done a meager online search of Stephie's symptoms after coming up negative with possibilities in her pediatric paperback. In addition, history had taught her "online" medicine was not the way to approach diagnosing real patients and real situations. Medical school was the proper way to learn what was needed.

She cocked her head. "Did the testing give you any answers?"

Dr. Gillespie cracked a smile, noting his success for being on the right track. "Let's go talk to Mr. Miller so I won't need to repeat everything."

Mr. Miller jumped up when they walked in, but Stephie remained next to him in a plastic chair, where her knees were bent into her chest.

"I brought my panda bear today," she said, extending the stuffed animal towards Annabel.

"She's beautiful, like you."

"There are panda cubs at the zoo, so Mommy bought me this one to take home."

Annabel squatted down, held her toy, and then gave it back. "Does he have a name?"

"Panda."

"He's easy to remember." She looked over at Dr. Gillespie, knowing she was digging into the time allotted for the office visit. However, she rationalized, if this little girl and her father were going to receive a bad diagnosis and prognosis, she should not go away remembering the entire appointment as being doom and gloom. No matter what, medicine should allow room or time for the little girl to continue what little girls do.

George Gillespie waited a moment. "Stephanie's urine that you collected over a twenty-four hour period was very important."

Mr. Miller continued standing, his muscular arms propped behind him on the examining table. He bit the inside of his lip. "Why?"

"I was looking for certain metabolic markers. Have you ever heard of catecholamines?"

"Sure. My wife and I split our care with Stephie. She works during the day, and later, I head to the gym. I'm a trainer and studied biology, so I know about the fight-or-flight response that stems from the catecholamines released in our body. Our sympathetic nervous system pumps up, increasing our heart rate. Sometimes I monitor my clients' heart rates so I don't overstress them. But that's all I know, doc. I don't remember what part of the body they come from."

"You understand their role, however. Better than starting from scratch."

"What does this all have to do with my daughter? Certainly children her age are not doing strenuous physical activity or exercise that would cause an outpouring of these 'metabolites,' as you call them."

Dr. Gillespie nodded. "As far as where they come from, catecholamines are hormones made by the adrenal glands, which are located in the abdomen, above the kidneys. There are three: epinephrine or adrenaline, norepinephrine, and dopamine. A urine test more accurately measures them than with a blood test. Unfortunately, two of the catecholamine metabolites called VMA and HVA, for short, are elevated in Stephanie's results."

Mr. Miller's concern grew and he shot a glance at his daughter. Annabel wasn't sure about the final diagnosis either.

"Stephanie's history, examination, and laboratory results are consistent with a neuroblastoma. It is not uncommon, Mr. Miller. It is the most prevalent solid tumor outside of the cranium in children." He waited, wanting the man to grasp the term "tumor," although not all tumors are malignant. He wanted Mr. Miller to ask the question.

"Tumor? What kind of tumor?"

"In all pediatric malignancies, neuroblastomas are the third most common, and almost all are diagnosed before the age of five." There. He said it, the word "malignancy."

The cast-iron man almost buckled at the knees. He clasped his hand over his mouth to hide his trembling lips. Stephie didn't understand why her father was all of a sudden sad and she stopped playing with her panda.

"My wife should be here. Spit it out. What do we have to look forward to?"

Annabel thought it best to distract Stephanie. She picked her up, sat on the chair, and put the child in her lap. Next, she whispered in her ear, "Does Panda like to dance?"

"A little bit. I'll show you." Stephie held the stuffed toy by both arms and popped him up and down on her lap.

Dr. Gillespie kept his voice low. "We should order imaging to ascertain the extent of the tumor and any impact on surrounding structures. We must stage the tumor, which will help guide our decision regarding any chemotherapy or radiation treatments along with surgical excision."

Mr. Miller grasped George's recommended plan, but he balked at the next, most important question.

"What are we talking here? What's her prognosis?" He tilted

over, close to George's ear. "Is there a chance she could die from this?"

Dr. Gillespie maintained his stoic expression. "Overall, the five-year survival rate is over ninety percent. However, for higher risk patients, the statistic reaches fifty percent."

Mr. Miller's mouth fell open. "Oh my God. I expected you to say something about twenty-five or fifty-year survival rates over ninety percent!"

The man quickly exited the room, as there was no containing the grief he felt and the sobbing that tried to rack his body. Dr. Gillespie followed and Annabel minded Stephanie. She had been close to a cancer patient before during internal medicine, but a young child was a different ball game.

She gave Stephanie a hug from behind. "I promise you I'm going to buy you another stuffed animal that can be best friends with Panda. How does that sound?"

A smile lit up her face. "I will give the present to my Daddy."

"You keep the new panda. We can get one for him too."

CHAPTER 12

Annabel opened the office door at the end of the day to a misty rain and low-lying clouds that floated above the taller buildings. Although her SUV was parked close, she made a quick dash, scooted in, and placed her things on the passenger seat. First order of business was to pick up Oliver from Bob's apartment since Bob was hauling an overnight call. She decided to dig in her backpack outside compartment for his key and put it in a cup holder.

Frustrated at the several zippered pouches, which mostly held extraneous items like extra pens and mints, she couldn't find the key. It was hard to suppress a smile sitting alone in the car, because all she could think of was Rowan Atkinson in *Rat Race*, exclaiming with bulging eyes to a baby on a plane, "The key! What did you do with the key?"

She suppressed the laughter. In essence, it was no fun not finding the key that she was supposed to have packed. She rolled her eyes at herself and grabbed her phone to text Bob.

"You can't believe what I did. Too stupid!"

There was no choice but to wait for his answer, but she still sat contemplating what to do next.

"I give up. What?" he finally responded.

"I forgot your key. I'm closer to the hospital than I am to my apartment. Can I drop by and steal yours?"

"Sure. And watch my team's real hospital pediatric medicine in action."

"I'll text when I arrive."

Annabel entered the back entrance to the hospital and scurried through the ER, where the pandemonium of the late day was palpable. She texted Bob at the elevator doors, which prompted a real call from him.

"Hey, come on up. My chief resident is going to conduct quick rounds soon, so I am set to hurriedly check on all my patients. I'm starting on the ortho ward, where I have one consult. Meet me there."

The doors opened and she got off on the fifth floor, where Bob was perched on the armrest of a lobby chair underneath a banner that stated "It's summer. Don't break your bones!" His index cards held him captive, so Annabel reached into her lab jacket, which she'd purposely left on, and pulled out the box of chocolate-covered blueberries she had stashed for him. She couldn't see his rich blue eyes yet, only his blonde locks. She had to admit they were a crowd pleaser in and of themselves.

"You plan on that, don't you?" she asked.

He jerked his head up. "Hey. Plan on what?"

She nodded above him.

"Ha! One medical problem in the last few months was enough, thank you. No broken bones for me." As he stood, he smiled, and then nodded towards the hallway.

"Walk with me."

"You're busy, I can tell, and the ER will most likely not give you a break tonight."

"It better. After all, we're going to the fair in the morning."

He dug in his pocket as they walked. Annabel did the same and they stopped outside Room 532, where the door was shut.

"We'll trade," Annabel said, handing him the box of chocolates. "A night on call will be blessed if you have these."

Bob's face lit up while he forked over the key. "Thanks. You can forget my apartment key any time."

"Except that stupid me is keeping Oliver waiting."

"He's lucky to have us. We're responsible dog owners."

The brown door popped open and a bespectacled woman came scurrying out. She ran straight into Bob and Annabel. "I guess all you students work together," Anne Owens said and looked specifically at Annabel. "Do you always come to the hospital after your medical student assignment in the pediatrician's office? I had no idea students have that much on their plates."

At first, Annabel couldn't place her. Then it came to her … a parent of one of Dr. Gillespie's patients that they'd seen earlier in the week. She wondered what she was doing here.

"Unlike my med student friend, Dr. Palmer, I won't be here long," Annabel responded.

Anne Owens nodded. "Toby is just not himself in there. I suppose that his leg fracture is a bigger deal than I thought."

"I'll check on him and my team will be around later," Bob said. "Are you leaving?"

"Yes, I'm heading home after being here all day. Plus, I need to eat a real dinner." She pushed her glasses up on the bridge of her nose and eyeballed each one of them.

"Will your husband be visiting Toby this evening?" Bob added.

"He'll be by in the morning, especially if Dr. Castle decides to discharge him. Jack owns and manages his own hardware store and, unfortunately, they stay open late on Friday night."

"Not a problem," Bob said.

"Good night, then." She turned and weaved her way past patients with crutches and wheelchairs.

Annabel faced Bob. "Leg fracture? Dr. Gillespie saw him on Monday for his school physical and gave him a clean bill of health."

"Last night, he was in the back seat of a car that got side-swept by another vehicle. Broke his fibula."

"What bad luck. Does your team or the orthopedic surgeon think it will jeopardize him starting school on time?"

"It really shouldn't. The only reason he's still here is that we're erring with caution to discharge him since he's running a fever, but I also don't know how his physical therapy went this afternoon."

Bob took a step. "I'm popping in. Come say hello."

The television volume was low in the room, set on an old Lassie black and white episode. Toby's eyes were at half-mast as he tried to maintain an attention span as good as the dog's.

"Toby," Bob said, "instead of one medical student visiting you, there are two."

The youth stirred and glanced over at Annabel.

"Remember me?" she asked. "At your pediatrician's office?"

Toby narrowed his eyes. "I do. Dr. Gillespie doesn't always have female medical students in the room with him. Mostly guys."

"That's changing. There are more women going into medicine."

"Like Dr. Clark. Recently, I suggested to my mom that she change me over to her as my doctor, but she said that would be tacky."

"Your mom knows best. Look at it this way. When you get older, you can pick and choose your own doctors."

Bob stood at the bottom of the bed and reread Toby's vital signs from the clipboard. "How did physical therapy go today?"

Toby shrugged his shoulders. "Not too good. She kidded me that I complained too much and that I was a slacker, but my legs were too tired to cooperate."

"She's the boss over that."

"Can I butt in?" Annabel asked.

Bob waved his hand forward and Annabel added, "You said 'legs.' I thought you only fractured one leg, which is enough. So what do you mean that your 'legs' were tired?"

"Like I told you the other day, my muscles are achy."

Annabel and Bob looked at each other and considered his statement. "Hmm," she mumbled. "You did."

"I'm going to listen to your chest in a minute," Bob said, "but I better walk Annabel to the door. She has to go mind our own Lassie, our own dog, at home."

"Oh, are you two married or something?"

Annabel tilted her head while Bob peeked over at her.

"Why? Do we look like a couple?" Bob's face lit up.

Annabel didn't wait for the boy's response. "Toby, nobody gets married during medical school!"

With indifference, Toby shrugged. "Well, if y'all take care of a dog together, I just thought …"

"It's okay," Bob said. "We understand. I'll be right back."

Annabel followed Bob to the hallway, a bit embarrassed about the marital remark. She realized that from his perspective, Toby's remark made sense. After all, how many households shared a dog between them?

"You're probably right," Bob said. "Not many students marry in medical school, but there are quite a few that tie the knot in residency." He searched her face.

Annabel sighed. At least the conversation had shifted to medical colleagues other than themselves. "I wonder how many of those work out in the long run." She glanced back to the room. "You know, with the aches he's been complaining about, maybe he's got some type of cold or early flu."

"It could be. Unfortunately, if it is, that will slow down the orthopedic agenda his surgeon has ordered for him."

She glanced at the key in the palm of her hand. "I better go give Oliver his walk before taking him home. To my place," she added with a smile. "Would you like to meet Oliver, Dustin, and me at eleven at the fairgrounds?"

"Sure, at the pet show registration table. I'll check with Nell if we're going to carpool or meet there. And please leave my key under the doormat."

"Sure thing. See you tomorrow morning." She turned while Bob went back into Toby's room. She hoped Bob would get some sleep on call or in the morning before showing up at the fair. Nell might be tired too, but if anyone was going to be up more during the night, she hoped it would be her and not Bob.

When Bob returned, he dangled his stethoscope from his hand, noticed the television was turned off, and that Toby's food tray was untouched. "You didn't finish your dinner, or I should say, you didn't even start it."

Toby gave him an imploring glance and waved his hand toward the emesis basin on the nightstand.

"Quick," Toby said and lurched his head forward just in time for Bob to propel the bucket in front of him.

Bob watched and waited, but what came up from Toby's gut wasn't much. It didn't surprise him, since he hadn't eaten anything. Bob handed him some tissues and removed the pan.

Toby wiped his lips and then narrowed his eyes. "Dr. Palmer, I'm getting a headache."

"Do you ever get headaches?"

"Not really."

"Let me examine you and then I'll ask my resident if we can order some labs on you.'

Bob checked Toby out even more thoroughly than his first H&P. His eyes, ears, and throat looked fine and his lungs sounded fine. His heart rate was up more than a resting heartrate.

"Chances are, you're dehydrated," Bob said. "We can also advise the orthopedic docs to restart the fluids you were receiving. I'm glad they kept that heplock in your hand."

Toby sighed. "For once in my life, I would like to start back to school. It would be better than being here." He clasped his hand over his forehead.

"I'm sorry you're having a rough time, Toby. We'll get you straightened out."

Bob hastened out the door. Dr. Mares was probably in the

ER. He needed to go pick his brain.

Annabel stuck her SUV into a tight spot at Bob's apartment complex and hurried. When she scurried down to his door and unlocked it, Oliver sat there with his big Australian Shepherd happy face.

"How come you can be so tolerant of us humans keeping you waiting to relieve yourself?" She glanced around as she grabbed his leash and didn't notice any accidental messes. "Oliver, you're such a sweetheart. Let's go."

They walked away from the apartments for a decent stroll and then decided to step back into the apartment and leave Bob a note. Oliver lapped from his water bowl as she scribbled on a piece of paper "Hope you got some sleep!" and left it on the counter.

The dog sniffed at his food bowl and looked up at her. "You poor thing. You're due for dinner and I kept you waiting on that too." She opened Bob's pantry, scooped out his dry food ration from the bag, and trickled the kibbles into his bowl. "Here you go." She gave him an emphatic "okay," and Oliver's muzzle lowered and began slurping up his meal.

Annabel stepped to Bob's oversized chair, nestled into the leather comfort, and plopped her legs on the ottoman. She had to laugh at how wonderful it felt, especially since Bob had bought secondhand furniture from a local on-line site.

Oliver ate every last morsel, came over to join her, and pushed his back against the chair. He nodded his head backwards towards her, demanding that she pet him. Her hand settled on his fur, and soon her fingers were immersed in his soft hair, rubbing with gentleness and love for the pet they had both taken into their lives.

It had been a hectic day, so she willingly welcomed the

peace and solitude. She closed her eyes and could not find the strength to reopen them.

In the ER, Bob clutched a handful of curtain and peered in the cubicle at Dr. Mares seeing a patient. Linnell stood on the other side of the stretcher, so he knew this was her admission to work up and follow. He was glad for that because, right now, he wanted to follow through with Toby Owens.

Rick looked over, stopped looking at a little boy's rash, and stepped outside the curtain.

"Sorry to barge in," Bob said.

"My team of medical students this time is very dependable. You would not have interrupted if you thought it wasn't important."

Bob felt like a higher-up on the totem pole because Rick Mares treated him like he was a resident. He wished all the chiefs treated their students like him.

"Dr. Mares, we thought Toby Owens was a straight-forward consult from the orthopedic department, but he may be turning out to be a quagmire."

"Tell me in medical terms, Dr. Palmer."

"Toby is still running a low fever and he's not eating. He vomited once or twice and continues to have muscle aches, which absolutely started earlier this week before his fracture. Annabel Tilson, a med student friend of mine, is rotating in the pediatrician's office and assured me of that because he went there for his school physical. Also, when I just saw him, he's complaining about a new onset headache."

"What do you suggest we do, Dr. Palmer?"

"First, I would order a full set of labs. Check his BUN and creatinine and see where he stands as far as hydration. Also a CBC. I did not see a note in the chart today mentioning the surgeon taking a look at the fracture site. Maybe they missed something after the closed fibular reduction; maybe there's an infection under his skin."

"Yes, order the labs and I'll co-sign your order. Don't write a note about your specific infection concern in the chart. Dr. Castle is thorough; he's on call tonight like us, so hunt him down and ask him about that. And, Dr. Palmer, don't be so surprised at my acknowledgment of your concern. You are beginning your fourth year of medical school, your residency specialty selection is imminent, and match day is right around the corner from that. You will be sharing more direct patient care sooner than you think."

Bob left with more purpose and mulled over Rick's words, which made him more confident. It had been months since he'd done his general surgery rotation and been near the OR, but it was the most likely place to find an on-call orthopedic surgeon on a Friday night.

The OR charge nurse at the desk pointed behind the OR doors. She read Bob's name tag. "If you must talk to Dr. Castle, Student Palmer, he's in Room 7."

Wanting to get his question answered, Bob changed into scrubs, donned a mask and bonnet, and entered the ortho room. Not being able to approach the sterile field, he lingered to the side. Anesthesia was busy at the head of the table, and there was a full group involved with the case.

"And who do we have here?" Dr. Castle asked from his peripheral vision.

"I'm Bob Palmer with pediatrics. Just a quick question. I've been writing medical students notes on Toby Owens. Not to be presumptuous, but he has a fever and some other vague flu-like symptoms. Just want to cross off the possibility of an infection at his fracture site."

"Looked at it myself today. All's well with his closed reduction and the area around it. Does Dr. Mares have you tied up right now? Want to watch an ORIF?"

"I haven't stood in on any ortho procedures and certainly not an open reduction and internal fixation. I'd love to. Until Dr. Mares calls me, of course."

A male adult patient was under anesthesia and his right leg was exposed between the sterile blue drapes. Bob gulped with the bloody mess and hardware, which made him think of an assembly line for parts in a car factory.

"This fellow's left tibia took the brunt of a free-for-all this afternoon at a soccer game. We use rods and plates, and metal screws and pins to fix the broken bone. A lot different than Toby's accident, where his fibula was set in a closed fashion."

Bob thought this was a lot more amazing than general surgery. He checked to absolutely make sure his beeper was on the waistline of his scrubs in case Dr. Mares needed him. During the next hour, he stood in awe of Dr. Castle's open reduction and internal fixation. It seemed like the chief resident and his first-year resident were also enjoying themselves; that their surgical efforts gave them utmost gratification by the end of the case. Their patient was brought out from under his anesthesia with hardware sticking out of his leg and on the way to a healed bone.

CHAPTER 13

Dustin Lowe absent-mindedly leaned against his desk with a cup of coffee instead of rolling out his chair and settling in front of the computer. The police station was busy for a three-to-eleven shift but not as hectic as a lot of typical Friday nights. Whoever had brewed the coffee made it extra strong and he was half bent on pouring it down the drain. He plucked his iPhone out of a snug shirt pocket, set it to the side of him, and tapped the screen. It came alive, but there was still no return text or call from Annabel.

Not hearing from her concerned him. After all, being a policeman made him highly alert for behaviors or routines that fell out of line from what was normal and expected. She had divulged her schedule to him for today because it had a bearing on the next morning's activity at the fair. She was still pulling days at the pediatrician's office, so she had no night-call duty, and she told him she had vowed to study. He had the impression that they would drive together to the dog show, but that had not been carved in stone.

He checked his outgoing texts and confirmed they were sent two hours apart. After a big frown, he began tapping his foot on the tile floor.

From the next desk, Sean watched his buddy with amusement and interest. "That foot beat you're doing," he said, "along with the agonizing monitoring of your phone, can't be related to work. It involves a woman. No other than Annabel Tilson."

Dustin swiped his phone off the top of the desk and stuck it back in his pocket. Hiding it away didn't change the fact that his partner readily understood his true thoughts, and he grinned over at Sean.

Sean leaned all the way back in his chair, which displayed

his potbelly. "I never prodded you after you failed to execute your proposal. Did you return the diamond or are you still keeping it in case you change your mind?"

"Of all things, my mother found it while she was visiting. Man, did that bring up a bunch of questions that I couldn't quite answer truthfully. I simply avoided telling her about my girlfriend's past with other men."

"I see. Soooo, the ring is still in your possession and maybe, just maybe, it will be on Annabel's finger one of these days?"

"Sean, don't ask me stuff I can't answer!"

Sean rose and stopped in front of Dustin. "Testy tonight?"

Dustin sighed. "Sorry. It's this muddy coffee."

Sean rolled his eyes. "I'm going to bring mine with me and follow up with the chief. It would do you some good to do the same. He signaled a minute ago through the window ... his 'Friday night trouble' hand signal."

Dustin pushed his chair in and beat Sean into the police chief's office as his boss thrust a piece of paper at him with a name and address. "Go check this out. A 911 call from a lady who says there's a disturbance next door, a possible domestic violence. She can't watch TV with all the screaming, yelling, and banging coming from her neighbor's place."

"And you," the chief said as Sean stepped in, "can go to an altercation at a sports bar a few blocks over. Have fun." Sean grabbed his paper as well and both men strutted out with a job to do.

Pressing his key fob, Dustin looked over the top of Sean's squad car. "I'll buzz you. Maybe we can meet for something to eat."

"I'm game, but you figured that already."

Dustin beat his colleague away from the station and took I-75 down to the south end of town. He turned west off the interstate and realized how close Annabel lived from the exit to the east.

He drove down the street, where aluminum and rubber garbage cans dotted the street. Some were snapped nicely shut and others were open, practically spilling their contents on the road. A mutt crossed the street and kept going.

To make sure, he glanced again at the address he was given, but as he pulled near and confirmed the address, which must be the "next-door neighbor," he knew he had pulled up to the correct household. He only then turned on his dark blue dash flashers.

Dustin scooted out and approached the front of a small house with porch lights on, a tidy front lawn, and a woman with her back to him, yelling at a man facing her.

"I'm telling you again," she hollered. "You're a stupid dumb shit, and you smell worse than that dumb-ass rotten pickled beer you drink." She wore denim shorts and a tucked-in T-shirt, and from the back, Dustin guessed her to be in her mid-thirties. She finally whirled around because his car lights could not be ignored.

As if giving up on the heated argument, she dropped her flailing arms. He continued paying strict attention. The man several feet from her gave testimony to her insult. He wavered on his feet, stumbled back to the front steps, and sat in an acceptable fashion.

He lessened the distance, all the while eyeing her clothes for the possibility of a weapon, and then did the same for the adult male on the front step. Standing between both of them, he introduced himself. "I'm Officer Lowe. You two are creating quite a disturbance."

"She started it," the male said.

Dustin waited. Often what people didn't say at a domestic situation was as important as what they did say. There was no evidence of physical abuse that he could tell; often, a woman would tell him when he arrived if she'd been hit, pushed, or punched.

"Of course I started it. What woman wouldn't if their lousy live-in boyfriend acted like you? The days you don't work, you get soused. You need a full-time real job. Not some redneck half-ass road worker thing."

"I should'a cracked that crappy flower vase you love with the pot I was holding when I had the chance."

"You know what? You need to leave."

"I'd be happy to." He scrunched his eyes at Dustin. "Officer, I'm leaving. But I promise to do it tomorrow. Gotta sleep off this beer."

Dustin glanced at the woman.

"Yeah, I guess so. He can sleep here one more night. We'll deal with it."

"You two have been disturbing the peace by carrying your argument into the front yard. How about we go inside? I need to get some names and assurances, and ask a few questions."

"Aren't you going to make him walk a straight line?"

"He isn't driving, ma'am."

"I'll show you a damn straight line." The man rose and weaved his way through the front door. The woman followed.

Dustin grabbed a clipboard from his vehicle and gave a wave to the neighbor next door who filed the complaint. "I'll be over in a few minutes."

Dustin filled in the blanks for his paperwork, and as the minutes ticked by, the couple became more restrained. When he left and visited the woman next door, she profusely thanked him for restoring the necessary peace on her street.

Dustin turned on the ignition and was about to pull away from the domestic dispute home, when he plucked out his iPhone. Annabel would be in bed by now, he figured; he needed to check again if she had left a text or voicemail after his earlier calls. He lit up the screen, only to find nothing back from her. He set his face in a deep frown. Especially since they had plans in the morning and he hadn't heard back from her, he grew more concerned.

His police instincts took hold and his idea was too easy. Her apartment house was a clean shot east over the interstate. He didn't think it out clearly, but it wouldn't hurt to drive by. If her light was out, she could be asleep. If lights were on, at least he would figure she was at home and not out in some kind of trouble. He could fit it right into his job before the next hour or two when his shift would finish.

He went straight, and on the other side of I-75, he turned up a one-way street and circled around to Annabel's road. He drove down her sleepy street at a slow pace. Going one way and looking ahead to the right, he saw the top floor was dark. He stopped out front just to be sure and stepped out of his car. Nothing but darkness up above, as well as the dark sky to the south over the Ohio River.

Well, if she's home, he thought, *her car should be around*. Usually, she procured a spot within a block or two of her street. He rode up and down to no avail and covered another two blocks north, east, and west for good measure. South of her street ended in highways and the Ohio, so he didn't need to worry about that direction. He stopped again in front of her place because he grappled with another new thought.

How could he even think of such a thing? What if she was over at her "good friend" Bob's place? Except for studying together, he pushed aside any reasoning why that might be. It would be better to simply rest his mind and check the guy's apartment complex parking lot for her car. After all, now he knew where Bob lived, which came in handy. If her car wasn't there, then any possible ideas he might harbor about them this night would be put to rest.

Dustin slowly accelerated, kept on side streets, and drove

north to Bob Palmer's neighborhood. When he arrived, and with the apartments looming in front of him, he circled around the street once to check the outer parking spots. Not finding her car, he rested more easily, and pulled into one of the entrances. He creeped behind the vehicles facing the fenced-in pool and braked suddenly.

His worst fear materialized. Next to his patrol car was a red Nissan SUV. In addition, he had no need to second guess the exact vehicle either. He was well aware of her license plate and the new bumper sticker she had stuck on, which announced "Dog on Board." There was no doubt he was staring at Annabel's car and that she was right now in Bob Palmer's apartment.

A flood of emotion swept over him. Yes, perhaps the possibility existed that this was some innocent "visit," but who was he kidding? Her not answering her texts and calls from him, and being here must attest to the fact that hanky-panky was going on between his girlfriend and Bob Palmer. He'd been denying how close they were to each other all along. Their relationship flooded over from the medical school rotation work that they were often doing side-by-side, straight into their personal lives.

Dustin felt like kicking himself. To think that he had almost proposed to her. Meeting that "boat" guy in his neighborhood restaurant one night who'd had a fling with her should have taught him something then and there!

Fortunately, no other vehicle crept into the lot, so he commiserated with himself silently in the car. At first, his index finger tapped the steering wheel in disbelief, but then he wrapped his hand around it and grasped it as hard as he could. He remained stunned, sad, and angry at the same time.

He startled as his phone rang. Any hope of a call from Annabel was dismissed as Sean's number lit up and he answered. "Hey," Dustin said.

"You free yet?"

"You could say that."

"You ready to snag a bite to eat?"

"I suppose."

"I'll take that as a yes. Meet you at our diner."

Sean beat his partner into the diner, so that when Dustin arrived, he sat in the booth facing away from the cash register and entrance. He wore an expression of pain and then pouted because he didn't sit in his favorite position.

Sean let out a sigh. "I'm thinking you want to eat by yourself."

"I'm sorry. I need to start my day all over again. What happened at the sports bar?"

"Two guys got into an altercation. They had some issues going on between them and, by accident, bumped into each other in a public place. Sparks were flying when I arrived and the beer they'd been drinking didn't help. What about you?"

"Beer involved in mine too. You know, a guy and a girl and a next-door neighbor wanting peace and quiet. Sometimes I feel like a baby-sitter when I go for those."

"Yeah, well, you know better because those situations can escalate."

"I hear you."

A waitress they weren't familiar with stopped. She flicked open a pad of paper and grinned. "Management told me sooner or later I would wait on cops. And here you are. I'm flattered. I love the police force. I want to join someday."

"Go for it," Sean said.

"Know what you want?"

"A straight bacon burger. Substitute chips for French fries."

She turned to Dustin.

"I'll take the same with coffee."

She left and Sean shifted his weight. "So spill it out. What now?"

Dustin wanted to bury his awful topic, yet Sean was great at giving advice. He bit the inside of his lip and treaded carefully. "I told you a bit earlier ... stuff with Annabel."

Sean squeezed a lemon into a glass of water and raised his eyebrows.

"I haven't mentioned it, but she has a close male medical school friend. They're thick as mud regarding their studies and clinical courses and sometimes have an ability to work symbiotically to solve medical problems."

"Besides all that clinical stuff, how 'tight' are they? Or the question really is, how would you be privy to how 'tight' they really are?"

Dustin scooted his hand into the front of his hair and then dropped it along his face. "Damn. That's the million-dollar question."

"Why are you so disturbed about this tonight?"

He slapped his phone on the table. "She's not answering my messages, even though we need to make arrangements for tomorrow morning. More importantly, she's not at home and her car is over at that male medical student's place."

"And you know this how?" Sean pried.

"Yeah, yeah, I admit it. I spied on her."

"Dustin, if you felt the need to spy on a girlfriend that you're considering marrying, that may be a bad sign. On the other hand, there may be a reasonable explanation for her car being there." He leaned into Dustin, ready to continue and tell his buddy the long fact of the matter.

"However," Sean began with one long breath, "Ms. Tilson may be hard pressed to provide you with a truthful answer as to why she was visiting her med school best guy friend on a Friday night while she ignores her boyfriend trying to get in touch with her."

CHAPTER 14

Aware of Oliver's moist nose poking at her hand, Annabel stirred. It was a wonderful new way of life for a dog to greet her after she woke up, but less so if he agitated her from her sleep. She started to make sense of the day as he swiped his wet tongue on the top of her hand.

With horror, she realized that she shouldn't be with Oliver and, secondarily, no way did she ever sleep in a semi-recumbent position in her bed. The sheet underneath her was no sheet. She patted the material ... definitely leather.

Annabel gasped out loud and blurted, "Oliver, oh no!" *What an idiot*, she thought. She'd fallen asleep at Bob's apartment. Obviously, she had been way overtired and overdue to crash for a solid long night, but it needed to be at her own place. She rose from the chair and hustled around the room and the kitchen in search of her cell phone.

"Oliver, I know you are ready for your walk. I'll take you before Bob gets home. But my phone. Oh geez, I left it in my car." She cut herself some slack because last night, when she entered his apartment, she had no reason to carry it. She stared at the dog, her dread ramping up even more. Dustin must be totally in the dark as far as their plans for the county fair. She never so much as gave him a text. She should have called him.

Annabel ran back to Bob's bathroom and, when she came out, Oliver darted to the apartment door as a knock sounded at the door. She grimaced and could hardly contain the anger she felt at herself; she never left last night, so she also never left the key outside for Bob. She swung open the door to find Bob with a question mark written all over his face.

Bob's expression smoothed into a smile. "You're giving our patient Toby more to think about as far as our relationship goes."

"My stupidity isn't funny. But I won't tell him if you don't."
Oliver shoved his way between them and greeted Bob.

"I'll grab his leash," Annabel said, "and I'll explain
everything."

Bob discarded his overnight backpack inside and Annabel
hooked Oliver to his leash. They stepped outside and headed to
the main sidewalk.

"I fed Oliver last night, sat on your cozy chair, and had no
awareness after that. I am so sorry, I didn't mean to squat at
your place like a homeless person. I must have been way too
tired."

"I find it amusing and my place is your place. Don't worry
about it."

"You're so sweet." She glanced over at him while Oliver
squatted. "Actually, you're home pretty early for after call."

"We hustled because the attending didn't show up for
rounds. I also told Dr. Mares that Nell and I were going to the
county fair this morning. He seemed quite supportive of
medical students doing something fun on their post-call day
besides sleeping and studying."

"You lucked out with your chief resident."

"I actually have massive news from last night." Bob took
Oliver's leash from Annabel as a mischievous smile crossed his
lips. "I stumbled on an illuminating realization."

What could it be, she wondered. Maybe something to do
with Nell? A spark of romance? "Are you going to stand there
with that silly grin or are you going to tell me?"

"I went back to the OR to touch base with Dr. Castle about
Toby Owens. Unlike Toby's closed procedure on his broken
leg, the orthopedic surgeon was doing an ORIF, an open
reduction and internal fixation. Playing soccer, his patient broke
his tibia."

Despite holding a dog's leash, Bob gesticulated with his
hands and his eyes grew wider. With a bounce to his step, they

began walking again.

"Anyway, I stayed until he finished. I mean, I could have gone to bed, but I stayed. I gave up sleeping in lieu of a surgical case!"

Annabel had never seen him so excited about anything in medicine before. "You must like putting things back together again. You found the case that stimulating?"

"I made up my mind!" He stopped short and faced her. "I'm going into orthopedic surgery."

"Wow. Congratulations on your middle-of-the-night epiphany. I'm happy for you. You seem one-hundred-percent sure."

They read each other's mind at the same time and, with no hesitation, they hugged. Oliver sat and cocked his head.

Annabel stepped back. "You'll need to start figuring out which schools have the best programs and where you want to apply for residency."

"But I often wonder what you will decide on too."

"I promise. You'll be the first to know."

They reached Bob's apartment and Annabel gritted her teeth. She needed to call Dustin.

"Why go home?" Bob asked. "We're both going to the fair, so why don't we go together? Maybe Dustin and Linnell can meet us there. By then, we must brush Oliver and make him handsome; make him shine and stand out."

"I should go home, Bob, and shower and change my clothes. I better rush."

"Okay. But take his brush from my counter and pack it with other things we may need for him. You'll do a better job with him when we get to the fair and I'll keep my arrangement with Nell."

"Congrats again. Now you're all set and don't need to worry about still having to make a decision about a specialty."

Bob and Oliver went inside and Annabel peeled away to her

car. She grabbed her iPhone right away and woke it up to find that last night Dustin had called and left text messages. From what she could make out, at first he seemed concerned about her whereabouts and why was she not getting back to him, but later, he seemed more miffed.

She took a minute to think through the situation. After taking a big breath, she called Dustin.

Dustin left the station and slid into bed by midnight, but it was all for naught. Sleep bordered between restless dreaming and fitful starts. At 2 a.m., he checked his iPhone to find no return message from Annabel. Why would she contact him? he scolded himself. She was most likely in a deep sleep after heavy sex with that medical student.

At 3 a.m., he woke again after a frightening REM sleep jolted his limbs so jarringly, he opened his eyes with a start. He dreamed he was in a long-term marriage and worked every weekend while his wife led a double life and had a family across the river in Kentucky. With further complexity, the other husband passed away, and he took in the children and adopted them as his own. The dream seemed so real that he called himself a fool for putting up with his wife and taking care of her kids.

At 6 a.m., he planted his feet on the bedroom floor and walked downstairs to the kitchen. Solar was in his cage and sluggishly bobbed his head. "What's your problem?"

"Lots," Dustin said, "but I can't trust you, Solar, with the information. You're such a blabbermouth." He opened the cage door and set fresh water inside and then worked on a pot of coffee.

"I'm a stupid fool, Solar. Remaining single has been fine up until now, so why did I consider rocking the boat? I'll tell you why. Because I'm crazy over Annabel Tilson. More than that, I've been in love with her.

"I guess our fair date no longer exists. I wish I had the wherewithal to figure out what to do, buddy. That must be part of being in love. I can't even make a logical decision; she clouds my brain cells despite doing me wrong."

Solar flew out of his cage and landed on the kitchen counter. He preened his wings for a minute while Dustin slipped a mug under the coffee dripping from the machine.

"Alexa, what's the temperature?" Solar asked.

"Right now, it's sixty-six degrees. Today, expect a high of seventy-eight degrees."

"Thanks, Solar and Alexa, but I don't need a weather forecast. I want a crystal ball to tell me what to do."

Dustin savored two cups of coffee and threw two pieces of bread in the toaster. He finally made up his mind. He had not attended a county fair in years; he was going to go no matter what his girlfriend and Bob Palmer were doing. Perhaps he could gawk at a ridiculously bizarre tractor pull, or a horse show with western saddles and cowboys. At the minimum, he'd be in the vicinity of a pet show, so if he wanted to watch it from the shadows, he could.

He had time, so he finished the toast, ate a banana, and jumped into the shower. By eight thirty, he appeared presentable in blue jeans and a denim shirt and, to his surprise, his cell phone rang.

"Dustin?"

"For months and months," he told Annabel, "I believed you owned a working cell phone."

"I can't tell you how sorry I am; I was going to call you about today and I fell asleep. Out cold like I had not slept in a month. My phone was not with me, so I never heard or saw your calls or texts."

Her voice sounded true and honest and sincere. He wanted

to give her the benefit of the doubt, but he vowed not to be irrational. When he attended high school and before his dad died a few years later, his father used to say, "Son, don't go through life letting people pull the wool over your eyes." His dad would roll over in his grave if he knew Dustin needed to apply that to the girl he almost proposed to.

Dustin sighed. He was dressed to go to the county fair. Maybe he could figure this out once and for all. It was a coward's way to make a final judgment via a telephone call.

"Do you still plan on going to the fair and enrolling Oliver in the show?"

"Yes, but if you are angry at me and don't want to come, I'll understand. However, I'd love for you to be there."

"Do you want me to pick you up?" He almost blurted out, "Should I pick you up at Bob's place?"

"That would be nice. Ten thirty okay?"

"I'll be there."

"I'll be outside on the stoop."

Annabel peered up at her favorite squirrel as he rustled about in his nest and she waited for Dustin. Next to her, she had a portable water bowl and bottle for Oliver as well as her own things in a canvas bag. They sat in the direction of the sun, unobscured by clouds. With no breeze, the temperature still made it perfect for an outdoor county fair. She thought it was the kind of day that kids would build memories on as they strolled through the livestock and agricultural exhibits eating a corn dog or a funnel cake.

Dustin's black Acura crept down the street, so she jumped up, stepped out between two parked cars, and slid into the front passenger seat.

"Good morning again," she said. "How did your shift go last

night?"

He studied her face for any indication of shame or guilt before taking his car out of park. He did not see any; she even seemed decompressed from tiredness or stress. But then again, Annabel Tilson always looked good or great, even after her hectic nights on call. He didn't know what to think about her appearance, but he knew what he knew concerning last night.

"A busy Friday night, but it could have been worse. How about you? I notice Oliver isn't with you, so you're not the one bringing him to the fair?"

Annabel slid her bag on the floor and shrugged. "Bob's bringing him. Today is his day with him, but we agreed I should be the one to prance him around the ring. I've never been to a real dog show, so I don't know what to expect."

"Don't sweat it. There must be significant differences between a professional dog show and an amateur one."

"That makes sense. You made me feel better already. When the time comes, will you take some pictures with my cell phone?"

"Be glad to."

"I don't see Solar in your car. You didn't bring him for the chance to amaze the judges and audience?"

"I was going to, but became too distracted this morning to get my act together and bring him."

Annabel squinted her eyes. "That's not like you. I apologize again for not getting back to you last night. I realized this morning how dreadfully tired I was, which is why I conked out so early." There was no way she would tell him that she accidentally fell asleep at Bob's.

"Shit happens," Dustin said, as if he was talking to Sean.

They soon pulled onto the street alongside the fairgrounds, where some lots were already filled to capacity. A man wearing a yellow vest directed them to a gravel road with a grass parking area off to the side. Dustin shut the engine and both of them headed to an entrance booth.

"What's your hurry?" he called out.

"You're right," she said and slowed down. "Registration began, but the show doesn't start until twelve."

They paid at the gate and asked for directions. As they strolled the aisles, the fast food vendors were hard at work and the smell of fried and grilled food filled the air.

"We'll have to indulge later," she said. "I could go for one of those chicken kabobs and a big fat old ice cream cone or a tall bag of kettle corn."

"A burger and double dipping into kettle corn would suit me just fine."

Annabel pointed. "The amusement park is way over on the other side. Any chance we could swing by and catch one of those rides?"

Dustin chuckled. "And lose what we eat? No thanks."

"That's the first time this morning you've loosened up, Dustin Lowe. That's worth more to me than jumping on that Ferris wheel ride in the skyline."

Dustin grinned as they came to the agricultural pavilion, a large, open-air building with aluminum benches and the ground covered with straw. Three people sat behind two folding tables and were taking the names of dogs and people in line. Annabel checked the short line and the people sitting with their dogs on the benches. Oliver, Bob, and Nell were not there yet, but Dustin tapped her elbow.

"They're coming this way," he said.

Bob walked Oliver and the dog tugged when he saw Annabel. "Sorry we're late," Bob said.

"Blame our tardiness on me," Nell said. "I wasn't ready when Bob showed up and I gave him a short tour of my place."

Dustin promised himself to listen attentively. At least now he was sure that this other medical student was a friend and she played no role in last night. After introductions, Annabel stood next in line.

"Who is your four-legged buddy and what's the name of the handler?" a friendly woman asked. She wore a red straw hat and her pen dangled between two fingers, poised to write.

"This is Oliver. I'm Annabel Tilson. There is a mixed breed group, isn't there?"

"Yes, sure is. It always has the most entries. Your Oliver looks like an Australian Shepherd, but not one hundred percent."

"You're right," Bob said. "We checked out his DNA."

"I enrolled both Annabel and Oliver. The competition will start soon." The woman peered again at Oliver with a wide smile and the group walked to an open bench in front of the show ring.

The color of the straw matched the primary colors of Oliver and, when he sat, the straw clung to his long hair and became one and the same with his coat. "Oh no," Annabel said. "Oliver will be littered with this stuff when it's his turn. Did you bring his brush?" She looked at Bob pleadingly.

Bob leaned over and plucked straw off Oliver's neck and glanced back at Annabel. "Yes. You left my place this morning without it."

Dustin's heart felt like someone kicked it. There ... he heard it ... and if he had had any doubt, it was gone. Bob was not in the hospital last night. They were together at his place. And Annabel had not said a word, keeping the information hidden from him, incriminating her that much more. His eyes fell on the dog because he couldn't look at either Annabel or Bob.

CHAPTER 15

The center filled up quickly as people signed in, and big and little, and furry, clipped, and short-haired dogs sat with their owners and family. A woman and her daughter sat next to them with a carriage. When she spread open the blanket, a bunny peered out and twitched his nose at Oliver, who wondered what kind of living thing it was.

Nell sat on the other side of Bob. Wearing sandals, leggings, and a loose top, she patted Oliver and tried tugging on his collar to bring him to her face, but he stayed too interested in the wide-eyed rabbit.

The red-hatted woman stepped in front of the tables. "We're kicking off our pet show with dogs, class one, sporting breeds. Please come forward with your dogs. Everyone walk around the ring in a large circle, and then come to a stop. Line up in a straight line and face us."

Coming from the sides of the pavilion and the aisles, all the dogs and handlers pranced in a large-looped circle. Annabel, Bob, and Nell watched setters, pointers, retrievers, and a Weimaraner walk exuberantly beside their humans. Dustin was fond of dogs, but his heart wasn't in it, for his heart was broken. If he didn't keep it in check, he could get very angry about the situation, but he told himself to be professional about a personal issue and act like he was an objective observer of a "situation" at work. Like the "domestic abuse" case he managed last night.

The man at the desk proved to be the official judge. He considered and calculated each dog's physical attributes and charm and stepped forward when they sat down in a line. Without showing any favoritism, he finished and spoke with the friendly lady. She announced the winners in reverse order. The winner was a yellow Labrador retriever.

"What grand dogs," Nell said to Bob. "Aren't you glad I

found out about this event? I can't think of a better way to spend the day away from medicine. We need to do things like this more often." Bob wore shorts, so she tapped his bare knee and flashed a smile.

"I'm curious about the herding breeds," Bob said, leaning more towards Annabel. "We can compare Oliver to pure-bred Australian Shepherds."

"Exactly. They're the fourth group." Annabel patted her hands together like an excited little kid.

The competition hosted the non-sporting and working breeds next and then the lady announced the herding group. Collies, regal German Shepherds, alert little Welsh Corgis, and Australian Shepherds came forward. "Those Aussies are handsome," Bob whispered to Annabel, "but not as gorgeous as our Oliver."

Annabel poked him. "We're a little bit prejudiced, don't you think?"

"Ha, you're right." Bob picked up the brush from between them. "I'll start de-strawing him and we'll touch up his coat again before they call his group." Bob leaned forward and brushed and brushed. The straw clung to Oliver like he was born with it.

In front of them, the judge had made his decision and they called the four winners again in reverse order. "And first place goes to Ripley, the Border Collie." The black dog with white markings cocked his head at his name and, for an amateurs' show, seemed to understand everything going on and what to expect.

Annabel's nervousness ramped up as the toy breeds and their handlers showed themselves off. A toy poodle with a giant attitude won first place.

Annabel stood up and pinned the paper with her entry number on her shirt. For the last time, she plucked the last stray pieces of straw off Oliver's neck.

"Next up are the mixed breeds," came the announcement.

"All the best to both of you," Dustin said.

"Knock 'em dead, you two," Bob said and patted Oliver's head. "Go strut your stuff."

Annabel started off with Oliver to her left, and since she was at the front, she led the pack as everyone else folded in behind her. She walked a quick pace around the side and straight past the judge and tables. The line behind her was longer than any of the previous categories. Handsome mixed dogs trotted along. One strutted hind legs like a German shepherd but had a face like a Corgi; another had a tail like an American Husky but a coat like an Irish Setter. As she closed in on the tail end of the line, it became one confluent circle of at least twenty dogs.

She made a full stop and became the first one to begin the stationary line-up. Oliver sat down without any prompting and they waited. The man came forward. He didn't give Annabel the time of day, but glued his eyes on Oliver and every dog next in line.

He spoke with the woman and she stepped forward. "Fourth place …"

Annabel held her breath, but the woman called someone else and presented them with their prize of a ribbon. She repeated the process and gave out another ribbon.

Phew, Annabel thought. The experience had been a blast but, for sure, they had not been serious about winning. The woman called second place and sure enough, Oliver didn't win. Annabel turned towards the bench where Bob, Dustin, and Nell watched, and she shrugged her shoulders and readied herself in her mind to walk over.

"And first place in the mixed breeds goes to number one hundred and thirty-one, Oliver with Annabel Tilson."

Annabel's jaw dropped and her eyes lit up like a Christmas tree. She was more shocked than if she scored higher than Stuart Schneider on a medical rotation test. Looking at the red-hatted lady, she pointed to herself. The woman nodded and waved her over. Applause ensued and she realized Oliver deserved the attention.

"You did it, boy!"

Oliver's happy face glanced up at her. The woman handed her the first-place prizes, a step up from second through fourth place. She placed a tall trophy in her hands with a metal dog statue on top, a blue ribbon, and five dollars.

"Thank you," Annabel said with as much pride as when she'd received her letter of acceptance to medical school.

At the bench, Bob locked eyes with Annabel. "We did it," he said as they gave each other a spontaneous hug. Then they both crouched down and loved on Oliver.

Dustin and Nell stole a glance at each other and Annabel stood back up.

"Congrats," Dustin said.

"Oliver deserved it!" She lowered her voice and nodded towards the ring. "I guess I better keep it down." The woman began announcing the novelty class for ducks, rabbits, and other less common pets. The lady nearby plucked her bunny out of the carriage.

"Is Oliver going to treat us to some junk food with the money he just won?" Nell asked.

"Ha," Bob said. "I think Annabel and I should put it towards his college education."

They sat petting Oliver while the novelty class and cat breed contest took place and the event officially finished. Dogs sniffed each other and tails wagged as everyone departed the pavilion.

"How about grabbing some food and strolling around for a while?" Annabel asked, addressing them all. They came to the asphalt path with a plethora of makeshift buildings and food vendors.

"Sounds good to me," Bob said.

"I could use a bite," Nell said, narrowing the space between her and Bob.

Annabel paused and turned to Dustin. His hair was not as curly as usual and the dimple in his chin was not highlighted above with his usual warm smile.

"What do you think?" Annabel asked.

Dustin turned sideways to talk to her. "Like you were last night, I'm overdue, overtired, and stressed from several days of working a late shift and not making up enough sleep during the day. Being out and about any more today is not a good idea for me. Sorry to say, but I'm backing out of any more adventure. I'm glad the three of you won. I'm sure Bob can take you home in his car."

Annabel stood motionless, stunned by his words. What he just said didn't fit the occasion. His words were like clouds raining over a child's birthday party. Her birthday party.

Dustin placed his hand on her arm for a moment, like reassuring her that she would be fine. Even if she knew what to say to him, she didn't have the opportunity. He stepped away, headed towards the entrance they came in before, and was gone.

"Should I order one that we can all share?" Bob's eyes studied a funnel cake stand and Nell answered.

"We can split one ourselves. Maybe Annabel and Dustin want something else."

Bob turned to Annabel for her response. Her eyebrows were furrowed, and a concerned expression had replaced her happiness. "Hey, our Oliver just won the top dog prize." He peeked behind and to both sides of her. "Where's Dustin?"

"He took off. He's been working too hard. Can you drop me off at my place on your way home?"

"Not a problem. Is everything okay?"

She hesitated. "As far as I know."

"Can I buy you a funnel cake?"

"I'll skip and eat a chicken kabob instead."

"I hope you give Oliver a morsel. He would love that."

She petted Oliver's forehead and his tail spun around in a circle. Not resisting his happy face, she crouched down and gave him a hug. After downing a few fast food items and checking out two exhibits, they made their way to Bob's car.

During the drive, Nell chatted away, but Bob glanced in the rearview mirror as much as he could. Annabel was not chipper like before the dog show, nor was she still excited about their win. He stopped the car next to her apartment and turned around. "If it's not a problem, I could leave Oliver with you today. After all, you and he had a special day."

"A deal is a deal. He stays with you today."

"Then for sure, take his trophy, his ribbon, and his five-dollar bill to display in your apartment."

"I can do that." She slid the items into her canvas bag and exited the car.

Annabel hung Oliver's blue ribbon on his trophy and placed them on the windowsill behind her desk. She stuffed his five dollars into an empty cookie jar. She had the rest of the day to contend with, with plenty of time to study. Even better, she was well rested and ready to absorb pediatric subjects she had not yet studied.

After kicking off her shoes and getting an iced tea, Annabel folded a leg under her and got comfortable on her desk chair. She first tackled salmonella food poisoning, for which the literature fiercely recommended frequent hand-washing practices for children, particularly at group functions and public places. Then she turned to head trauma, an awful subject to think about in the pediatric population. At least she had a fine grasp of that area, such as subdural hematomas, because of her neurosurgeon father who, over the years, told the family a thing or two about head injuries and intracranial pressure.

Several hours ticked by. Her glass was empty and she stretched her legs. That was solid studying this afternoon, she thought, and she pulled it off not by happenstance. She had deliberately pushed Dustin to the back of her mind because something was just not right with him. Winning the mixed breed event with Oliver and Bob was special to her, but Dustin seemed to be an uninvolved spectator and barely acted like they were boyfriend and girlfriend.

And he left in a strange way.

Annabel rose and padded to the kitchen. She glanced at her iPhone to find no messages. She perched herself on a stool and peeled a banana. What was she thinking? If she were in his shoes, she'd be annoyed at her too. She didn't mean to fall asleep early last night, but the way it all evolved was not right. She did care about him and needed to take credit for being inconsiderate, maybe even flippant, about acknowledging his side of the issue. He was a good man; underneath it all, she had a deep sense, an enlightenment, that she'd done him wrong by not contacting him back. In her defense, however, she felt he was taking her bad social behavior much more critically than what it deserved. Over the course of the next few days, she figured she would know by his actions, or lack of actions, one way or another.

Although Linnell made innuendos to Bob that they spend more time together the rest of the day, Bob dropped her off at her place. He wanted time to study and wanted to appreciate a few dog walks and bonding with Oliver.

After he pulled into his apartment complex, he half trotted

on a walk with Oliver. The last twenty-four hours were so eventful, his blood acted like it had been spit through a purifier and sent happy hormones to his brain. When they burst into his apartment, he gave Oliver a new rawhide bone for his win and then studied for a few hours. As he grew tired early after having no nap, he nonetheless began a preliminary search for orthopedic residencies.

Then it dawned on him. He and Annabel might sustain a long-term friendship, but with different residency programs in different cities or entire opposite ends of the country, that would more than likely terminate his hope to get together with her. He might always love her, but any chance of them getting hitched as boyfriend and girlfriend in the near future would die and be buried.

He realized starting a residency somewhere would mean the end of seeing her on a regular basis. He admonished himself for the next selfish thought. When she left for a residency program, that would more than likely end her present relationship with Dustin Lowe. He was sure that would not be to her and the policeman's liking.

In essence, both men would most likely lose her for good.

CHAPTER 16

Sunday morning, Bob got up extra early, put on a pair of trousers and a shirt, and enthusiastically gave Oliver a walk. He only needed to go into the hospital for morning rounds because the on-call team for the day would cover all pediatric patients for the rest of the day after each team made their own rounds.

The apartment complex was quiet with only one other dog walker, and Oliver made his mark on shrubs and trees before Bob went back inside and fed him.

"You mind the apartment, Oliver. I'll see you later."

He made his exit and individually saw each of his patients on the pediatric ward, leaving his consult for last. He liked to leave extra time for Toby; he hated for the youth to be strapped with his flu-like symptoms while he was nursing a leg fracture and a cast. Any eleven-year-old kid concerned about not starting back to school on time had his attention and respect. Bob thought back to that age, at which time he was in no way conscientious. In fact, he remembered, once in a while, he faked symptoms to his mother to avoid going to school.

Bob stopped first at the nurses' station and read all the orthopedic and nurses' notes on Toby's chart since yesterday morning when he left post-call. The ortho team mainly reported on their patient's orthopedic progress and slow going with physical therapy. The nurses' notes were dotted with additions of "still complaining of a headache and Tylenol given," and "Phenergan was ordered for nausea and vomiting."

A nurse passed him and noticed him with Toby's chart. "You pediatricians need to do something about him."

Bob frowned and nodded. "You know how medical care slows down on the weekend, but I'll see to it."

She smiled and added a big "thank you."

Bob entered Toby's room and opened the blinds to halfway.

The morning light aimed at the floor and made the room less dreary.

Toby's arm moved to the edge of the bed and he groaned. "Don't open them any more. The light is bothering my eyes."

"Good morning, young man." Bob tweaked the blinds a little less open.

"Dr. Palmer, I'm glad someone came to visit me."

"Nurses were in during the night, Toby."

"That doesn't count. I was asleep. Now it really matters because my neck aches."

Bob glanced at the new set of vital signs on the bedside chart and, although Toby still had a low-grade fever, he figured it was dampened by the Tylenol he was getting for his aches and pains.

"What do you mean, you have a neck ache?"

Toby used his hands to scoot up, trailing his casted leg with him. He turned his head from side to side. "My neck is stiff as a board. Aren't old people the only ones who get stiff necks from sleeping funny?"

Bob stepped over. "I wish there was some truth to that, Toby. How about a headache? Is it still there?"

"Yeah, but they keep giving me pain and headache medicine. My muscles ache too."

"Did you eat anything last night?"

Toby started to shake his head but grimaced. "No. The nurse told me at least I was getting something to drink in my IV."

After examining him, he assured Toby the team would stop by, and scurried to the office, where his teammates had assembled.

"I just told everyone your dog won yesterday," Nell said.

"Great job," Dr. Mares said. "I'm proud of the way you two spent some time out of the hospital. Of course, give your dog an extra biscuit for his accomplishment."

"I certainly will."

"Let's huddle around the table and run through our patients' lists and then do quick bedside visits. Afterwards, students are ordered to go home and study." Rick cracked a smile.

The chief resident listened to each student report on their patients as they drained a pot of coffee. As the last order of business, Rick asked, "What about our consult, Bob?"

"Toby Owens' vital signs have statistically not changed. Since yesterday, he continues to have nausea, little vomiting, muscle aches, a headache, and now a stiff neck."

"A stiff neck?" Bob had Rick's undivided attention.

"Yes. I may be a medical student with a lot to learn, Dr. Mares, but these symptoms are screaming out to me that Toby may have meningitis."

"A smart presumptive diagnosis, Dr. Palmer. What would be the next step?"

"A lumbar puncture."

"You need to finish your train of thought. Why?"

"To take a sample of the fluid that surrounds the brain and analyze it to confirm our suspicions."

"The fluid may or may not be diagnostic of the type of meningitis, if he does indeed have it, but it is absolutely needed for diagnosis. Also, his other lab work has proved not to be enlightening.

"All right, then. Are you all tanked up with enough coffee?"

All four students rose and nodded. They would skip more coffee if it meant rounding and going home sooner.

At the nurses' station, the students rounded up their patients' charts. Bob finished quickly and decided to text Annabel. Even if she wasn't up yet, she'd get his text later in the morning.

"Good morning, dog winner. Guess what? Toby Owens may have meningitis. We may do a lumbar puncture on him."

As they walked to the far end of the hallway, his phone flashed a return message. *"Darn. Poor kid. Would your chief resident mind if I was there too?"*

"Are you crazy? On a day off?"

"Not crazy. I've been following him from the beginning. It makes sense and I'm interested."

"Anybody ever tell you how dedicated you are?"

"You just did."

Bob texted an emoji smile. *"If we're going to do the spinal tap, I'll ask Rick."*

Annabel countered with a happy emoji as well and waited. She was up and going through her second cup of hazelnut coffee. Bob's Keurig machine present to her continued to be used daily.

At last the team stood in Bob's patient's room and, after evaluating him, Rick said, "I'm giving your mom and dad a call, Toby. We would like to do a procedure, one which may give us important information and be diagnostic."

"What procedure?" Toby asked. He had a bad feeling about this.

Through experience, if Rick could help it, he had learned not to tell all patients the names of procedures. The technical terms only served to scare younger ones more than needed. He, however, did tell parents the name, description, risks, and other information of any procedure he performed on their child.

"We want to insert a needle between the bones in your spine and take out a small amount of fluid for analysis. I'll go talk to your parents about it and be back."

Rick turned to Bob. "You can stay with Toby for a few minutes. The rest of the team, go write your progress notes and be back bright and early tomorrow."

"Dr. Mares," Bob added tentatively, "Annabel Tilson would like to be here. Is that okay with you and Toby?"

Rick's eyebrows rose. "Fine with me." Toby nodded an okay.

Bob sat next to Toby's bed and texted Annabel. *"You're welcome to come. Dr. Mares is getting parental permission, which shouldn't be a problem."*

"I'm on my way."

Toby's forearm trembled. For the last few days, he had done everything possible to tolerate his situation, not complain, and act like a grown-up person. Which he wasn't. Missing the familiarity of his own bed and room, he was reduced to sleeping in a hospital. Nights were scary and uncomfortable and laden with strange sounds and strange people in the hallways. Most were hospital employees, but they came and went like he was some object of their eight-hour shift.

Besides the bulky cast on his leg and the futile attempts at physical therapy, he felt like crap and it was only getting worse. And within the last few minutes, he was stupefied about what Dr. Mares had said, but now, as he began processing it, he started to freak out. It was bad enough when the technicians were drawing blood from him and when the nurse had slipped in an IV, but the fear of having a needle stuck into his back was terrifying.

Bob remained silent. At least someone was with him, Toby thought, but the youth could no longer contain his worry over what would happen to him. His head and neck hurt and he wished he were home and buying school supplies like everyone else his age. No longer able to hold back his emotion, he started to cry.

Bob leaned in, propping his elbows on the bed. He patted the boy's forearm. "Toby, what? What is it?"

"I'm scared. I want to go home."

"I promise, we'll take extra special care of you. First, we must find out what's wrong, fix it, and then send you home. We must."

"I don't like needles."

"I hear you. But this may be easier than you think. As

opposed to the other needles you've had so far, Dr. Mares can use a baby needle to put some numbing medicine under your skin before he puts in the next needle to draw the fluid he needs. It'll be a snap and Annabel and I will be with you the whole time."

Toby grabbed a handful of his bed sheet and wiped his eyes. "Here," Bob said, and handed him a tissue from the nightstand. The youth took a deep breath and his sobbing lessened. The more they waited for Rick and Annabel to appear, the more Toby calmed down.

Annabel slipped in the door with the spinal tap tray and other medical necessities for Toby's procedure

"Hi, you two," she said. "Dr. Mares is waiting for your parents to arrive, Toby. They want to wait in the lounge while you have your procedure. And Dr. Mares asked me, since I was headed this way, to tell you something." She looked at Bob, who nodded and placed the kit on the tray table.

"Do you mind if I tell him, Bob?"

"Absolutely not."

"Dr. Mares and Dr. Palmer believe you have meningitis." She paused to let the word sink in. Maybe or maybe not, Toby had heard the word before.

"That sounds bad. What does that mean?"

"Meningitis is an inflammation of the membranes that enclose your brain and spinal cord, inside your skull and the bony canal in your back."

"Which is caused by an infection, Toby," Bob added.

"Oh. So some germ is multiplying inside my head? That's dangerous, isn't it?"

"We're right here with you," Bob said, "and we'll get to the bottom of what is causing it and what we can do about it. We want to nip it in the bud. How does that sound?"

"You better." Toby kept from crying. He liked the fact that both medical students he liked and trusted were explaining it to him so that he could understand.

"One more thing," Annabel added, "because the team thinks meningitis is the problem, but they don't know what kind, they are going to restrict the number of visitors and you'll be quarantined."

"What do you mean?"

"You will be isolated from other patients or many visitors," Annabel said.

"So that other people don't accidentally catch what you may have," Bob said.

When Dr. Mares came in, he began to set up for the procedure. Toby's leg in a cast didn't help matters, but with Annabel and Bob helping out, he managed to drain Toby's cerebrospinal fluid into the necessary vials and hastened it off to the laboratory himself, ordering Bob and Annabel to leave and possibly go study.

"You must be thinking what I'm thinking," Bob said after both students stepped out from the hospital's revolving doors to the sidewalk.

She glanced over. "I'm wondering if he has a bacterial meningitis, in which case Toby Owens could possibly die."

"Haven't we learned that with a bacterial meningitis, it's onset would be quicker? In other words, he had symptoms a few days. If it were bacterial, he'd be much sicker already."

"But we can't exclude the possibility. Not everything is textbook. And what about the Powassan virus that the national park ranger had on our internal medicine rotation?"

"Possible but unlikely, since it's really, really rare. Chances of two cases here in the area in such a short time would be crazy."

"True. Let's not jump to conclusions until the results of the spinal tap are back."

"I'm going to walk Oliver when I get home. Want to come? Then I'm going to study; maybe you'd like to join me. After all, we're both studying the same stuff. Unless, of course, you're spending part of the day with Dustin."

"You're on." She ignored the inclusion of Dustin in the conversation.

Annabel pushed aside her sandwich plate with leftover kettle chips and picked her head up from a book while Bob made a chart inside a notebook. They methodically covered all the types of bacterial meningitis they could lay their hands on outside Pete's Café. Oliver basked in the sunshine, tethered to the fence beside their table.

"This is the perfect day to do this," Bob remarked. "Chances are, autumn will be here before we know it and this will be our last opportunity."

"It is nice, isn't it?"

"This is the perfect weekend."

Annabel glanced down. *Maybe not that perfect,* she thought.

"Let's look at your list of the most prevalent types of bacterial meningitis and then categorize them in the pediatric population."

Bob read the five most common and Annabel dived into the specific incidence in young age populations. They rewrote what they came up with.

"Group B strep, strep pneumonia, Listeria monocytogenes, and E. coli are most prevalent in newborns," Annabel said.

"So we'll skip the newborn list since we're dealing with an

eleven-year-old. And babies and kids are again Group B strep, strep pneumonia and, in addition, Neisseria meningitides, and Hemophilus influenza type b."

"Teens and adults are again Neisseria meningitides and strep pneumonia."

"And they are still extremely prevalent in the older adult population, but we don't need that information. In all probability, we can discount E. coli and Listeria monocytogenes in the newborn list too."

Annabel drew an asterisk star beside what they had left. "If Toby has a bacterial etiology, then we're down to primarily strep pneumonia, and Neisseria meningitides, and secondarily, H flu, and Group B strep."

Oliver stood up and wagged his tail while sticking his head through the fence. "I can't resist him," Bob said. He plucked a residual piece of burger from his plate, leaned over, and opened his hand to the dog. The meat disappeared and Oliver continued to lick Bob's hand.

Annabel laughed. "You asked for it."

"That I did." She handed him a napkin and he wiped off his hand.

"We need to go back to an important point, one which we talk about all the time, and that is risk factors. What are Toby's risk factors for any of these infections?"

"Says here," Bob said, "babies are at a huge disadvantage as far as a risk for bacterial meningitis, but more important to us would be if Toby had been involved in a crowded community setting."

"Such as school, especially boarding at a college campus. But school hasn't started for him yet. However, did you miss something in his history?"

"Good point. I have to go back over his history. What if he went to some huge concert at a large venue in the last month? Or stayed at a summer camp for a week?"

"Exactly. Then there are medical procedures and conditions that would make a patient more likely to acquire it, but I don't think his leg fracture or cast would be related, do you?"

Bob shook his head and peered at her textbook. "Last one is travel. Going somewhere a person doesn't normally go, especially abroad."

"Did you get any history about that? Actually ..." Annabel stared across at Oliver and narrowed her eyes. "It's not exactly like the family went to Belize, but Toby wore a Florida T-shirt the day he came into Dr. Gillespie's office." She gasped and put her hand to her mouth. "And his mother mentioned something."

"What?"

"Toby mentioned muscle aches to Dr. Gillespie. His mother said she knew he didn't want to miss any sports activities during the last few days of summer vacation but, at home, he had mentioned muscle pains since they returned from their Florida vacation."

The two students pondered it over. "I agree," Bob said. "Florida isn't exactly exotic. But who knows what went on down there."

CHAPTER 17

Heather Clark couldn't decide on which miniature scone to select from the platter. "Becky, you're too kind to start our Monday morning with these. The problem is which flavor to sample.

"You're welcome, Dr. Clark. Don't 'sample.' Just eat them whole. Making y'all happy right off the bat makes my job easier."

Popping one in her mouth, Heather's already full cheek puffed out even more. She chewed quickly as she focused on pouring a cup of coffee.

"I'm trying a blueberry," Annabel said."That was predictable," Stuart said after he gulped down one with cranberries and nuts.

"Sometimes I am. We've been spending too much time on rotations together, Stuart. But I bet you would not have guessed this. Oliver won the mixed-breed dog show on Saturday. I had so much fun prancing him around the ring and what everyone kept saying about him turned out to be true. He's a beautiful dog. Now Bob and I have bragging rights."

"No way!" Heather spun around. "My sister shows dogs and hasn't even won a ribbon in two years."

Annabel chased down a bite with coffee. "Maybe it was beginner's luck."

"Did you and Bob celebrate or did you and Dustin celebrate?" Stuart asked.

"Dustin went home to de-stress from his work week, and Bob, Nell, and I ate junk food at the fair. Bob and I even ate at Pete's and studied yesterday. So you could say we mixed business with pleasure all weekend. However, another striking event occurred this weekend too."

Stuart gave her a long look as he held a second scone.

"Bob made up his mind. He was on call Friday night and popped into an orthopedic case because he needed to talk to the surgeon about a consult. Engrossed, he was able to watch an ORIF. Fell in love. Just like that. He says he's going into orthopedics."

"Get out. That wasn't even on his list of possibilities."

"Tell me about it."

"Sometimes a certain specialty impresses you when you least expect it," Heather said. "What about you two?"

"I need to do some soul searching because I'm not sure," Annabel said. "And I'm running out of time. I'll speak up for Stuart because he's been bent on psychiatry all along."

Stuart rinsed his hands at the sink. He turned sideways, his frame thin as a dime, and seemed to contemplate what he was going to say. "Over the weekend, I thought about changing."

Annabel, Heather, and Becky stared at him.

"I like your patient population, Dr. Clark, as well as the specific area of medicine. I'm thinking of going into pediatrics or pediatric psychiatry."

Annabel's jaw dropped. "You are another surprise."

"I'm tickled to death," Dr. Clark said. "I hope my mentoring has made a difference in your decision."

"You are an inspiration," Stuart said, "as well as the kids who come to your office."

"I'll speak for the doctors," Becky said, "when I say that you are invited to come back here to do elective time. Especially before you send in your residency applications."

"I may take you up on that. I have plenty of elective time left in my schedule."

Becky stepped to the doorway and motioned to Annabel. "Dr. Gillespie is here and is picking up the first patient's chart. Better go join him."

Annabel dumped the rest of her coffee down the sink,

slipped on her white jacket, and trotted down the hallway. Dr. Gillespie peered over the chart at her and mumbled, "Another school physical. This one's for a seventh grader."

The exam room door opened and an overweight woman wearing an array of costume jewelry almost bumped into them.

"Hey, Dr. Gillespie. No use in staying in there; I didn't stay for Aaron's physical last year either. He's old enough to see a doctor by himself and he'll be driving before I know it too." The mother of the patient nodded at Annabel and began scrolling through her iPhone as she took a seat in the waiting room.

Dr. Gillespie waddled in. "Welcome to your seventh grade physical, Aaron. Any complaints or health problems since the last time I saw you?"

"I'm great, Dr. Gillespie. Nothing's wrong with me at all." The long-limbed boy grinned and ran his hands through his hair like tossing a salad. He put an iPad to the side as George went through his record.

"This is Annabel," Dr. Gillespie finally said. "She's an advanced medical student learning about the field of pediatrics." He put the chart down and gave the boy a long look for the "general appearance" of the physical exam and then examined his ears, nose, and throat. The youth wore nothing but a short gown and his lower legs dangled from bony knees at the end of the table.

"What sports have you been playing?" George asked as he picked up a reflex hammer.

Aaron smiled for the first time. "Over the summer, mostly basketball with my buddies."

George nodded and tapped on Aaron's knees with the hammer to evaluate his deep tendon reflexes. "Besides a short neuro evaluation," he said to Annabel, "I spend a little extra time examining kids' joints if they're more involved with athletics."

Annabel stayed by the back wall. "That must mean most kids Aaron's age."

"Pretty much." Dr. Gillespie went on to check Aaron's heart, lungs, and abdomen and asked him to stand down.

Annabel sighed. She hated to think it, but another somewhat boring school physical, which needed to be done, was out of the way. She took a baby step sideways to leave the room, and paused for Dr. Gillespie to give the okay.

But he wasn't finished.

"You can lean over the table," Dr. Gillespie said to Aaron. He put on a glove, unscrewed the cap off a lubricant tube on the counter, and squirted some on his glove. The boy's gown was tied in the back and the pediatrician widened the space between the cloth, below the tied bow.

Annabel began feeling terribly awkward as it became apparent what the senior doctor was going to do. She stepped from one foot to the other and couldn't help but grimace. The adolescent placed his elbows on the examination table and bent his head down to stare at the black upholstery. He also grimaced in advance and Annabel gathered that Aaron was schooled in what was to come. It was not his first time.

Dr. Gillespie's eyes widened. He began slowly and quietly humming. His vocals droned louder as he inserted his gloved, lubricated index finger into Aaron's rectum and palpated.

Aaron squirmed and Annabel's heart thumped against her chest with distress. The youth's exam turned into a painful show, upsetting and disturbing her as she pinned herself against the wall. She wanted to focus on what she knew about pediatric healthy, routine physical exams because nowhere did she remember reading that a rectal exam was part of it.

But she couldn't get past the scenario in front of her in the confined space of Dr. Gillespie's exam room. Gillespie's eyes appeared hungry and he seemed like he was ready to explode with excitement.

When Dr. Gillespie left the exam room, he made a left turn and headed to his office. Annabel slinked to the room next to the kitchen and hurriedly opened her manual to the physical exam. Maybe she had missed something. She read and reread the systematic parts of the pediatric exam and nowhere did it mention a digital rectal exam for these patients unless, of course, there were specific complaints such as constipation, gastrointestinal bleeding, an abdominal mass, etc.

She poked her head around the corner. George's office door still did not open, so she lowered herself into a chair while still holding the book. Reading the chapter highlights again shed no more light on the exact office circumstance she had just witnessed.

"You seemed glum when you first walked in this morning, but now you're downright sulky." Stuart leaned against the door frame, his hand jammed in his pocket.

"You are becoming more street smart and inquisitive, Stuart."

"Hmm. There may be some truth to that. Interesting, because I had not recognized that." Stuart turned the second chair to face her and sat. "What's the matter?"

"To utter what I am thinking would be defamatory."

Stuart cocked his head. "I am as trustworthy as they come."

"No doubt. I am simply uncomfortable about something going on in this office and that's not grounds to jump to conclusions about someone's character."

Stuart narrowed his eyes and then looked away.

"See that," she said. "I've probably said too much already."

"Annabel, I don't have many friends, but you are one of them. Whatever you don't like about this place, it's water under the bridge. We only have the rest of this week to follow these docs around and be with their office staff, then we're off to the wards."

Annabel sighed. "Yes, I see your point. Outward and onward, so they say."

She forced a smile as they both went to look at their next patients' charts.

"What's your problem?" Solar said from the top of the refrigerator.

Dustin grumbled while he cleaned out the bird's cage and then washed his hands. "It's funny you ask, Solar, because I do have a problem. However, much to the detriment of my heart, my relationship with Annabel Tilson is resolved. Well, almost. I don't know how to tell her it's over, or even if I should. Being the gentleman that I am, I should let her know. After all, it's not like I'm some kind of teenager or something. I already walked away from her, but definitive closure would be best."

He turned around and rolled his eyes. "Damn, I'm talking to a bird."

Solar flapped down to the kitchen counter and pecked at Dustin's hand.

"I'm sorry, fella. You're more than the average bird, otherwise, you wouldn't be here. Now I have to get ready for work. I'm swinging back to a day shift." He went upstairs, changed into his uniform, and vowed to start Monday morning off on a positive note. At the door, he looked back. "Solar, you mind the house. If you don't mind, I'm going to get my break-up advice from Sean today because you can't help me."

Dustin first pulled through a coffee shop drive-thru lane one block away from work, then parked in a perpendicular spot in front of the station and popped the lid off his Americano. He took a swig as Sean stepped up to his vehicle, his fist ready to rap on the driver's window.

Dustin smiled, opened the door, but stayed seated. "How

was your day off?"

"More decent than usual."

"Why's that?"

"My 'honey-do' list was shorter than normal, but you wouldn't know about those lists yet."

"May never know about them. I'm breaking up with Annabel. No ifs, ands, or buts about it. I only need to tell her, although my walking away from her at the fair on Saturday was a clear signal."

"Here we go again. Even if you do officially break up, how are you going to get her out of your system?"

Dustin reached over to the other cup holder and wrapped his hand around another coffee. "Here, I bought one for you too."

Sean extended his hand but stopped as he watched an old red sedan come around the courthouse square. The window was down and a man with a narrow face and bags under his eyes took a double take in their direction. The man jerked the vehicle into a perpendicular spot across the street. As the car door flew open, he grabbed the pistol beside him. The spry man was out and in the middle of the road in a flash.

"Fascist pig!" he screamed. He fired his shotgun and Sean jolted where he stood.

Sean tried to hold Dustin's left arm as he crumpled down to the ground and blood oozed from his chest.

Dustin hunched his head down as he put his revolver in his hand. He had no time to think, so he lurched over Sean, and found the man racing back to his car. He fired his first shot as the man's car door slammed. Dustin continued his pursuit. The car screeched backwards, missing Dustin, but the driver couldn't outdrive the police officer's next shot. Straight to the head.

As shots rang out, the officer at the front desk inside sprang to her feet and bounded outside. The red car plunged into a parked car, the assailant slumped over the steering wheel. Dustin cautiously approached the vehicle and verified the man was no threat and was probably dead. The woman crouched over Sean and other officers from inside came out to the scene.

Dustin ran back to Sean. Unconscious, his colleague was losing blood fast, too fast. The hospital in the vicinity sent paramedics to the scene before he even stood. As they worked in unison to both treat Sean and load him on a stretcher and into the ambulance, the captain grabbed Dustin by the arm. "Go with him."

Dustin slid in, and hunched over Sean, he mumbled, "You're gonna make it, buddy. Hang in there." The back doors slammed. Dustin grabbed the edge of the seat as the vehicle sped away. As a cop, he was used to reaching a destination in a hurry, but this driver cut corners like a Hollywood stunt driver.

The back doors of the ambulance flew open when they reached the ER and Sean became the major case to hit the trauma room. The door stayed open and Dustin watched the chaos. Doctors and nurses flew into the room from each direction. No one asked him one question. It was simple. They knew what needed to be done without knowing if Sean still had his appendix, a history of arthritis, or any other similar history.

"Call the OR," a tall, slender doctor shouted. "Tell them we're coming straight up."

After gathering all the ancillary equipment attached to Sean, a group of people in scrubs wheeled the stretcher past Dustin. Blood hung from one pole and went straight into a large bore IV in Sean's prominent vein in front of his elbow. An endotracheal tube jutted out from his mouth and a respiratory therapist squeezed on an Ambu bag to deliver oxygen to his lungs. But there was so much blood on the sheets, Dustin couldn't fathom how much remained circulating around to the major organs of his best friend.

They rode an elevator to the second floor and Dustin stopped short as Sean and the ensemble disappeared behind the main door of the OR. He wrung his hands so tight, he glanced down to check for skin damage.

Soon Sean's wife arrived and Dustin told her what happened and consoled her. But as the minutes ticked by, more family members appeared, so he slithered to the background, letting them have their space. After two hours of pacing and then sitting and jumping up every time someone exited the OR doors, he sat more still and his cell phone rang from his captain.

"How is he?"

"He's in surgery and I don't have one update." Dustin clenched his jaw. He had never killed a man and dreaded asking the question. "What about the guy I shot?"

"He's dead, Dustin. Taken to the morgue. He was a thirty-five-year-old. Going to the courthouse to pay his annual property taxes; apparently had a beef with the police over being temporarily locked up in the past for a domestic violence charge. We just learned he had a minor psychiatric history as well. He came around that bend to park and I guess he just snapped when he saw you two because of his beef with cops. You and Sean were in the wrong place at the wrong time."

"Sean was." Dustin turned and talked facing the window. "If I hadn't been giving him a cup of coffee and discussing our weekends, we would have been in the station already. And that lunatic would have missed his opportunity."

"Thinking about 'what ifs' won't help you. So drop that train of thought. Shit happens or doesn't happen and it has nothing to do with whether we make a right or a left turn."

He let a silence pass. "I'll call if the doctors tell me anything."

Dustin hung up, sat in the corner, and hunched over looking

at the tile floor. He placed his phone on the seat next to him, but it immediately dinged with a text message. He grabbed it and stared. It was from Annabel.

"Sorry you were so tired and stressed on Saturday. Hope I didn't add to it because of dragging you to the dog show. Maybe you caught up yesterday with some R&R? Are you okay?"

He shook his head. *You are sleeping with someone else,* he thought, *who you actually flaunt in front of me, and my best friend has been shot in the chest and may not live. No, I'm not okay.* Dustin squeezed his eyes shut and covered his face. His lips trembled and he quietly sobbed into his own hands.

CHAPTER 18

Becky rounded up Annabel and Stuart in the hallway and asked them to take their lunch hour. They threw their white jackets on a chair, opened the front door, and stepped out to appreciate the fresh air.

"Those scones didn't hold me very long," Stuart said. "I'm ready for a fat burger."

"Not me," Annabel said. "I'm going light. Maybe their lunch special will grab my attention. All I know is that it feels revitalizing to get outside for a walk, away from strep throats and runny noses." She inhaled and exhaled two big breaths.

"Are you over whatever was disturbing you?"

Annabel turned her head sideways and scowled.

"You're right. We only have four more days to tolerate Gillespie."

"So it is Gillespie?"

"Me and my big mouth. Being a student, I've often wondered about this. The board-certified, practicing physicians that teach and mentor us are approved staff through different university departments. They are human just like everybody else, and there are bad apples who shouldn't be in the positions they have. I bet it's political just like everything else is. What if you suspect a doc of not being on the up and up? I bet it would take an act of God to 'fire' them or let them go in a non-accusatory manner."

"But, Annabel, there are lots of doctors we won't like and patients won't like either. Their practices don't rise to the top. Their reputation and word of mouth about them spreads and serves to cull them out."

They crossed an intersection, and when they came to their lunch place, they settled in a booth. "However, I bet you're correct. Bad, dangerous, or inept doctors probably keep practicing way longer than they should before they are somehow weeded out."

"My dad knew a surgeon who quit medicine after a huge malpractice suit."

"There you go. I hope, however, he wasn't a decent doc unjustly sued."

"According to my dad, he deserved it."

Annabel checked out the lunch special and then remained silent waiting for the waitress. She still had not heard from Dustin, but who contacted who during their relationship was never an issue. He should be back on day shift this week and maybe it was time that she pop him a hello and get a sense if anything was wrong. After all, she perceived a problem, but sensing it didn't make it true.

The waitress appeared and Annabel ordered the special of grilled shrimp and pasta. She took out her phone and texted Dustin while Stuart ordered.

"Sorry you were so tired and stressed on Saturday. Hope I didn't add to it because of dragging you to the dog show. Did you catch up yesterday with some R&R? Are you okay?"

After pressing "send," she did not regret sending it. By ending it with a question, the message required a response. She took a deep breath and set the phone next to her placemat. Based on Dustin's history, she should hear back from him by the time she and Stuart landed back at the pediatrician's practice.

Stuart kept his head low while he ate his burger and Annabel savored the tasty shrimp. Her thoughts kept flashing back to the private exam she witnessed earlier as well as other moments when she disliked being in the exam room with Gillespie. On top of it, her mind darted to Dustin and monitoring her phone. *Darn,* she thought, why couldn't she eat in peace and let her troubles take a backseat?

When they finished, Annabel and Stuart paid at the register. Uneasy and fidgety, she pocketed her iPhone after no communication from anyone. Maybe Dustin was wrapped up with work. *Fat chance,* she thought. *It only takes a minute break to read a message and text someone.*

The students stepped outside from the restaurant to an overcast sky and a sultry afternoon. As they approached the corner, Annabel stopped. "I just remembered something. Remember my neuroblastoma patient from last week, Stephanie Miller?"

"I believe so. The father brought in his daughter's urine sample."

"She's first on the afternoon schedule. Things got rough for her and her father last week and I vowed I'd give her a stuffed animal to add to the one she carries around." She pulled at her long, wavy hair and looked around.

"This area is not a shopping mecca," Stuart frowned.

"What about that card and stationery store across the street? They sell small gift items."

"It's worth a try. Let's hurry or we'll be late."

They bounded across when the coast was clear, admired the storefront, and went in. Two shelves in one aisle were filled with small to medium-sized stuffed animals. "She had a panda, so I want to find something that would be a good match. I also promised her something she could give to her father."

"Doubly kind," Stuart said. "Good thing you remembered."

A white leg with a black foot stuck out from a pile and Annabel plucked the rest of it out. "A baby cow with a cute face."

"How about this one? An owl with big expressive eyes."

Annabel nodded and paid in a hurry at the counter.

"You may be the first medical student," Stuart said back on the sidewalk, "to buy a small outpatient child a present, as well as a parent."

"The circumstances presented themselves. It'll never happen again, I'm sure."

"There should be two points extra credit at the end of our pediatric test for this question, 'Did you do any philanthropy for a patient during your rotation?'"

"Leave it to you to bring up a test!"

They came to the post with a prominent sign, "George Gillespie, M.D. and Heather Clark, M.D." and stepped into the office. The waiting room buzzed with infants crying and young children playing.

Stephanie Miller stood between her father's legs, patting on his knees. She grabbed her panda from the chair beside him as Annabel and Stuart approached.

The students nodded at Mr. Miller first. Annabel put the bag in front of her and crouched down. "Look what we brought you, just like I promised ... two stuffed animals." She lowered her voice. "One for you and one that you can give your dad."

She filtered through the tissue paper in the bag and pulled out the animals. "A baby cow and an owl."

Stephanie glued her eyes on the toys, which lit up her face. She studied them first and then took them in her arms and cuddled all three stuffed animals at the same time. Stuart lowered himself to their level and he said in a whisper, "Which one are you going to give to your dad?"

"The cow. I heard Mommy say that Daddy isn't eating or drinking enough because I'm sick. Cows give milk, so my new baby cow can give him pretend milk."

"You're an amazing little girl," Annabel said.

The door opened and a nurse called Mr. Miller and his daughter back into an exam room. "Thank you," Mr. Miller said, looking back at Annabel.

"You're welcome."

Annabel and Stuart followed, peeled into their small room,

and put their jackets back on.

"Now comes the part where Dr. Gillespie doles out more test results to them," Annabel said.

"Then those stuffed animals you just gave her are worth their weight in gold."

The students stopped speaking to each other as they diligently followed their attendings into the first afternoon appointments. Stephie was up on the table pointing her two animals at the cow in her father's lap.

"The MRI results are back," Dr. Gillespie said. "Fortunately, there is no indication that Stephanie's tumor is more advanced than we thought. Her orbital bones are involved, which I suspected because of the bluish color around her eyes. In summary, it is not a low-grade tumor where surgical excision alone would suffice, yet it hasn't majorly progressed either. I'm going to recommend her to a pediatric oncologist where, I believe, she only needs minimal treatment with chemotherapy and/or radiation to decrease the tumor size. After that, we have the best surgeon with the university who can remove the rest of the tumor."

Mr. Miller wrinkled his brow. "She doesn't deserve this."

"You're right about that. But, Mr. Miller, one of the most important goals with a neuroblastoma is to make a timely diagnosis and to try and alleviate the potential for more metastatic disease. We are doing that." He glanced over at Stephie, who stayed absorbed with her toys.

Stephie's father let out a loud sigh. "Okay, I guess we have no choice."

"My office will call the oncologist's office about the referral and they will call you to make an appointment. I want to continue seeing Stephie to manage her primary care and progress." He stole a glance at his patient. "My role will be as the captain of the ship."

Stephanie smiled at him. "I can jump off of here," she said.

Annabel stepped over. "Here, Stephie, hop down on the step."

The three-year-old slipped off to the step and bounced to the floor. She stared wide-eyed at Annabel.

"I won't see you again," Annabel said, "because I don't work here like the doctors and other people. You be brave about your medical treatments. Bring panda and owl with you for your appointments because you can hug them whenever you feel like it."

Stephie gently placed her stuffed animals back on the table and gave her a hug. Annabel closed her eyes as she embraced the little girl back. She wished she could do more, like have her come face-to-face with Oliver and be licked in the face.

"Thank you so much," Mr. Miller said. "You're going to make a fine doctor."

Annabel only smiled. All she wished for them was that Stephie zipped through the medical care and surgical removal of her neuroblastoma and got to enjoy life like a three-year-old should.

Because of Dustin's career so far, he had more insight than most laypeople into the dynamics of trauma cases that fled into the OR. Loved ones would accumulate in the waiting room and a waiting game would begin. Heads would turn whenever OR personnel came out to talk to someone and fingers would cross as visitors hoped no terrible news was headed their way.

And so it was for Dustin. More than two hours had elapsed since Sean vanished into the bowels of the OR with more physician and nurse manpower hanging on to his stretcher than he had ever witnessed. He tried to rationalize the amount of time his colleague was gone. He was hopeful because staff was back there still trying to remedy his colleague's condition as best as possible. On the other hand, perhaps the situation was taking so long because the damage done was too extensive and they kept running into more and more trouble with his case.

Dustin sat and crossed one foot over his knee and eyeballed the sole of his shoe. He swore, in the last few hours, he caused measurable wear to both of them by pacing back and forth. Even the tile floor had dirty rubber sole marks. After some time, a janitor came by, emptied the trash cans, and mopped the floor. He swished the wet mop a second time over Dustin's footprints.

He went over to the fake plants and leaned against the wall, thinking how much Sean meant to him. His friendship rated high on his list, along with his mother, and as much as Annabel had meant to him. With consolation, he thought about Solar. At least at home he had someone to talk to. It might be viewed as crazy, he thought, but yes, his bird mattered.

But no one could replace Sean. And, obviously, no matter what, his buddy would not be fit for work for quite some time. A bullet to the chest could have damaged his lungs or ribs, or worse than that, his heart. But no one could survive a bullet straight into heart muscle and right into the "chambers." The shots must not have pierced Sean's heart.

Whether his colleague stayed in the hospital in the near future, or at home, he must carve out lots of time to go visit him. Hopefully, Sean's wife would understand and be supportive of him sitting by his bedside a good deal of the time.

Dustin spotted him coming out, his demeanor unmistakable. The head trauma surgeon in charge of Sean's team swung through the doors and lowered his mask like a flag being lowered to half mast. It was all he had to see to know the terminal fact, as the man in blue scrubs with clues of blood on them, approached Sean's wife. He said little to her and she broke down with pitiful crying. Immediately, she was surrounded in a circle by loved ones.

Dustin's heartbeat slowed in mourning. He fought to be

brave and not shed a tear when the surgeon came over.

"I'm sorry," the surgeon said. "We did everything we could. Sean was hit in the chest, the bullet grazing major blood vessels. Give my condolences to the police force." He lingered appropriately, waiting if Dustin had any questions.

Dustin extended his arm for a handshake. "Thank you."

The surgeon left while the family moved to the "family room," where they would have more privacy. He sank into the cold chair and took out his iPhone. Right away, Annabel's message popped back up. Her communication was the last thing he wanted to see as he called the captain and reported the bad news.

As he headed back to his car, and the short drive back to the station, the day's events echoed in his head like an exploding bomb. He passed the coffee shop and wished he had never stopped there earlier. But "what ifs" served no purpose, like his captain said.

He hated to think this way, but Sean was also his main confidant, who stuck by him through thick and thin. His partner doled out personal advice better than his own mother who, after all, he couldn't tell everything. They would have had another "Annabel" discussion today had it not been for the mad man's shooting.

That was it. He would try and bury his relationship and his memories of Annabel along with his best friend. Physically, they would be gone, but emotionally … that would take some time.

CHAPTER 19

It was mid-afternoon and the pace in the office had not let up. Since Stephie Miller and her father had left, kids with colds and allergies and skin infections had come and gone. Annabel ran cold water into a Styrofoam cup and drank the whole thing. She had a view of the hallway where a nine year-old girl stood on the scale and the nurse wrote down her weight.

Dr. Gillespie stopped outside the door. "Aren't you beautiful!" he exclaimed to the girl. The nurse walked ahead and George tapped the girl's ponytail. The youngster smiled and mother and daughter followed his staff straight into a room.

George waddled through the hallway and examined the girl's chart outside the door. "New patient," he said to Annabel. "Let's introduce ourselves to Mrs. Klondike and her daughter, Tabitha." He sprang into the room before she acknowledged him.

Tabitha sat sideways on the exam table. A sketchpad the size of an iPad was in her hands and one hand was busy moving about a pencil.

"Wow," said her mother, Margaret. "We used to wait in Tabitha's old pediatrician's office at least a half hour."

Tabitha glanced up and paused doing her artwork.

"I'm sorry to hear that," Dr. Gillespie said. "Tabitha is too special to wait for a doctor." He diverted his attention to the young girl. "You are a stunning nine-year-old. Are you drawing something?"

"Nothing great." She shrugged.

George put his finger on the sketchpad and lowered it. The picture was a work-in-progress of a country field with cattle and bales of hay. Trees dotted the background and the girl so far had a decent start on perspective and depth.

"Wow!" George proclaimed. "You are more talented than

the famous French artist, Claude Monet. His work was what they called impressionistic, but yours is what nature really looks like." He put his hand on the side of her hair and patted.

Tabitha had vivid amber eyes and rosy cheeks. She gave the new doctor a half-smile while her mother reached over for the pencil and pad and the girl passed them to her.

"Anyway, I'm Dr. Gillespie and this is one of the University medical students, Annabel Tilson. What brought you in today?" He looked at Tabitha more than Mrs. Klondike, but she launched into the reason for the visit.

"We just moved to the Cincinnati area from up north. The timing was terrible because Tabitha was diagnosed and treated for asthma one month ago in the middle of our move. Her pediatrician insisted on our establishing a new doctor as soon as we were able to. He said she needed testing and possibly chronic medications."

"Did you bring any prior medical records with you?"

"No, but I gave your nurse his name and information so our old doctor could electronically send it."

"Perfect. So Tabitha did not take a test called spirometry to evaluate her pulmonary function?"

"No, but they did take a chest X-ray."

"They said my heart looked okay," Tabitha chimed in.

"Excellent," Dr. Gillespie said, "because you'll need that heart someday to break some young man's heart."

Margaret furrowed her brow. "Don't get ahead of things."

George stuck to the rest of the history and physical, which Annabel could relate to because of her older sister's history. Since Tabitha was having no symptoms, he decided to wait for the records and the results of spirometry to prescribe her anything in the interim. He wrote orders in the chart and on the electronic medical record and went back to staring at Tabitha.

"Like you, that picture you are in the process of drawing is exquisite. Would you mind very much if I snapped a picture of it with my iPhone?"

Amused, Tabitha grinned and grabbed the pad on the empty chair next to her mother. She opened it to her black and white sketch.

George took his phone from his pocket and stepped close. He clicked a photo and touched her ponytail again. "Thank you so much. I will treasure this, a landscape from a beautiful girl up north, now a resident of Ohio."

Annabel and George peeled out of the room first and when the Klondikes passed them in the hallway, George stood at the front desk. Annabel held her breath, expecting him to rub his oily hands on Tabitha's hair again. But he didn't. He seemed to be transferring information from her chart into his private cell phone.

Annabel monitored the head count in the waiting room and Becky concurred what she thought. Gillespie's last patient for the day was a no-show. She crossed her fingers that he'd let her go early and not make her sit in the side room twiddling her thumbs or studying.

"He's in his office," Becky said. "I'll rap on the door and tell him the news." She lowered her voice. "And put in a word to let you go home."

She came back quickly. "You're out of here."

"I owe you."

"Students are already in debt. Don't promise something that will take you twenty years to pay back."

Annabel gathered her things and wished she could say good-night to Stuart, but he was with Dr. Clark and they still had one more patient to be seen. She left and had driven her own car that morning so she had no Uber driver to call. After scrambling into her car, she texted Bob.

"Hey, how's your day? After all our studying about meningitis, any results back yet on Toby?"

She rapped her fingers on her steering wheel and waited. She'd had Oliver since late Sunday when she and Bob parted, but she didn't feel the urge to race home. It was earlier than her usual pediatric days.

"Results weren't ready earlier in the day .. I can recheck soon. Day's been half-crazy."

"I'll pop over. I'm out already. I want to ask your opinion about something. Maybe visit Toby?! I'll walk Oliver right away after leaving the hospital."

"Text me when you're here. I shouldn't be too late either."

Annabel closed with a thumbs-up emoji and went about her way. Soon she strolled through the revolving doors and into the hospital lobby and re-texted him.

After a five-minute message silence, Bob spoke up behind her. "You should earn a double grade for taking part in a pediatric office and a hospital rotation at the same time."

Annabel swung around. "Ha, I'll need two clinical grades because Dr. Gillespie is probably not too impressed with me. It works both ways, however. I'm not enthralled by his bedside manner."

"What now?" The students stepped aside from the entrance and took cover behind an artificial tree.

"Since you began your hospital rotation, did you see any of the residents give a rectal exam on a kid?"

Bob glanced down for a second. "Not that I recall."

"Or use a magnifying glass to examine genitals?"

"Annabel, that sounds quirky."

"I find it as peculiar to be a spectator watching these things as it probably was for the youth who suffered a finger up his butt."

"I see your point."

Annabel sighed. "Just remember, you'll follow in my

footsteps and end up in Gillespie's office next week."

"Based on your discomfort, I'm hoping I get to work with Dr. Clark. I have a fifty-fifty chance, since I'll be with Nell next week."

"Linnell's been assigned with you?"

"Yeah, I thought you knew."

Annabel stared blankly at him. "Maybe you could say something up front that you'd like to shadow Dr. Clark."

"I could try. However, they may automatically pair us up as a male student to a male doctor and the female with the female, as biased as that sounds."

"Could be. Dr. Gillespie may, however, prefer a female student with him." She thought a moment and then shook her head. "But maybe it doesn't matter what a student's sex is who's beside him. It would take a shrink to figure him out."

"What does Stuart think?"

"He said we only have a few more days in Gillespie's office. We can't like every attending or his or her ways of doing things, each and every time. We'll be out of there before we know it, meaning I should grin and bear his behavior."

Bob nodded his head slowly. "Good advice, Annabel. There are bigger burdens on our shoulders and you still have not figured out what you're going to write down on your residency application." He thought ahead and took a chance with adding one more point. "Not only what type of medicine you want to practice the rest of your life, but also what city you want to train in."

"That's a no-brainer. At least I know that, or at least what my first choice would be no matter what I apply for. Because all their programs are excellent."

Bob kept his excitement to find out subdued. "Oh ... your hometown."

"It's been productive going to medical school somewhere other than Nashville and home, but for my training, that's another story. I can only hope that I match at Vanderbilt."

"Smart. I envy you."

"No you don't. Good friends can't envy each other."

"I mean I envy you because you had it figured out already."

"It would be heartwarming to have family around again. Since you've met them, you can understand where I'm coming from. My mom and dad, and uncle and aunt, even my stupid sister, are important to me. During the transition, I can even stay at their house ... my original grandparents' house. The one you visited."

Bob started to sadden, and it showed on his face. She'd be gone and back to a life filled on a daily basis with love and support. There would be no room for him, perhaps not even enough room for Dustin.

"I'm sorry," she said. "I guess all of us in medical school will be going our own ways." Her expression also turned forlorn. "In a way, it will be sad to graduate next year and to fully realize that med school was a stepping stone to more training.

"But what am I saying? Don't you realize we have another major exam to pass before we proceed? I better stop thinking about Gillespie because we still need to take the Step 2 two-day test of the United States Medical Licensing Exam board or we're not going ahead with anything."

"Yes, that test will be our major obstacle to date." He stared past her to the elevators, to the here and now and Toby Owens. "I'd better get to the lab on the top floor."

"I'm coming with you."

Upstairs, a slender woman with a buttoned-up lab coat and round glasses walked to the end of the laboratory counter loaded with machines and faced Bob.

"When med students come up here, they're waiting for something more important than usual, and results that are hot off my machine. Who are you inquiring about?"

Bob told her with an imploring voice, "Toby Owens. We did a lumbar puncture on him."

"Ahh. Vital lab work. I'm happy to assist." She traced back her steps and took but a second. "Just in time. Here you go." She waved a sheet in the air before handing it over. "Your resident and attending are going to want to know about this one."

Bob read without watching where he walked and Annabel opened the door. "Says here the normal white blood cell count in cerebrospinal fluid is zero or no more than five WBCs per cubic millimeter of CSF. Toby's count is two hundred and eighty-two!"

Annabel gasped. "We suspected as much. He has meningitis."

"Those disease-fighting white blood cells are needed because they're fighting off whatever the hell bacteria it is. I'll tell Rick Mares."

Bob stopped outside the elevator and texted his chief resident. *"Toby has a high white blood cell count in his spinal tap results."*

"Meningitis," Rick responded. *"If you see him before me, you can confirm that to him. I need to evaluate the whole report before you leave."*

"Annabel is here. We'll tell him."

"Do you still want to see Toby?" Bob asked her.

"Sure. We can both assure him that he's going to be fine."

They rode the elevator down to the orthopedics floor and hurried straight to Room 532.

"It was smart thinking that Dr. Mares isolated Toby already," Bob said. "There may be a risk of spreading whatever infectious disease he may have." They squirted sanitizer on their hands from the bottle on the cart outside the door and rubbed their hands. Annabel cracked the door open and frowned.

"Toby's mom is in there and another boy."

Bob followed Annabel in and first said hello to Toby. "It's nice to see your mom here as well as another visitor."

Toby lay still; his neck didn't budge, and his casted leg lay like a brick on the bed. He grimaced and grasped Bob's hand, but it was a feeble attempt. The youth was both bored with his hospitalization and very tired from his illness. "You two coming in makes four visitors. Lucky me."

"This is Toby's friend Jonathon," Anne Owens said.

The dark-haired youth continued sitting in the bedside chair, his large sneakers pointed in. "Hi. I go to school with Toby too."

"Nice to meet you, Jonathon," Bob said. "Bet you two play basketball together as well."

"Not lately," Jonathon lamented.

"Is it all right if I talk freely about Toby's medical condition?" Bob asked. He walked to the other side of the bed and rested a hand on Toby's shoulder.

Mrs. Owen stepped between the bed and Jonathon. "Sure. We are all aware that the doctors believe that Toby has meningitis. Do you have an update?"

"The results of his spinal tap do confirm that diagnosis."

"It figures," Toby said.

"Why does he have such a headache?" Jonathon wondered aloud.

"Simply put," Bob said, "with meningitis, there's an inflammation of the membranes in a person's brain, which causes swelling. That's what triggers the symptoms in a patient's head and neck."

"Oh," Jonathon said.

"This is quite insane," Anne said, pushing her glasses up on her nose. "Where on earth could my son pick up this infection? All he does is stay home, play basketball, and hang out with

Jonathon. We rarely *do* anything."

Bob and Annabel couldn't interrupt as Anne Owens spilled out the thoughts that had been troubling her.

"And why does he have it and none of us do? Toby is a good kid. He never does anything crazy."

While shaking her head, Mrs. Owens aborted her rant. Jonathon made a little laugh from the sideline and leaned over closer to Toby.

"Except while we were in Florida and you ate that disgusting slug."

"What?" Anne asked.

Jonathan realized he said something in front of her that he shouldn't have.

"Toby, what is Jonathan talking about?"

Toby gritted his teeth and shot Jonathon a dirty look. His mother put her hands on her hips and waited. It appeared he had no choice but to divulge what happened.

"We were waiting outside that lunch restaurant on the boardwalk while you and Jonathon's mom were still shopping. Two local boys, older than us, tried to gross us out by telling us about mudbugs, and then they dared me to eat a slug that was right there on the steps. Mom, it doesn't matter. It didn't taste that bad."

Mrs. Owens eyes grew big and Jonathan added, "But they had to pay Toby six dollars because they lost the bet."

Anne Owens couldn't restrain herself. She turned to Toby, as sick as he was, and clunked him on the side of his head. "What the hell's the matter with you!"

"Ouch. You're not going to tell Dad, are you?"

"Probably not. He'll wonder what kind of mothers Mrs. Harmon and I were on vacation ... letting you eat slugs!"

CHAPTER 20

George Gillespie stuffed papers into his old-fashioned briefcase and closed the door to his office. He strutted down the hallway, ready to go home.

Becky was the only person left at the front desk, and he made a point of stopping. "Enjoy your evening, Becky."

"You too, sir."

After unlocking his car door, he dug his hand in his pocket one more time to make sure he remembered his cell phone. Rest assured, he drove the twenty-minute drive home, looking forward to his wife's cooking. She always conjured up something decent on Monday night because she counted on the leftovers for him on Tuesday when she always had a meeting.

George's wife, Marlene, was a busy physician's wife. George often heard hospital gossip from her because she worked part-time in the administrative offices. The rest of the time, she donated her time heavily to charitable children's organizations, where most of the money went to the medical care of children at their very hospital for families that couldn't afford it.

Marlene, in her late forties, was aging very well. She kept a shapely figure and actually stood an inch higher than her shorter husband. Her rosy lipstick was her trademark, which accentuated her full lips and bleached white smile.

In Marlene's mind, it was a strange marriage, which she had finally come to terms with and had decided to go about with her own life. Which, of course, was comfortable. It was not as if George made a ton of money, but she lived as cozy as other spouses of thriving physicians, and she did enjoy her philanthropic endeavors of helping children.

She often admitted to herself that, when she married him, the writing was on the wall and she had a clear premonition that their sexual relationship did not seem normal. It was one thing to get a sense of how other relationships worked, but she also had her own past history as a foundation. Each and every past relationship she had had with a man was a pleasant, if not awesome sexual experience. It was not only intercourse itself, but the *desire* for sex had percolated in her male partners. They would make physical advances that were appropriate and she would do the same. Sometimes it turned out to be hot and wild.

Sex was important to her and, yet, she had married someone with a scant libido. At least for her. And it hurt her feelings.

For years, in the beginning, she egged her husband on to engage in sex because he showed no initiative. Then, in the middle years, she stopped practicing her neediness because he was down to no initiative whatsoever. They attended one session with a marriage counselor, during which George proclaimed, "It's just not enjoyable for me."

On top of this, he kept handy tubes of lubricant on his nightstand as well as next to his toiletries in the bathroom. The contents would slowly disappear and then the tubes would be replaced. That spoke for itself.

All of this really hurt her feelings, yet she knew enough to not take it personally. *He must be gay*, she figured, and he was either aware of that fact or he was the last one to realize it. At that point, she thought about throwing in the towel, but her wedding vows were for life and divorce was a terrible concept she didn't want to try.

Marlene heard the garage door open and her husband came in with his usual restrained personality. She followed him to his front room office. "How was your day?"

George put down his briefcase. "Just like the other three hundred and sixty-four. Parents and kids come and go and I help solve some of their problems. Medical ones."

George placed his iPhone on the edge of the desk, took off

his sport coat, and slipped into the bathroom. Marlene hesitated and decided to go for it … pick up his phone and glance at his recent pictures. Over recent months, she happened to stumble on a dozen pictures of his patients, which she found odd. Interestingly enough, they were sweet photos of kids, and they, or their parents, must have allowed him to snap them. Maybe he was compiling a bulletin board of his happy patients for the waiting room or something like that.

She tapped on "photos" and, since last week, the only picture that showed up appeared to be a half-finished black-and-white sketch. She shook her head at why he bothered to take a picture of it, but it was none of her business.

Marlene went to the kitchen and doled out a stir-fry chicken dish for dinner.

"I liked that," George said when he finished. "New recipe?"

"Yes, and I made extra." Although she had nowhere to go the rest of the evening, she reapplied her lipstick when she got up to do the dishes. George helped her bus the plates to the sink and then went straight back to his office.

He had brought home no medical paperwork that needed attention. After reaching for his phone, he opened up the pictures and stared at Tabitha Klondike's sketch. More importantly, he went to his list of contacts and scrolled to the Klondikes … the entry he had discreetly entered as they left the office.

He stared off into space and formulated what he would say on the phone and placed a call.

Margaret Klondike answered. "Hello?"

"Mrs. Klondike, this is Dr. Gillespie. Every once in a while, I call a patient and the family in the evening to make sure there were no problems with their appointment in my office during the day. Like a post-medical call survey. Were the girls at the front desk friendly, etc., etc.?"

Margaret took a few seconds to process the reason for his

call. "The visit went smoothly, thank you."

"I picked your visit specifically tonight because your family is brand new to the area. I want to make sure you are satisfied with your beautiful daughter's new medical care."

"Yes, like I said, everything was fine."

"I wish I could thank your daughter for letting me snap a picture of her lovely sketch."

"She's around here somewhere."

George waited. He heard noise and voices in the background and then the sweet voice of Tabitha Klondike sounded in his ears.

"Hello? Dr. Gillespie?"

"Tabitha, honey, I wanted to personally thank you. Your sketch on my phone is your personal present to me. It's the most glorious photo in my whole collection. On your next visit, please do show me the finished project."

Tabitha beamed with delight. No one had ever made a big deal about her artwork like him before. "I will finish it before my mom brings me again."

George's free hand went to his crotch. His hardened crotch.

"I look forward to it."

He couldn't keep talking and taking care of his crotch at the same time. "Bye, then," he said, and hurried into the bathroom.

Annabel and Bob left Toby with his mother and friend Jonathon, and went to the nurses' station. Bob first made a copy of his patient's LP results and then stuck the original in the lab results section of his chart. Both students huddled at the side of the counter.

"I'm pretty sure I would not have taken that Florida kid up on his dare," Annabel said. "Kids do crazy things to avoid humiliation."

"At his age, I might've," Bob said. "It is possible to chuck something small down your throat really fast, like a slug or a snail, and avoid tasting it."

"Not only are they disgusting, but think where they've been."

"What's disgusting?" Rick Mares asked, stepping up behind them.

"Eating a slug or a snail," Bob answered.

"Surely neither of you lost your mind and did such a thing. Mollusks are distasteful, I'm sure, and gross. Slugs secrete a film of mucus for their own protection ... to keep stupid human beings from eating them."

Annabel cocked her head at him and he said, "I graduated from college with honors in biology. My studies included terrestrial mollusks. Come on, let's sit somewhere. Bring Toby's lab sheet."

"It's dinnertime," Bob said. "Any objection to going to the doctors' lounge? I rarely make it in there to eat scrumptious free food."

"Excellent idea. However, did you tell Toby about his confirmed diagnosis?"

"We did, along with his mom and friend."

Rick nodded and peeled down the hallway in front of them with his long stride and opened the door. "This is a great time of day to go in here. It will be half as busy as lunchtime."

A round center table inside was stocked with cheese and crackers and fruit, but two tables against the wall had hot food and soup. They fixed a plate, grabbed drinks, and gathered around their own table. Only a handful of doctors remained, some watching the news. Nell was hidden from view on the couch and popped up.

"Hey," she said. "Can I join you? And are we otherwise done for the day, Dr. Mares?" She half sneered at Annabel while she placed two cookies on the empty spot on her plate.

"Yes, you can go," Rick said. "We're finished, except for my discussion with Bob regarding his consult."

"Then I'd love to stay. Toby Owens is the only possible pediatric case of meningitis I've seen."

"For all of you," Rick said, "now a confirmed case." He tapped his finger on the table and Bob immediately produced his copy of Toby's results.

"Miss Linnell, Bob's patient's CSF white count is two hundred and eighty-two."

"Did we prescribe the correct antibiotic?" Bob wondered. "One that we can keep using on Toby?"

Wide-eyed, Rick stared at the sheet and dropped his fork.

"What's wrong, Dr. Mares?" Annabel asked.

He raised his head slowly and turned solely to Bob. "You neglected to tell me the breakdown percentages of the type of white blood cells in Toby's fluid. I have never seen this before."

Bob ducked his head and tapped his forehead in disapproval of himself. Obviously, he goofed up.

"No harm done," Rick said. "I am simply flabbergasted and this is an opportunity for the three of you to review the basics. So what are the five types of white blood cells?"

Bob was still making amends with himself and Nell had stuffed half a cookie in her mouth, so Annabel took the gamble. "Basophils, lymphocytes, monocytes, eosinophils, and neutrophils."

"Correct. Now, which cells are disproportionately increased above normal values during a bacterial infection?"

"Neutrophils," Bob said.

"And which cells are increased during a viral infection?"

"Lymphocytes."

"Toby does not have higher numbers of either in his cerebrospinal fluid, flat out eliminating a bacterial meningitis *or* a viral meningitis. So, in answer to your question, Bob, the IV antibiotic Toby is receiving is incorrect because it is meant to stampede out a bacterial infection."

"So which other type of white blood cell is increased?" Annabel asked. "What on earth strange infection does he have?"

"The differential shows thirty-two percent eosinophils. He has an eosinophilic meningitis! Even I am going to need to investigate this further, because high eosinophils point to one thing. And one thing only – parasites!"

Rick suddenly got up. "I must go write an order to discontinue the antibiotic and leave a note on Toby's chart. Have a good night."

"I'm leaving," Nell said. "Bob, are you coming?"

"Annabel isn't finished with her chicken sandwich. I'll catch you tomorrow."

Linnell stopped at the center table, wrapped up some snacks to-go, and flashed a final smile at Bob.

Annabel grinned. "We'll be like Rick one of these days. Residents pull longer hours than we do. It's like their work never ends."

"Are you saying that we better enjoy medical school while we still can?"

"Something like that. I better get going too. Poor Oliver must be waiting patiently." She chewed the last bite while Bob contemplated.

"Rick seems stumped by Toby Owens. We should have talked about calling in an infectious disease specialist."

"You're right. And you and I don't have the resources to figure out rare medical conditions. I wish we were close by to the campus medical library."

Bob turned around. "Doctors and foundations do lend books in here."

"I forgot about that. I'm rarely in this lounge." She also

turned to take note of the book shelves on half the wall on the other side of the room.

"Wonder how old some of them are."

"Let's check." The students bused their trash and studied the spines of the textbooks. Annabel opened a few. "The publishing dates are relatively new and the older ones are recently edited."

"Here's an option." Bob pulled out a navy blue text. "Modern Infectious Diseases."

"Perfect," Annabel said. "Another option is checking with the government disease control site."

"I'll do one and you do the other and we can compare notes."

"I'll snuggle with Oliver and the book later tonight after I walk him and do some other pediatric reading."

"I can come over and snuggle with the two of you too," he chanced saying.

"My bed isn't big enough for three."

"Actually, Oliver can stretch out and hoard an entire bed just by himself!

Annabel bounded up the two flights of stairs and inserted her key in the door. It was a normal occurrence when Oliver stayed with her. Before she even cracked open the door, the biggest smile of her day would spread across her mouth.

She pushed straight in with her bag and textbook from the doctors' lounge. "Oliver, look at you! You are an impeccable young watch dog." After giving him an exuberant petting and taking a walk, they went back to the apartment.

Annabel changed and settled by the headboard of her bed and was grateful not to cook or to heat up leftovers for dinner. "Come on up, Oliver. Curl up next to me and watch for our Mr. Squirrel outside the window. I must research a nasty disease." Oliver had no problem heeding her request and he turned belly up with his snout nuzzling her.

It took time, but Annabel finally weeded out a pertinent eosinophilic disease from the book and then remembered it from medical school. Called "cysticercosis," it was an infection caused by the adult tapeworm, *Taenia solium*, acquired through poor hygiene and eating raw pork. What she had forgotten was that it could affect the central nervous system and then it was called neurocysticercosis.

However, she thought, there was a slim chance that Toby had this one. The disease was most prevalent in Africa, China, India, and Latin America and seventy to ninety percent of the patients presented with seizures. Toby had no history of seizures since his illness began.

Annabel's hand rested on Oliver's fur as she indexed another eosinophilic meningitis. The diseases were rare and she had never heard of the next one. Maybe because it reared its ugly head in Asia, Central America, and South America, and particular spots in Africa, and not the United States. Called "gnathostomiasis, the disease was caused by parasitic worms acquired by eating undercooked or raw reptiles, birds, frogs, eels, and freshwater fish.

She pondered over the food sources and wondered if a slug would count. However, on further reading, she eliminated it as Toby's disease. The most common symptoms were migratory swellings under the skin and Toby had no dermatologic manifestations. One other awful symptom was when the nematode entered a patient's eyes, causing blindness. She shook her head. At least, thankfully, Toby did not have gnathostomiasis meningitis.

The sun had long set and only a street light illuminated her favorite tree outside. She slinked off the bed without disturbing Oliver and closed the blinds, but her true intent was to check her phone. She left it in place on the kitchen counter and pressed messages. The last ones were between her and Bob. There was still no return message from Dustin after she had texted him during lunchtime.

CHAPTER 21

Dustin Lowe's night couldn't be worse. Death and violence was part of his job, but he was always the objective observer to other peoples' losses. His partner's death, however, made him just like everybody else he consoled, especially when folks had told him late in the day, "I'm sorry for your loss."

He felt especially alone. Not in the mood to eat any dinner, he grabbed a container of milk, measured two scoops of protein powder, and mixed the drink in the blender. He sipped it over a half hour on his most comfortable chair and, for the time being, didn't even feel like talking to Solar.

The bird pranced around on the table in the middle of the room. When he commented, "What's your problem," Dustin closed his eyes. Never before was the bird's question so relevant.

"Too much for you to listen to, Solar. I can't handle Sean's death and breaking up with Annabel all in one week. You just go about having a bird's life with nothing to worry about."

He felt doubly saddened by the fact that he had spent the most amount of time with Sean than anyone else and, yet, he would have no say in his funeral arrangements. Of course, families took care of those details, but he would love to know if they were contemplating cremating or burying him. He and Sean had once jokingly talked about death and his partner mentioned how petrified he was of fire. "After my life is dead and gone," he said, "no way do I want my dead body to face burning flames."

Dustin wondered if Sean ever said anything like that to his wife. Long after he finished his protein shake, he thought of all the advice Sean had given him. He hoped he had been as good a friend to him in return. His heart also yearned to call Annabel to tell her what happened, especially each time he re-read her message from earlier in the day. But the relationship was over and he wasn't yet ready to confront her or call her to make that crystal clear. At present, he was too vulnerable.

He could depend on his mom. She'd still be awake, especially since a thunderstorm approached both their locations from the south; she would be affected as well. The telltale signs of a stormy night were already present with distant rumbling skies and lightning, so he decided to call.

"It's late," she said when answering. "Is everything okay?"

"No, Ma, far from it. The worst thing happened today. If it weren't for me buying my partner a cup of coffee, something might not have happened ... "

It seemed like Annabel found the most medically known, yet rarest, eosinophilic parasitic brain offenders, so she canned her search for the next hour and read from the rotation-assigned pediatric book. With disappointment, she glanced over at the clock; it was past bedtime. To show up at a private practice in the morning looking like some post-call medical student would not be professional.

She jumped into the shower, but as she dried herself off, rumbles sounded, coming from the direction of the river. When she opened the bathroom door, she needed to shove it a bit, and found Oliver standing in the way. He wore a frightened appearance. Since lightning and thunder was headed their way, his quivering had begun.

"Oh, no, Oliver. Bad timing." She grimaced as she pulled a pajama top over her head. "Actually, since I'm a doctor-in-training, no timing will ever be appropriate."

After she pulled on the other half of her pajamas, she crouched down in front of him. "Don't get me wrong, boy. I don't hold a grudge. Your characteristics are embedded in your

DNA and we can't change that. I'll take care of you through thick and thin. Even when you're old, tired, and arthritic."

Oliver plowed past her and walked into the wet shower stall. He circled around and, finding no better security against the pressure change and approaching storm, he exited with wet paws.

Annabel then remembered. "Bob bought you something that may help!" She bit her lower lip; where the heck did she put it?

Her apartment was too small to lose anything, so she opened the closet accordion doors and remembered throwing the Thunder shirt box on the top shelf. After she grabbed the end, it fell to the floor. She let Oliver stay cowering in the closet while she read the instructions and straightened out the material. After grabbing him by the collar and closing the doors, she put the article on the dog step-by-step. He made no fuss and didn't seem to mind.

The thunderstorm ramped up as Annabel climbed back into bed and Oliver again took to her mattress and nervously circled. Over the next half hour, the storm continued to grow worse, but the dog's panting didn't.

Her phone dinged and she scurried past Oliver. Hoping beyond any other wish, she wanted to see a message from Dustin. But no such luck. A weather alert pinged for severe weather in her area. *No kidding*, she thought.

She scrambled back and, in time, she realized that both the thunder shirt and paying attention to him helped Oliver better tolerate the noise and light show.

Sleep for her, however, was useless. Her mind wandered back to the two parasitic diseases she had read about earlier, the first one involving the pork tapeworm. But the idea of the second one, the gnathostomiasis, nagged at her. For some reason, there seemed to be some fact she had overlooked, she had missed. Something not to be disregarded.

"You idiot," she said clearly. The undercooked or raw

sources of the parasitic worms, especially the frogs and eels, was the important piece to the puzzle. The etiology of Toby's problem may have been stark and evident, handed over to her and Bob in outright dialogue in Toby's hospital room earlier in the day, like a spoiler alert to a murder mystery novel.

"A Florida raw slug!" she exclaimed to Oliver.

It was midnight, but the search had just begun.

The last few years, George Gillespie's bedtime routine stayed prim and proper and as dependable as a faithful employee who never took a day off. He went to bed at nine o'clock whether he attended an evening meeting or not, and always after showering and a last look at his computer.

George and Marlene's master bathroom was extra spacious, but he had made it clear earlier in their marital years that bathrooms were for one person at a time.

Marlene thought her husband's privacy issues were indeed strange. After all, doctors were the ones who trained and worked with naked or semi-naked people all the time. So, in her opinion, there should be little to no modesty issues for a physician. If anybody understood that human beings all had the same body parts, it was them. His behavior was odd.

George showered and padded into the bedroom wearing his favorite pajamas. Marlene closed her reading device and swung her legs to the side of the bed. "You finished?"

"Sure. I'll be in my office for a little while."

Marlene went into the bathroom. George's iPhone was on the shelf next to the sink. She picked it up and poked her head out the door. "You forgot your phone." The screen woke up as she passed it to him, and Tabitha Klondike's picture popped up.

"Did you take a picture of a picture?" she asked.

George took the device and turned it face down. "Yes, I did.

A lovely female patient of mine drew that sketch. I complimented her on her creativity and artistry. Even snapped the picture, letting her know that people may desire her work."

Marlene smiled. "You are the best pediatrician, adding such personal touches to the doctor-patient relationship. I bet she was thrilled."

With a wide grin, her husband nodded. "I try to be."

"Well, you are. Whenever I visit your office, I see that side of you."

Pleased with her remarks, George left for his home office. She showered as well and went back to bed, this time to sleep and not read. Her husband had made it to bed as well, and within minutes, he began to lightly snore.

But sleep would not come, especially since a thunderstorm added to the situation. Marlene hated when she couldn't sleep, mostly because her activities the next day would suffer and she'd be too tired to focus correctly. And tomorrow morning, she needed to put hours in at the hospital. She read two more chapters of her current sci-fi fantasy and closed the cover of her eBook device.

Time to turn to a sleeping aid, she thought. She ambled to the kitchen and contemplated the over-the-counter pill containers in the cabinet. Although rarely needed, a white one combined with a pink one was her "color code" to sleep, so she grabbed an acetaminophen and diphenhydramine and chased them down with water. Now she waited for their effect and, in the interim, turned to go back to bed.

Marlene glanced at the hallway towards the front door. Her husband's office door was always closed, but it was cracked open and a dim light shone from inside. *That's a first*, she thought, and decided to turn off any lights.

She creaked open the door. It was only the desk lamp that was on, so she passed the other sparse furnishings and rolled the desk chair out of the way. George's laptop cover was open. She still had a few minutes to kill, so she figured, what the heck. Perhaps a current news breaking story would pop up on the screen. She settled her fingers on the mouse touchpad and the screen came alive.

But in a second, she furrowed her brow and gasped. How could a news agency be so explicit! She was horrified at a naked young girl in a lewd posture.

Without thinking about it, Marlene hit the forward key to eliminate the story in front of her, but as she did so, she realized what she saw had no text or information.

Another picture popped up. A male youth was also without clothing and the shot appeared to be taken in a barn. The boy's expression showed discomfort, as if someone was behind the camera making sure he did what was asked of him.

Finding it unacceptable and obscene, Marlene wanted to throw up. She couldn't look at the boy's act for another second, and placed her index finger on the laptop tab.

"Oh my God," she cried, realizing she had discovered a cache of child pornography.

Her heart pounded with disgust and uncertainty about what the material in front of her meant. Some pages had more than one photo, and there was no discrimination over sex or ethnicity. Worse than that, all pediatric ages were exemplified, from infants to boys and girls more likely in their years of puberty. A huge thunderclap sounded, but it didn't rattle her because the images in front of her gave her a jolt and took precedence.

Marlene left the computer just like she found it, turned off the desk light, and hurried to the bathroom attached to the office. She cried over the sink and trembled. For every young child she had seen, her body quaked like it was beset by a natural disaster.

How horrid, she thought. The material she witnessed was the result of poor, innocent children being used or abused by sick adults for their perverse enjoyment. And the bottom line most likely had to do with money. An illicit money-making industry where the perpetrators' wrongful material was sold through porn sites or private websites like underground illegal drugs.

So what the hell was her husband doing with it? Her husband, a pediatrician? Her quivering subsided as she began to get hold of herself and her own stupidity. What she had failed to admit to herself was that, for years, she suspected his behavior was more amiss than she acknowledged.

Yes, she was guilty of being in denial that her own husband was a certifiable pedophile. Her chest heaved. Should she consider herself an enabler and somewhat responsible?

No, she told herself. But now what? She had found the material by accident; this was his own private affair and computer. If it had not been for the light on in the room, she would have never entered.

Minutes slowly ticked by and Marlene finally got hold of her emotions. She slipped out and into the hallway where a night light guided her back to the master bedroom.

She had two issues to grapple with as she slid under the covers. First, what to do about what she found. Was there some action she was *supposed* to take? Not that she was aware of. She was also not going to confront George. In essence, their relationship was off a bell-shaped curve already, so she should leave it unchanged.

Secondly, and worse for her, she had to keep those images from popping back into her head like some kind of child abuse pornography PTSD. Under these circumstances, even a whole bottle of acetaminophen and diphenhydramine wouldn't be able to put her to sleep.

Throughout the dark morning hours, Marlene stared up at the dark ceiling. She was afraid to close her eyes and have her mind invaded by those images as lightning lit up the sky outside.

Bob was never the medical sleuth that Annabel was, but tonight his blood simmered with exhilaration as he dove into the medical and scientific world of published articles in obscure, as well as important, journals. He was deep into researching medical illnesses with high eosinophil counts in blood and spinal fluid.

He was snug in his overstuffed leather chair and ottoman with the drape open to the sliding door. The thunderstorm was the perfect backdrop for his endeavors and one that helped deter him from going to bed.

A huge clap of thunder boomed and he startled. *Oh no*, he realized. Another night with a significant summer storm and Annabel had storm-phobic Oliver. Bad timing, he thought, because it should be his turn to deal with and comfort Oliver. And get no sleep because of it.

He grinned because at least he had bought the dog a thunder shirt and perhaps she would be using it on him for the first time. He wondered if he should call her to ask if it was helping, but it was already 11 p.m. Maybe, just maybe, she was getting some sleep.

Bob straightened his laptop on his thighs and focused again on a paper he just stumbled on. It was a historical accounting more than anything else, published in China, and written several years ago by multiple authors.

Here it was; the first reported human case of the particular type of eosinophilic meningitis they found, discovered in Canton, China in 1933. And the parasite responsible was first detected in rats!

CHAPTER 22

"The dare, that's it," Annabel continued. Oliver was huddled beside her on the bed and paid no attention to her. The stormy weather was more important.

"A stupid kid's dare. I swear Toby is sick because of that slug he tossed down his throat! Now all I have to do is prove it."

She went back to the literature regarding neurocysticercosis, caused from ingestion of eggs from the adult tapeworm, *Taenia solium,* and then gnathostomiasis caused by several species of parasitic worms in the genus *Gnathostoma.* After assuring herself that both eosinophilic meningitises were not what Toby had, based on geography, etiology, and other parameters, she became more resolved to find a link to raw slugs.

By midnight, Annabel exhausted the use of the textbook she borrowed from the doctors' lounge.

"Oliver, sweetheart, I'll be right back."

The dog nevertheless followed her. When they settled again, she sat cross-legged on the bed, resting her laptop on a thin pillow. She wasn't bothered one bit about the time because Oliver needed her anyway. Tomorrow, she chuckled, Bob deserved some flack for somehow avoiding Oliver's storm nights and leaving him with her.

Now it was time to dig into the massive volume of information so graciously available to every person in the entire world. She whittled down her search to "rare infectious disease," and dived pretty far, but never pinpointed an entity quite like Toby's illness. Soon she narrowed things down to scientific journals reporting "tropical" diseases.

Luckily, she stumbled on an American journal mainly dealing with tropical medicine and thumbed through indexes looking for the keywords of mollusks such as slugs or snails.

Oliver's panting increased with a close thunderclap and she managed to keep him lying next to her using her left arm.

Her eyes again rested on the computer screen to find an article with an important subtitle: "A parasitic nematode that is transmitted between rats and mollusks in its natural life cycle."

She flipped the pages to the article and began speed reading: "Humans are accidental hosts. They do not transmit this infection to others."

So far, as much as the medical team knew, no one else contracted the illness from Toby. She kept scanning and, finally, she came across something awful: "Eosinophilic meningitis caused by a lung worm of rats."

"Oh my God, Oliver, listen up." The poor dog startled, but she continued. "A lung worm of rats was first reported on the Gulf Coast only in 1985 and researchers think it came from infected rats. Rats scrambling off ships that docked in New Orleans!

"It says here this lung worm of rats is the principal etiologic agent of human eosinophilic meningitis, *Angiostrongylus cantonensis.*"

Annabel's left arm left Oliver's back and raised toward the ceiling. "Bingo! Now we're talking!"

Ambitious to find out more, Annabel behaved like a sponge and absorbed everything presently known about angiostrongyliasis. Very few cases had been reported in the United States, the first one being a youth in a Louisiana hospital in the 1990s.

She pushed her head back into the pillow shoved against the headboard. The storm was muted and heading north, and it was time to undress Oliver from his thunder shirt. She undid the Velcro and unwrapped the material. After giving him a hug, he jumped off the bed.

"I'm finished, Oliver. I can't read another word." Her excitement over the information she had unearthed was only muted by tiredness. Bob was definitely asleep, but if she texted him, he'd see it first thing in the morning. She grabbed her phone:

"I think I found it ... Toby's disease. Angiostrongylus cantonensis. *Rats are the definitive hosts of the parasite, and snails or slugs are the intermediate hosts. And, hell, humans are not supposed to be eating raw mollusks!"*

The text zoomed off with a swish. As she wiggled under the covers, she heard a return "ding." *That can't be,* she thought. She reached again for the phone. Bob must be crazy to still be up.

"Darn you, Annabel. I found out a lot too. And btw, I hope Oliver was not too much of a burden Again!"

"Your thunder shirt helped a lot. And no, he's a love, not a burden." She paused to think about it. *"Actually, good work comes out of my storm nights with Oliver."*

"How about that?!? Good night," he added.

"Good night as well."

Her eyes were so tired, but she forced them to look at one more thing on her phone, but there was still no word from Dustin.

Annabel woke, aggravated as hell at her alarm clock, but, of course, it was her own fault why she was too tired to scramble up and start moving. Oliver made it impossible to catch another five minutes of rest because his snout was in her face. The morning left no residue of a storm in the sky and he wanted his walk.

She hurried getting dressed and took him downstairs. The street and sidewalk showed an aftermath of the night's weather, with twigs, sticks, and leaves littering the wet ground. Oliver had more to sniff and was back to his normal self.

After the walk, she put on a single serving cup of coffee and began packing up for the day, when her phone dinged. Her heart rapidly beat. It must be Dustin.

No such luck. She quelled her disappointment, because at least it was Bob. Since he was on the hospital rotation, he started earlier than her, both for his own rounds on his patients and team rounds as well.

"I told Dr. Mares what we both found regarding eosinophilic meningitis. Would Dr. Gillespie excuse you for a few hours to come enlighten him/us with your input?"

"I would love to, but I'd have to ask him. I'll get back to you."

What fun, she thought and called the office. At least Becky should be in the office this early. She did Annabel a favor and called George at home.

Annabel texted Bob after receiving her attending's okay. *"I'll be there."*

He stuck in a "thumbs-up" emoji and wrote, *"Find us in the team's office."*

She gave Oliver a big kiss on his head. "Mind the house, boy."

With the notes she wrote in the middle of the night, her normal backpack material, and a reused fast-food coffee cup with her brew, she rushed out the door and took her own car, knowing there was no time to call a car service.

Inside the lobby of the hospital, she chucked her empty coffee cup and went upstairs. With purpose to her steps, she came around the pediatric nurses' station and heard the team conversing inside.

"Annabel Tilson," Dr. Mares said, "welcome again. Thank Dr. Gillespie for me. It was thoughtful of him to share you with us."

Annabel pulled out a chair. Bob smiled at her. Three other students were there, including Linnell. The team's white board on the wall was crammed with names of their patients. At the bottom was Toby's name listed as "orthopedic consult."

"I'm happy to be here." She put down her dependable notebook.

"Toby Owens, your original patient, is still worthy of our attention. I hunkered down with the subject of meningitis caused by parasites last night as well, but was deviated by calls from the hospital. Share with us what you found in the literature. Bob highlighted his end of it, but you can start from the beginning."

The team all had coffee cups. Donuts dusted with white powdered sugar sat in the middle of the table.

"They are small enough to eat by the handful," Rick said. "Help yourself."

Bob popped up and poured her a coffee. She thanked him and, with two bites, ate one donut.

"From what I've heard," Rick said, "you're a damn smart medical student. If you don't mind, in the essence of time, I'll ask you in stages what we need to know. If you know it, that is.

"Such as ... what are the risk factors and epidemiology for an angiostrongylus infection?"

"Bob and I learned yesterday that Toby ate a raw slug in Florida on a dare. That's a red flag, since the actual reported risks are the ingestion of undercooked or raw snails or slugs infected with the parasite. It can even be pieces of those that accidentally end up in vegetables or salads, or foods contaminated by their slime.

"The epidemiology is creepy because this parasite is a worm, a rat lung worm, that is transmitted between rats and mollusks in its natural life cycle. Humans can't transmit the disease; they are unfortunate accidental hosts. Reports indicate that *Angiostrongylus cantonensis* has been spread to around thirty countries, mostly because of rats transported on ships."

Annabel took a sip of coffee. She was tired from lack of

sleep, but the coffee, subject matter, and audience helped boost her eyes open.

"Bob told us about rats with the parasite from the early nineteen hundreds," Rick said, "first discovered in China. It's making its way around the globe."

"But very few cases have been discovered in the U.S., and only in the south. Terrible cases have ended up in children's hospitals near the Gulf Coast of Louisiana and Mississippi. Perhaps this is the first case more east, but I'm not sure. The CDC does recommend that these patients get reported, but it is not a mandatory reportable disease."

Rick nodded. "Absolutely. If Toby has it, we will call it in. And his case would be a clear example of how a person's travel history is important and how a traveler could pick this up when outside the country."

Bob shook his head. "Like on a Caribbean vacation."

Annabel nodded. "Yes, the parasite has been found there."

"Ugh. Maybe I should reconsider my medical school graduation trip."

"If you can get it in Florida," Rick said, "I wouldn't change my plans."

Bob laughed "Just kidding; a trip there is wishful thinking."

Nell pulled her braid forward and stroked the end. "Does this parasite have anything to do with a rat's lungs or do they just call it that?"

Annabel thought about another donut but waited to pick one up. "The adult worms live in their pulmonary arteries."

"Too gross," one of the other students said.

"I agree. The females lay eggs, they hatch into larvae, which travel to the pharynx. There, they are swallowed and eventually pass into feces. Next, they either penetrate or are ingested by the intermediate host … our snails or snugs." She opened her notebook and checked the second page. "In a definitive host, a third-stage larvae migrate to the brain, eventually to become young adults."

She shook her head. "Long story short, Nell, the life cycle is way complicated."

"Not to worry," Rick said. "I doubt if anything about Angiostrongyliasis is going to be on your rotation final exam. Unless, of course, some chief resident asks the test writer to throw in an extra credit question." He winked at Annabel. "Let's get back to humans. How do Toby's symptoms compare to what is reported?"

Annabel turned her head towards Bob.

"Patients present just like they have a bacterial meningitis," he said. "Which is what we thought initially. He's had the correct symptoms of nausea, vomiting, a stiff neck, and headaches. After his trip to Florida, the incubation period fit into the timeline too. Anywhere from a day to six weeks."

"He complained about muscle aches," Rick said.

"Which are included as well."

"We're down to what is most important for our young patient. We have the high eosinophilic count from his spinal tap, but are there any tests to make a definitive diagnosis? And how are we going to treat him? The beginning of school is looming any day for this lad."

"Sixth grade," Bob said. "I can't remember that far back."

"You old man," Annabel said with a laugh.

Rick reached for a donut and Annabel swigged down more coffee.

"I only saw mention of this in one scientific paper," she said. "In the case in Louisiana in the 1990s, they did a serologic test. A. cantonensis was diagnosed, proved positive by enzyme immunoassay."

"Hmm. I will have to look into that. In any case, I will report our suspicions to the CDC and they can help us out with testing if the hospital's lab can't."

"Dr. Mares," Bob said. "You probably guessed already. The

only treatment for this parasitic meningitis is supportive care."

"Why won't antibiotics work in this case?" Rick asked Nell.

"Because it's not a bacterial disease," she answered.

"Also," Annabel added, "other countries have tried anti-helminthic drugs without any success."

"I read if those drugs do kill worms," Bob said, "those dying worms could exacerbate a patient's neurologic symptoms."

"Yuck," Nell chimed in.

Rick pointed to the box. "Finish the donuts. We're going to go see Toby Owens."

Rick Mares rubbed his undersized chin as he forced the students to keep up with his lengthy stride down the pediatric ward. He looked over his shoulder. "Anne Owens spent another night with her son. I hope she's still here."

Annabel and the team geared up outside Toby's room and Rick went in first after he finished tying on a mask. Both parents were with their son.

"I stopped by on the way to work," Jack Owens said, standing alongside the bed. He rubbed his hands together like he wanted to play ball with his son. "I'm glad I'm here. Maybe you can give us an update on Toby's condition."

Anne moved an afghan and got up from the cot placed beside the other side of the bed. She held a small travel pillow.

"I really am awake," Toby said from the bed. "Headache and all."

"I swear his red hair looks like it's being tossed around from that headache," Anne said.

"No, Ma. It hasn't been combed in days." He let out a big sigh and turned his attention back to Rick. "Dr. Mares, I'm so tired of this."

"You have every right to be, Toby. Since yesterday, we've

dug up some information that we believe pertains to your case."

Anne and Jack sidled closer to each side of the bed, waiting for Rick's explanation. Toby cocked his head.

"We think you may have what's called *Angiostrongylus cantonensis,* the parasite responsible for your eosinophilic meningitis."

"What on earth is that?" Jack Owens blurted out.

Rick gritted his teeth. He was trying to brush over giving them some of the sordid details, such as being a lung worm of rats.

"That bad, huh?" Jack asked, not getting a response.

"We are going to inquire about a special test to confirm the diagnosis, to be certain."

"Come on, doc," Anne said. "How did our son get this angio parasite?"

"Probably that slug he ate."

Anne's motherly fury showed on her taut lips and she popped the pillow on Toby's head.

"Ma, would you quit hitting me on the head!"

"You deserve it. Jonathon wasn't crazy enough to eat a slime ball. What were you thinking?"

CHAPTER 23

Dr. Mares corralled his team outside Toby's room, where he addressed Annabel first. "Thank you for your input. Now go have a productive day in Dr. Gillespie's office."

"You're welcome. I'll never forget this meningitis. My dad's a neurosurgeon and deals with 'head' cases all the time, so I'll be sure to tell him about it."

Rick nodded, and with a hand wave, guided his team to finish rounds.

Lastly, Bob turned. "Talk to you later."

"For sure." Annabel put a mask back on and poked her head back into Toby's room.

"Come on in," Mrs. Owens said.

"I'm leaving," Jack Owens said. "My hardware store doesn't function without me." He patted his son on the shoulder and gave Annabel a smile as he left.

At least he didn't clunk his son on the head, she thought. "Toby, when you eventually leave the hospital, I'm sure they'll give you a follow-up appointment with your pediatrician. I won't see you again at Dr. Gillespie's office because I will only be there a few more days. Then I'll be here in the hospital. I'm sure you'll be discharged by then. I want to wish you luck and a smooth recovery."

"Thanks a lot. Can you be my doctor later, when I grow up?"

"How sweet. I wish, but I'll probably be leaving Ohio."

"Oh," he said sadly and looked down at his leg. "I hope when I change to a grown-up's doctor, he or she quits checking my private parts."

Anne Owens scowled over at him. "Doctors know what they're doing, Toby, and some exams are tailored for the individual. When men get older, they need what's called a prostate exam, which are done for cancer screening. Exams are for your own good."

"There are many doctors around in every specialty," Annabel said. "Sometimes the trick is finding one who is an excellent at his or her field of medicine, but you also like them as a person; you feel comfortable with their bedside manner. Sometimes it's difficult to find both."

Toby scrutinized his leg. "You haven't signed my cast."

"It would be an honor."

"There's a black magic marker over there."

Annabel fumbled through the items on the nightstand and picked it up. She hovered over his leg about what to write.

"Mom, I'm serious about this." Toby's red freckles seemed to grow larger on his cheeks as he continued with authority in his voice. "Please change my doctor to Dr. Clark. I like her so much better. Jonathon goes to her too."

For a few moments, Mrs. Owens stared at him. "That will make for an uncomfortable situation with Dr. Gillespie, but I'll talk to Becky. Yes, if that is what you prefer, I'll make it happen."

Annabel smiled at him. "Your office records are all in the same place, so that makes it easy. If you would like, I can subtly ask Becky to make the transfer when I go back."

"Thanks, Dr. Annabel," Toby said as his mom nodded.

She glanced down and wrote in cursive: *"GET BETTER and best of luck in 6th grade. Maybe someday you can be that exemplary pediatrician that you seek!"*

Toby beamed. He had never thought about that. His eyes sparkled as he looked at Annabel.

"If you can get through this, even medical school will be a snap." She winked, nodded at Anne Owens, and left. It was time to show up at Dr. Gillespie's office.

Annabel hummed to the music in her car on the way out of the parking lot. The sunshine was bold and bright and the Cincinnati sky was blue and free of even a wisp of a cloud. She wished she could look into a crystal ball and find out what young Toby Owens would do with his future. Now experienced with his own surgical and medical problems, perhaps it would make an impression on him to grow up and be on the other side of patient care.

She changed channels once, sampling both country music and top pop. Parking in the back of the lot when she arrived, she left spaces out front for parents and kids.

With her lab jacket draped over her arm and carrying the rest of her gear, Annabel entered the waiting room of Gillespie and Clark's pediatric office. Notably, there was a lack of babies in mothers' arms, which made for a quieter area than normal. Three young children were grouped around the square rug sharing toys and a toddler played against the wall with a tall doll.

She slipped into the front office and approached Becky.

"How did it go? Was your morning as mentally stimulating as this place?" Becky slipped a file into the vertical folders on a tall shelf. Her bun was tighter than normal and swirled to hide much of her premature gray.

"Kind of. Dr. Gillespie's patient, Toby Owens, is in the hospital with an interesting meningitis from a parasite. He also has a leg fracture. When it rains, it pours."

"My goodness. I've known that family for some time. Poor Toby. Nice kid. Are they taking good care of him?"

"Yes, and Toby and his mom have a request for after his discharge, that you switch over his records and future care to Dr. Clark. Toby would prefer not using Dr. Gillespie anymore; you may confirm that with them. I'm only the messenger, the middle-man."

"Hmm. These days, I'm thinking of switching the order of

their names on the sign outside to 'Heather Clark, M.D. and George Gillespie, M.D.'"

Annabel narrowed her eyes.

"Every once in a while, a mother or older pediatric patient finds his behavior unpalatable," Becky whispered. "The Owens are not the first family to switch care."

Becky sat and Annabel wanted to ask her more, but it was not her place. She repeated her recent mantra to herself. "Only a few more days."

"Is Stuart in a room with a patient?" she asked.

Becky craned her neck to the hallway. "I believe so. Dr. Clark is sharp as a tack this morning. We've phoned several prescriptions into pharmacies, admitted a girl to the hospital, and Xeroxed a bucket load of back-to-school paperwork for her patients."

"I'm sharing Toby's case with him because we students are learning pediatrics together. I'll tell Stuart later."

The fax machine on the desk came alive and a report started streaming out. The paper landed face down and Becky took a peek. "George is waiting for this one. He'll be out of his office soon to check if it's here."

Becky stood and glimpsed over the counter. A four-year-old was dwarfed in the seat of a chair, grasping an iPad. The volume was up and game music roared across the waiting room. The child's mother sat next to him, but she isolated herself from the problem. She was plugged in with earbuds to her iPhone hung on her waist.

Other parents rolled their eyes and a stir of remarks filtered through the room. "How rude that we must listen to this," a woman said to her husband. "Some people don't care what their kids do," he replied.

"As long as it doesn't affect her," she said. She stuffed the magazine she tried to read back in the rack and picked up her toddler.

Becky sighed as she lowered herself back in the chair. "During my twelve years working here, I have watched first-hand the decline of public social manners. But the descent is everywhere. Have you taken a flight recently? Waiting for a plane is an exercise in futility. Some guy will get on his cell phone a half an aisle away from you and will talk so loud that his private conversation is broadcast publicly. You can't read a book or a magazine, or think straight to use your own phone for a quiet call or a text message."

She cleared her throat and went to the door. "Sweetheart, would you mind turning that down a bit?"

The little boy looked confused and continued on just the same. Becky shook her head, turned, and looked down the hallway. "Annabel, on second thought, please go back to Dr. Gillespie's office, let him know you're here, and hand this fax to him. Wait and see … then he'll be up here in a jiffy to tell me what to do about this." She waved the paper once and handed it over.

Annabel slipped out. As she went down the hallway, she passed two of George's exam rooms with half open doors and patients. Although she was surprised that Becky confided in her about a few of Dr. Gillespie's patients, the woman's remarks did not shock her. But the best news was that the office staff could transfer Toby's care without a hassle.

Annabel fully rapped on George Gillespie's door.

"Come in."

When she stepped in, George popped his head from around his computer screen and gazed fixedly at her. "You're back."

"Yes, and Dr. Mares said 'thank you' for letting me join their medical team this morning."

"Anything in the name of a medical student's education." He cleared his throat. "I'll be out in a moment. We have patients waiting for us."

"Becky sent this in for you." She marched to the edge of his desk and handed it over.

Dr. Gillespie held the paper. "I'll join you in the hallway. First, I'll attend to this." He popped out of his chair and wobbled out the door, but as he did so, a pile of papers fell to the floor.

Annabel hesitated but didn't want to disturb him. She could place the papers back up on his desk herself. She stepped around to the other side and crouched down on the floor mat of the rolling chair. After tucking the folders and loose papers neatly together, she stood and slid them on the empty space.

Her eyes fell on the laptop screen. *What the hell?* She gasped. It took only a moment to wrap her head around the video in front of her. Not just any film clip, but a live video, in a physician's office.

For there was Stuart in his white jacket along with Dr. Clark in her doctor's coat.

Additionally, a young girl approximately six years old was on the exam table and a mother was standing by the door.

Heather had a stethoscope on the girl's chest and was asking her to take a deep breath. The sound was muted so that Annabel had not picked up on it before.

How creepy, she thought. *Does Dr. Clark know that her partner is watching her physical exams of children? Do families know their children are being recorded and viewed by another person ... the other doctor in the office?*

She was frozen with fear at the implications of what she saw. As she stepped away, it felt like her legs were dragging lead weights.

Annabel kept her eyes peeled for Stuart, but Dr. Gillespie was soon ready to see the next patient. Although she accompanied him into the room, her mind was still blindsided by the video streaming on his laptop. The patient's chief complaint, as reported by her father, went over her head.

The problem, she thought, might be a bigger issue in her mind than it really was. But she had no idea. It would be best to talk to Dr. Clark, but maybe that was not even appropriate. She should talk to Stuart first. Was he told at the beginning of the rotation that any or all of the exam rooms were being spied on? She wasn't told any such thing. Perhaps Dr. Clark had video access to Dr. Gillespie's rooms as well?

The afternoon wore on. Finally, during a short break when she grabbed a cup of tea and opened a book in the tiny room beside the kitchen, Stuart walked in.

"Hey," he said. "How did this morning go?"

"In a nutshell, fine." She focused past him, and seeing no one close at hand, she said, "Close the door."

Stuart scrunched up his face and shut the door silently. "What's up?"

"Just between you and me, I found something disturbing. When we started here the beginning of last week, did anyone tell you that any of the rooms are monitored by video cameras?"

Surprised by the question, Stuart fumbled for an answer. "Not at all."

Annabel bit her bottom lip. "Do you think you could ask Dr. Clark a question really subtly? Like work it into a conversation without making her suspicious or sound an alarm off in her brain?"

"Depends on what it is, Annabel. You're talking pretty cryptic."

"Look, somehow find out if she knows about any videotaping in the office. For instance, if she has video access to Dr. Gillespie's exam rooms or he has a camera on her rooms and can see her examine patients. If I ask her, she would think I'm crazy or the questions would raise a red flag. You're the one shadowing her."

"You're wigging me out, but I can try. These questions must

be important to you."

"As significant as each and every child that comes to this office."

"You're serious. Okay." Stuart focused on the floor. "I have an idea; how to ask her without raising suspicion about whatever you're suspicious about."

Annabel chuckled. "Stuart Schneider, the Dr. Columbo of Medicine."

Alongside Heather Clark, Stuart peered at the folder that she had open on their next patient. She was chewing on the last piece of vanilla cookie in her mouth, so Stuart saw an opportunity to talk.

"Leukemia is unfair for anyone to deal with, but especially for your next patient so young. Looks like you've been seeing her for some time."

Heather swallowed. She licked her lips and agreed. "Two years, to be exact."

"I learn a lot from your patients with sorrowful diagnoses. It would be interesting, as a student, to see the progression of her care. Do you or Dr. Gillespie ever do anything like videotape patients' visits? It could serve as a record, a teaching tool to students, or as documentation."

Dr. Clark closed the file. A nurse, patient, and parent walked by them and entered the next room, giving her adequate time to reflect on Stuart's question.

"What an interesting concept, Stuart, but I don't think worthwhile. Over and above the clinical time students put in, and their book work, videos of patients' visits would take too long for students to watch.

"Also, in answer to your question, my partner and I have never done such a thing and I would never ask that of families.

Who wants to be scrutinized on camera? Children are shy enough without knowing they are on camera. What about when they get older? How would they feel about being filmed half nude when they were little? What if a taped exam somehow leaked out to social media? I myself would cringe if we allowed monitors in the office." She smiled but continued.

"Sorry about the rant. I would never put cameras in our rooms. I even dislike the fact that we find it necessary to use the security cameras that face the parking lot outside."

When they went into the exam room, Stuart held the little girl's interest while Dr. Clark did a routine follow-up exam on her. "Come back in two months," Heather said when she was finished and handed the family a note for the front desk to make an appointment.

Dr. Clark lingered in the room to enter a note in the electronic medical record. Stuart raced off to find Annabel. He found her in the kitchen grabbing one of the cookies that Heather had brought in for staff.

Stuart flashed an affirmative nod like his good deed questions were asked and answered.

Annabel was full of anticipation. "Well?"

"An emphatic 'no.'" He lowered his voice as much as practical. "Dr. Clark and her partner have never done such a thing and would never ask that of their patients and patients' families. Annabel, there is no known videotaping going on in this office. Or video spying without anyone's knowledge. She's sure."

Stuart leaned close, the closest he ever sidled up to her.

"What do you know? Is there?"

CHAPTER 24

Annabel's next heartbeat thumped against her chest like a knock at the door. Stuart grimaced. She was tongue-tied and finally caught her breath.

"I'd better not talk about it, Stuart. This is a tricky situation and we're just students here as a courtesy because these doctors are affiliated with the university. This is a privilege to be in a private office observing pediatric medical care. I better shut up about what I saw for right now. In essence, I'll try to make inquiries about the matter outside of the office."

"Annabel, I'm not a gossiper. If you change your mind, I'm here to add my two cents worth."

"I appreciate that, as well as you asking Dr. Clark my questions."

Becky scurried in, straight to the table. "Both docs are ready for their next patients. You two better hurry up."

"Sorry to make you hunt us down," Annabel said.

"No problem. I wanted to come in here anyway." She picked up a cookie, and then a second one, and smiled.

Annabel found Dr. Gillespie reading a chart. "Ever do a dermatology elective?"

"No, and I don't believe I can fit that in before graduation."

"You see lots of cancer in derm, especially since a chunk of our society is negligent about sun protection."

He handed over the file and Annabel took a quick glance at the next patient's chief complaint - "strange skin growth." The twelve-year-old girl's name was Molly.

Inside, the girl was on the exam table with an upper body paper gown that opened in the front. Small for her age, she nevertheless appeared healthy. She flashed a quick, bright smile.

"Hi, Molly," Dr. Gillespie said. "Is your mom or dad in the

waiting room?"

"My dad brought me. Yup, he's outside."

"Perfect. This is Dr. Tilson, a medical student."

"Hi, Molly," Annabel said.

"Your hair is pretty and long," the girl said. "I wish mine shined like that."

"If yours was like mine, you'd wish for hair like yours."

The girl scrunched her forehead.

"We aren't satisfied with what God gave us, but want something else. You have wonderful locks of curls and I wish mine bunched up like those curls."

"Oh," she said. "Thanks." She twirled a finger behind her ear and smiled.

"I don't wish for waves or curls," Dr. Gillespie said. "I just wish for more hair! Now, it says here, you came in about a 'skin growth.' What's that about, Molly?"

"I have a blackish bump on my chest."

"How long has it been there?"

"I'm not sure. Maybe a few months, but it wasn't so dark before."

"Show me."

The top was loosely tied at the neck, and Molly spread it open.

Surprised, George said, "You're wearing a bra."

"I'm old enough."

"You don't need to wear one when you come see me. I mean, especially since your lesion is on your chest."

Molly's cheeks blushed. "But it's above my bra."

"Better to check your upper body for more," he said, irritated.

"It's the only one I have. I'm sure about it. My mom wanted you to check it out."

Dr. Gillespie's lips tightened in a thin grimace. "Let's take a look."

Molly pointed to her right chest above her bra where she had a lesion smaller than a thumbtack. The color varied between dark brown and black and the round border was irregular.

Annabel moved to the other side and noted the slightly raised skin lesion while Dr. Gillespie hovered in front of Molly's chest. Her breasts, although small under her bra, already qualified as a young lady's. Like an insect in motion, a low hum began from George's throat.

"I would like to take a sample of this irritating bump. Let me get permission from your dad. We'll be right back."

"Molly's lesion is suspicious for a malignant melanoma," George said as they approached the waiting room. "If that's the case, early diagnosis is imperative. We rarely diagnose those, however, because less than two percent of all melanomas occur during childhood and, besides that, girls are also less apt to develop it than boys."

Molly's father stood while Dr. Gillespie briefly explained. "Taking a snippet of your daughter's skin problem shouldn't hurt. I'll give the area a bit of numbing medicine. It would be best if I send the removed skin piece to the lab so we can figure out what it is. It does concern me."

"Please do what you think best," the man said. "She's our only daughter."

George told him the few minor risks. Back in the room, one of the nurses joined them as George cleaned the area and injected some lidocaine. Molly didn't move a muscle while he took a scalpel and excised a sample. His nurse readied it for the lab and took off.

"You can get dressed," Dr. Gillespie said with a smile, "and just to let you know, you're going to have a beautiful figure. Actually, you are already worthy of winning first place in a beauty pageant."

Molly blushed again. "Thanks, Dr. Gillespie. Nobody's told me that before."

"You're welcome, darling."

George pulled the door closed behind him and shrugged. "I try to boost the ego of the girls going through puberty because it's a sensitive time for them."

Annabel didn't want to touch that one and kept quiet.

At home, Annabel geared up for a serious run. Bob was on call for the night and she was glad she still had Oliver. The poor dog needed exercise as much as she did.

Downstairs, she made a right and, after he did his business, she started off in a trot. All the flowers in the park overlooking the river were in full bloom and the benches were half occupied. She nodded at folks, but their eyes settled on Oliver and not her.

Annabel had another reason for rushing out to run. The spike in endorphins would do her brain some good; she needed more clarity about the behavior of Dr. Gillespie and the situation she had witnessed in his office. If Dr. Clark had no knowledge of videos in the office filming her and her patients, were those recordings permissible?

She was no police officer to know such things for certain. Police officer, she thought. Dustin still hadn't answered her text from yesterday and she was painfully aware of how he abruptly left the fair on Saturday.

Annabel rushed down the steps to the pass over the major road leading to the path along the Ohio River. Oliver trotted with enthusiasm and kept perfect pace. Perhaps Dustin had his reasons for Saturday's exit, but not answering her message perplexed her further.

Although she played a diversionary tactic to keep her mind off him, she'd sorely missed him the last three days ... his voice, his dimple, his smile, his concern for her, and listening to his enthusiasm about his job.

Clearly, they worked in different fields, and often she could not share things with him like she did with Bob. For one thing, he might not understand the "medicine" part of what she told him, but there was also patient confidentiality. And the dynamics of what she did with medical colleagues and teams would probably bore him.

No different, she thought. Dustin did not reiterate the dynamics of the officers working together at the station. However, she realized, he did quite often talk about his faithful partner, Sean.

She did long for him, emotionally and physically. It was worth a shot to contact him again, but this time, she'd call him. She wanted to hear his voice and again try to find out what might be wrong.

In addition, she did not know who to turn to; he was the best resource she could think of. If she mentioned her attending's behavior to the pediatric department chairperson, she could suffer repercussions. She had to talk to someone outside of medicine. She would go mad if she didn't.

George Gillespie was throwing up too many red flags.

Annabel and Oliver went the whole distance and ran along the river road. She allowed the drone of the bridge traffic from the Kentucky to Ohio side to stifle her racing thoughts. The sunset was fogged over and a humid mist increased and swirled in the air. They slowed their pace, and when Annabel arrived back in front of her apartment, Oliver made a gentle tug towards the entrance.

"I need a treat, Oliver, besides the run. Let's go to Pete's Café and I'll grab dinner."

They walked the rest of the way and she tethered Oliver to the fence. Customers were sparse but consistent as she went from the outdoors to the inside.

"Hey, Pete," she said. He stood behind the counter wearing a baseball cap with the name of his café. "New hat?"

"It is. A subtle advertisement. Like it?"

"Sure thing, and it looks handsome on you."

"You're too kind. What'll you have?"

"Your half sandwich and salad mix. Make it tuna."

"Where you sitting?"

"Outside with Oliver."

She paid and Pete brought her combo out in a short while. He handed Oliver a biscuit.

"You earned a friend for life."

"He's a keeper, that one."

"He won first place in the county fair mixed breeds dog competition."

"Like I said, he's a keeper for life. And you and your friend saved him from probable extinction at the shelter."

"We did." Annabel opened the napkin with utensils while Pete placed a glass of water down from his tray. "Can I ask you something?"

"My waitress is behind the counter in there, so you sure can."

"What if a chef acted so strange that his behavior bothered the customers? Or he filmed other employees without their knowledge? What would you do about that, if anything?"

"Hmm. I presume this is a hypothetical question that needs an answer. As far as the restaurant industry, we are inspected and rated by the Health Department. However, yes, another employee or a customer can report a problem to them if they are concerned.

"As far as filming, if a chef had a camera on co-workers and they had no knowledge about it, that might be an issue to take up with the police department."

Annabel bit her lip. "Thanks, Pete. You're very helpful."

He laughed and tilted his cap. "You're not reporting me, are you?"

"No way. This looks too tasty."

Pete patted Oliver. "Where's that boyfriend of yours tonight?"

"Good question."

Before she hunkered down to study at home, Annabel knew she must call Dustin. Pete's advice had made her certain. Not a text or an email, but a real old-fashioned phone call.

She picked up her iPhone and deliberated what she would say while looking at Oliver, who was flopped out on his bed with his legs jerking. He was engaged in a deep REM sleep after the evening's activities.

She went to "favorites" and pressed Dustin's number. Most likely, she figured, her call would go to voicemail. She hated that it did.

"Dustin, it's Annabel. My thick skull finally tells me that you're ignoring me. I'm sorry if I said or did something to offend you. Please at least give me an explanation." She took a deep breath, trying to compose herself. She wanted to tell him how much their relationship meant to her, but she couldn't. If she could, she would rather do it in person.

"There is also an issue I am faced with regarding the pediatric doctor I mentioned to you, the one I'm working with for two weeks, George Gillespie. I consider it my duty to ask a police officer about what I've seen in his office, or downright report it. Please, Dustin, call me."

Dustin walked out of the nearby movie theater and headed for his car. After a short walk to the wrong area, he let out an expletive under his breath. His black Acura was two aisles over and he was not thinking straight. Or thinking at all. The mindless flick he had just watched drowned his sorrows for two hours by diverting his attention, but now he needed to face his own realities.

Personal losses of loved ones took time to get over, he told himself over and over again. The magic number was one year, especially with a death of a close family member like a parent. But to him, it also included a breakup between a guy and a girl whose relationship could have been marriage material, the death of a partner in the police force, and the death of a beloved dog or pet.

Arriving at his car, he slithered in and turned the volume back up on his phone to find it ringing. The incoming call came from his captain and he swiftly swiped to answer.

"Hey, cap, perfect timing."

"Sorry to disturb you, but Sean's wife called the station after most of us left for the day. Sean's memorial service is one night, tomorrow, from five thirty to nine o'clock. I thought us day shift officers could go after work."

"That would work for me. However, that seems speedy for a funeral home to prepare a dead body that quickly for a service and a subsequent burial."

"He's being cremated in the morning."

Dustin bit his tongue. *Damn,* he thought.

"You still there?" asked the captain.

"Yeah, but I tell you, if I find out about any more bad news, I'm going to dive into the Ohio."

"Dustin, that would be a dirty swim. You wouldn't make it far, however, because a barge or the current would push you to the mucky bottom."

"Yeah, well, I guess I'll live another day."

"You keep talking like that and I'll ask one of the three-to-eleven shift officers to take you to a suicide prevention doc."

"Don't worry about me. See you tomorrow."

He closed the call and noticed a new voicemail, which raised the hair on his neck. It came from Annabel, and he didn't want to listen because he might not believe whatever she had to say. She always sounded innocent and trustworthy, dependable and smart. And he couldn't believe the innocent and trustworthy part.

Besides, he just found out that his partner, who never wanted to face fire and be cremated, was indeed going to face both. Yes, Sean might be dead, but his wishes were what was important. Either his desires were not known or were being ignored. Sadness over his partner delayed him from starting the ignition as he felt emotion gather on his face and in his heart.

Dustin let his feelings play out as couples passed going to their cars. He made a rash decision. What harm could be done to listen to Annabel's message. She sounded sincere, as usual.

"Dustin, it's Annabel. My thick skull finally tells me that you're ignoring me. I'm sorry if I said or did something to offend you. Please at least give me an explanation.

"There is also an issue I am faced with regarding the pediatric doctor I mentioned to you, the one I'm working with for two weeks, George Gillespie. It's my duty to ask the correct authority about what I've seen in his office, or downright report it. Please, Dustin, call me."

He listened more attentively to the first part of her message, and after the whole thing played, he put his phone on the passenger seat. Maybe one of these days when he felt up to it, he'd at least say "good-bye." And as far as he was concerned, he had nothing to do with whatever Annabel was perplexed about with some doctor named George Gillespie.

CHAPTER 25

Before getting ready for bed, Dustin cleaned out Solar's cage while the bird stood steadfast on the top of the refrigerator. Why did he always get the impression, he thought, that his two-legged friend snickered at his human master cleaning up after him?

"Solar, I wish you would make yourself more useful around here and tidy up after me!"

Dustin threw dirty newspapers in the trash bucket. "At least you're not hurling any back talk at me."

"What's your problem?" Solar said.

"Come on down here and keep me company. I could use it now. Even if you give me grief."

The bird cocked his head and, to Dustin's amazement, Solar took a short flight to the counter. Instead of going upstairs to the bedroom, he considered the fact that all evening he had only eaten popcorn at the movie theatre. He poured a bowl of cereal and smothered it with milk.

As he made his way through the Cheerios, Annabel's voicemail came to mind. Now he was thinking more clearly than earlier in the evening. *She must be working with a strange doctor who makes her uncomfortable.* At least that was the way she sounded.

He put his laptop next to him, and with a mouthful, he typed in George Gillespie's name for a Google search. A box showed up in the upper right hand corner with the man's Cincinnati practice address, a tab for directions, and phone number. Reviews and medical biography information sites showed up as well. Other doctors around the country with the same name also surfaced. Dustin spent time reading about the guy and also learned he practiced with a female physician named Heather Clark.

As he expected, the doctor's information all seemed flawless. He finished the cereal and thought about flipping down the cover. He never left it open when not in use, just in case Solar walked across the keyboard.

Instead, he grabbed a banana, which he should have cut up in the cereal to begin with, and went to YouTube. It couldn't hurt, he thought, and typed in George Gillespie's name. An account for that name appeared, but he gave little credence to it being for the man in question.

The account was registered as "public," and Dustin counted seven boxes with videos ready to be viewed. He clicked on the first one with a running time under three minutes. The headline said, "Knockout girls having summer fun."

With no geographic location listed, it could have been any community public pool. Several children frolicked in the shallow end of a pool in their bathing suits. Some made an attempt to swim. Two girls climbed out from the steps and walked on the slippery surface to the edge, where the camera zoomed in on their little behinds. When they turned, the video zoomed generously close up to their bodies.

Except for kids squealing and splashing, the camera person had nothing to say. Dustin shrugged. He went to the rest of the recordings, of similar content, except that both sexes were represented. The kids all seemed under ten years old.

Finally, he gathered the content came from different geographic locations, and whoever this Gillespie was, he had simply reposted content from somewhere else. His other captions boasted similar headlines: kids were "sensational" and one clip proclaimed the girl filmed would be the "next, best upcoming wife a guy could ask for!" The one he disliked the most said "Hot Dog!" It went further than the others and came close to crossing the line into child pornography.

However, he thought, it didn't. Plus, it was a public account and surely someone went a little overboard in posting little girls in their bathing suits. After all, no content showed any nudity.

He said good-night to Solar and went to bed. His curiosity over Annabel's message, however, increased. If his "ex-girlfriend's" attending doctor was a weirdo, he most probably was a strange person for a long time. First, Dustin needed to attend Sean's family service tomorrow evening, which would be a very sorrowful event. If he spoke to Annabel sometime in the next few days, however, he would be curious to know if the YouTube videos he watched were put on the internet by the same man she shadowed in her pediatric rotation.

Officer Kendrick and one other undercover cop sat in the remotest area of the Cincinnati police station, which gave them the distinction of being referred to as "out of sight and out of mind." Kendrick didn't mind because he could better focus on his job. When he needed a break, he either pranced over to keep the coffee pot going or he was ready to go out in the real world and follow a lead that was coming to fruition.

No one suspected Kendrick of being a police officer because of his slight build. It was as if he had stopped growing when he turned fourteen. He'd been around in the same Cincinnati station for his whole career and had seen officers come and go.

And for different reasons. Like Sean, some had died in the line of work, and that strengthened his resolve even more that police work was more valuable to the general public than any other job on the planet.

Most of his hours were spent at a desk but, to him, what he did never bored him. For one thing, the need for his specialization had grown, just like the vast worldwide internet had overgrown. Of course, in his line of work, he focused on the territory associated with the station's geographic area, but if he did stumble on something that officers in northern Ohio or other states would appreciate knowing about, he was more than ready to supply the information.

For him, unearthing the perverted, degrading, and illegal material on secluded websites gave him purpose. And even though the FBI and a host of other criminal investigators had taken down Backpage.com, there was as much work in the aftermath as there was before. The service, second only to Craigslist in business, had been huge, but content in its classified advertising had gotten a slew of officials arrested. Every time he thought of the erotic material hidden in automotive services and real estate and job listings, it made his blood boil.

Now, in the aftermath of the site's demise and removal of its content related to human trafficking, prostitution, and pornography, Officer Kendrick was like a sniffer dog going in after a building's collapse. Material from the site had been downloaded to personal computers and also subtle, small new sites had hatched to take Backpage.com's place.

What Kendrick hated the most was all the crap out there that involved minors. As the years went by, he came to categorize child pornography into two classes, which he thought of as the "creators" and the "end users." The damn creators took innocent children and used them to shoot the still photography or video content, thereby making the kids like slaves and emotionally and maybe physically damaging them forever. The vulgar "end users" bought and/or streamed the content, thereby keeping the trade alive. Both types of people were despicable and it was not possible to have one without the other. For every lead from him that led to an arrest in the Cincinnati area, he took immense pleasure. As an overly religious man with kids, he wanted the dangerous perverts to be put away for life, which was simply wishful thinking.

This week alone, Officer Kendrick was hot on the trail of child pornography, which he believed originated from the old site and, on Wednesday, he honed in on an IP address.

After a brief stroll around the office and a walk to the coffee pot, he sat down one more time. Soon the office would be emptying out to leave for Sean's funeral home service but, by God, he was going to attach a name to this newfound IP address if it killed him.

Police officers filtered into the funeral home for Sean's memorial service from many other police stations besides the one he had worked in. Men and women in blue milled around everywhere and it warmed Dustin's heart. Family members, especially Sean's wife, were given deep condolences for their loss, but it surprised Dustin how many attendees gave him sympathy as well. Police bonded to one another with strong ties, especially when it came to partners.

After several short eulogies by family members, the captain said a few words and then added, "Sean's partner, Dustin Lowe, will conclude for the police department."

Dustin nodded at the captain and walked through an aisle of people to the podium. Sean's ashes were laid to rest nearby in a special cremation urn, on a table surrounded by flowers. Additional tables held pictures and snippets of his life.

He gazed out at the room of faces, the larger percentage of people being his family of law officers.

"I had the honor of working on a daily basis with this man who we lost too early. Sean was dependable, hard-working, thoughtful, and always put himself in the line of duty to protect citizens. I know for a fact that his passion for protecting the public ran over into his off-duty hours. For me, I've lost a true friend who always had my back, both professionally and personally. He taught and advised me more than I deserved.

"But I'll shut up about the loss we all feel. Now I would like to commemorate and celebrate his life with a big smile because, having known him, he would want us to carry on with the happy memories we hold in our hearts about him."

Dustin eased into a warm smile. One of the officers in the crowd yelled, "Yeah! Sean, we love you, buddy."

Dustin countered, "Rest in peace, Sean."

An hour later, many officers left Sean's service, but the group from his police station still stayed. The double doors to the room stood open and many of the remaining cops filtered out to the reception area outside. Couches and chairs clustered in arrangements for intimate sitting groups. Dustin poured a decaf from a setup in the hallway and then took a spot at the end of a couch.

"Sorry you lost your partner," Officer Kendrick said as he settled into the adjacent chair. "Sean was one of the best. Had a sense of humor too."

"Tell me about it." Dustin sighed. "I didn't say anything about this in that miniscule tribute I just gave, but I feel responsible for what occurred."

"I came out of the office on Monday when it happened. Dustin, you can't blame yourself. We all know that spontaneous, random shootings occur, whether they're directed at police officers or the general public."

"You're right, unfortunately," he said and took a swig of coffee.

"Coffee any good?"

"Better than I expected. So how's life with the undercover snooping on illegal drug sites and money laundering? Not to mention prostitution, porn, and all the rest of the crap that human beings are so sleazy about?"

"Busy as usual. If it weren't for all that sleaze, I wouldn't have a job. Yet, if I could snap my fingers and bring all the perpetrators and end-users to justice, and put myself out a job, I would." He gasped at the idea and Dustin nodded.

"Like some dirtbag I honed in on today," Kendrick said. "I gotta dig more, but he may have loaded up on child pornography around the time the law enforcement agencies cracked down on that Backpage.com. Somebody local, as far as I can tell."

"You getting a search warrant yet to confirm your suspicions?"

"Maybe. Before I go begging down at the courthouse, I gotta dot my i's and cross my t's so they don't send me away with my tail between my legs. Nothing worse than getting real close in an investigation only to have it blow up in your face. No, I want this perp, George Gillespie, caught before he goes any further with his salacious desire for child pornography."

Dustin's breath caught in his throat. "Did you say George Gillespie?"

"Yeah."

Dustin's blood raced in his veins. He leaned over to Kendrick and lowered his voice. "You and I need to talk. Last night, I looked him up. He has a YouTube account with video clips, all involving kids. All sexually suggestive in their own way."

Kendrick tilted his head. "Hell, yeah, we need to compare notes. But what made you look the guy up?"

Dustin widened his eyes. "My girlfriend, I mean, my ex-girlfriend." He rose suddenly from the chair and grabbed his coffee from the table. Kendrick followed his lead and popped up.

"What's the matter?" Kendrick said.

"This guy, George Gillespie. He's a pediatrician."

Dustin corralled Kendrick outside on the porch of the funeral home. Pillars lined the porch, and a few people, including officers, glued their ears to cell phones. A couple sat on a bench.

"How do you know he's a pediatrician?" Kendrick asked.

"Again, from my ex-girlfriend. Now I have to call her. She left me a message about him yesterday, but I didn't respond."

"Your love life sounds complicated, Lowe, but this case is sounding more plausible to present before a judge and procure a search warrant. You better the hell call her so we can find out what she has to say."

Dustin rubbed his hand over his eyes. "Yeah. She's an 'ex-girlfriend' whom I have not officially broken up with yet."

Kendrick sighed. "Why not?"

"Because I'm a coward."

"In the best interest of this doctor's little young patients, call her right now. However, please don't complicate matters by breaking up with her now. We must hear what she has to report about this Gillespie guy." Kendrick stared him down.

Dustin pulled his iPhone out of his front pocket. Now he hoped she wouldn't ignore his call. After all, he thought, he had disregarded hers for days.

CHAPTER 26

Wednesday morning, Annabel dropped Oliver off at Bob's apartment after walking and feeding him. Bob was not home yet from his night on call, so she made sure the dog had water and that his fluffy bed was nearby. Because of the dog's transfer, she had her own car, and first texted Bob before starting the ignition.

"Oliver's all set, already bunked down in his bed. How'd your night on call go?"

"Wild, but I survived. Will only need a short nap this afternoon. How about some study time together tonight (if you're not seeing Dustin)."

She gaped at the message, the part about Dustin. *No worries there,* she thought. She would surely not be seeing him.

"Sure. Let's make it a serious study binge."

"How about my place, which is bigger than yours, and Oliver is already there."

"Okay. Why don't I bring in some take-out food?"

"Don't go through any trouble. Just something on the way. Anything is fine with me."

"Later, then ..."

Both smiling faces and tearful, sick children watched Annabel as she walked through the waiting room of Drs. Gillespie and Clark. Becky pulled her into the front desk area immediately.

"Dr. Gillespie has a meeting this morning at the pediatric department," she said. "He wants you to shadow Dr. Clark."

Annabel tried to keep her enthusiasm about the news low-key. She found Heather and Stuart in the hallway and slipped on her student jacket. "Sorry for the intrusion. I'm supposed to tag along with you two this morning."

"No problem," Heather said. "Two students are better than one. We're getting started because we may need to see a few of Dr. Gillespie's patients as well."

Heather took down the chart in the rack, read for a moment, and they all piled into the room. A woman with her nine-year-old daughter were inside. After introductions, the girl spoke up after a prompt from her mother.

"I am sick of being the littlest kid in my class. It makes them all make fun of me."

"Do you mean the shortest?" Heather asked.

The girl nodded.

The girl's mother spoke next. "I agreed to bring Wendy in because her father and I are a bit concerned as well. He and I are fairly tall, so it doesn't make sense that Wendy is the shortest kid in her class."

Heather narrowed her eyes. "Any weight loss, abdominal pain, vomiting, poor appetite?"

Wendy and her mom both shook no.

"Any other problems you can think of? Her records are here, so I can check some statistics."

"No," Wendy answered. She wore summer clothing and Heather listened to her heart and lungs through her T-shirt, checked her abdomen with her shorts unbuttoned, and reviewed her head, neck, and limbs.

Dr. Clark sat at the desk and swiveled the chair around to talk to them all.

"I totally understand the concern you both have for Wendy's short stature." She opened up the chart and reevaluated the girl's growth chart, especially for the last few years. "Here's my concern. Although Wendy was in the lower growth tier of this chart for the last several years ... around the thirtieth percentile ... now she has slacked off to less than the tenth percentile.

Fortunately, her weight has remained appropriate."

Heather thoughtfully showed everyone in the room the chart in her hands.

"Let's snap some radiographs, which will tell us if Wendy's bone age is delayed."

"So there is something wrong," Wendy's mom said, and put her hands to her mouth.

"My suspicion is a growth hormone deficiency. I will order some screening tests and we'll get to the bottom of this." She glanced at the students. "For instance, we'll run a CBC analysis, which will tell us if Wendy is anemic; and electrolytes, chemistries, thyroid function tests, and a urinalysis. And especially for a growth hormone deficiency, an IGF-1."

Dr. Clark turned to the family. "Our lab here in the office will start the ball rolling. We'll have more answers when all these tests come back."

"What if she does have the deficiency?" Wendy's mom asked.

"A pediatric endocrinologist can take over. I will make the referral."

Heather gave Wendy a wide smile. "You are going to be fine. In any case, be proud of whatever height God has given you, even if you have some catching up to do."

With a scurry out the door, they all left. Wendy went to give blood and Heather kept the students for a moment. "We're in a time crunch, but any questions?"

Annabel pulled out a memo pad and wrote down "growth hormone deficiency." "Not from me, Dr. Clark. I'll look up cases tonight, but I really appreciate working with you today, or at least this morning."

As they went into the next room, Annabel realized that even she was being filmed in Dr. Gillespie's secret tapings. She tried to shrug it off because working with Dr. Clark gave her a sense of normalcy about the way a pediatrician should behave.

Annabel handed a brown bag with dinner food over to Bob in the doorway and shuffled back to her car for her books. Oliver wagged his tail, happy to be free, and trotted behind her.

"Did you end up getting any sleep?" Annabel asked after stepping into Bob's apartment.

Bob nodded as he unpacked the containers. "A two-hour nap and then a long walk with Oliver. Thanks for bringing the food. I'll split the bill with you."

"Absolutely not. Next time."

They unwrapped beef brisket sandwiches and salad and sat across from each other at the kitchen counter.

"Dr. Gillespie was absent this morning, so I saw patients with Dr. Clark and Stuart. Boy, was that refreshing."

"Sounds like it. Anything interesting?"

"I put it on our bucket list to review tonight. A nine-year-old with a working diagnosis of growth hormone deficiency. Her case made me realize how important growth curves are even after the first and second years of life."

"Interesting. I didn't know that either. I guess it goes with the territory of being a pediatrician."

Annabel drizzled dressing on the salad. "Dr. Clark is referring the girl to a pediatric endocrinologist but ordered the necessary lab workup besides films."

Bob shook his head. "There are so many subspecialties in medicine, it's mind boggling. I'm relieved I made up my mind about orthopedics and don't need to worry about which field of residency to apply to."

"But you still must decide about which programs are the best and where to apply. Geography will be important. Say, Nashville has top medical residency programs in just about everything. Why don't you apply in my hometown?"

Bob practically choked on his sandwich because she also wanted to go back home for residency and, this year, he was constantly troubled knowing he wouldn't see her any more after medical school.

"Cat got your tongue?" she asked. "Maybe I've grown on your nerves and you want to be as far away as possible from me." She gave him a big smile, hoping that was not the case.

"Are you kidding? Being at the same University for residency would be awesome. There are still so many training years in front of us, at least we could be nearby for some of them."

"Bob, thanks. I don't mean to sound immature but, presently, you qualify as my very best friend." She glanced at her iPhone at the edge of the counter. "I have an idea. Don't get angry at me, but I could mention something to my dad about you and your desire for orthopedics. Believe me, he can't get you into a residency program in Nashville, but he can be an added recommendation, especially since he's met you. As you know, he is well respected and his opinion counts."

Bob's pulse bounded at his wrist. The residency programs there would be stellar. He was surprised at her willingness to help out.

"Is that a yes?"

"Yes. When the time comes, I would be so grateful."

"Nothing stops me from saying something right now." Annabel picked up her phone and placed a call, taking a gamble her father would be home already from the hospital. Danny answered the call.

"Hey, Dad, I'm glad I caught you."

"Your sister handed me the phone because she doesn't want to talk to you. You two better settle your differences one of these days. How is your rotation coming along?"

"There is a lot going on, Dad, not related to my education. I don't like the attending I'm working with, mostly because his behavior seems inappropriate."

"In what way?"

"I don't want to burden you at the moment. Besides, I'm with Bob, we're eating dinner, and we're going to hit the books tonight. I called for another reason."

"Okay, then. Shoot."

"Bob is further ahead than me; he came to a decision about residency. He wants orthopedics."

"Wise choice."

"I told him, for sure, to apply to the program in Nashville."

"One of the best."

"Since you know him, and you know I vouch for him, can you talk to someone in the department ahead of time? As a verbal recommendation regarding his character and work? They would see his fine grades and major test scores sooner or later with his application."

"I would be happy to. He's a wonderful young man."

"Thanks, Dad."

Bob patted Annabel's hand and waved for the phone.

"Here, you talk to him," she said.

"Dr. Tilson, thank you so much. I don't mean to be a burden."

"No trouble at all. Just like their neurosurgery program, the more information they receive about a candidate, the better they can make decisions. In the end, however, a lot comes down to the paper application and the residency interview. But my recommendation will be taken into account if you are high on their list."

"Thank you, sir. Thank you so much."

"Not to mention it. And prompt that daughter of mine to make up her mind soon as well." Danny laughed. "So how is sharing Oliver working out for the two of you?"

"Better than we thought. We love him to death. He's probably getting spoiled rotten going from one place to another."

"One of these days, Sara and I must meet him."

"I'll tell Annabel. Thanks again."

Annabel grasped the phone. "Dad, thanks for your help. I'll call you and Mom by the weekend before I transition to the pediatric wards."

"Bye, honey."

"That was easy," Annabel said.

"Every little bit counts. We better start studying so my grades are stellar on my residency application."

"That goes for both of us."

Bob opened a book to the side of his sandwich. "I'm looking up the particulars of a pediatric growth hormone deficiency."

Annabel nodded as her phone buzzed with an incoming call. She glanced at the incoming number and bobbed her head back. Dustin was calling her back after all these days, she thought. Was he calling because of the big deal she made on the last voicemail message about a possible police matter? Or was he calling her because of their relationship? Or both?

She answered, put the phone to her ear, but realized it would be more difficult to talk privately with Bob sitting in front of her. "Hey, I was beginning to worry if something happened to you or if you weren't receiving my messages."

"Your voicemail was intriguing. I'm with a colleague at the moment and, as it turns out, the name of that doctor you mentioned, Gillespie, came up."

Annabel's heart sank. He sounded impersonal and spoke straight to the point. Perhaps there was nothing personal about his call at all. "A colleague," she stuttered. "Then say hello to Sean."

His silence was deafening as Bob turned a page. "Can you tell me what you were concerned about with him?" Dustin asked, ignoring her comment about Sean.

Annabel gulped. Finally, she could hand over the

information and feel better about getting it off her chest.

"Don't get me wrong. This doctor has not overtly done anything outright physically or sexually intimidating with his pediatric patients that I'm aware of, but in my opinion, he goes overboard with his private examinations and comments to them. You and Sean may not be the resource I need to talk to, but if I comment to the department chairman or the medical board of licensing as a student, I may be out of line. Dustin, I just don't know who to tell." Her head raised and she looked at Bob.

"Annabel, I had no idea this situation was so bad," Bob interjected.

"I am trying to keep quiet and not spread possible false accusations in the department."

She redirected the conversation back to Dustin. "Sorry, I was just filling Bob in. We're studying together."

Dustin and Kendrick still stood outside the funeral home. Dustin shook his head. Studying wasn't the only thing they did together. His disapproval ramped up and he clenched his free hand.

"Do you have any concrete information on this Gillespie at all?"

"I hope so. He works with a female doctor named Heather Clark and he planted a video camera in one of her examination rooms. He's taping everything that goes on … Dr. Clark, her patients, and physical exams. I learned that Heather has no knowledge of the camera or that she's being taped. Isn't that unlawful?"

Dustin opened his mouth in surprise. "What'd she say?" Kendrick asked.

"I'll tell you, Kendrick. Hold on."

"Anything else you can tell us?"

"Maybe it doesn't seem like much, however, he absolutely gives me the creeps. My gut instinct tells me he's as dangerous as a venomous snake waiting in the underbrush for the next prey to walk by."

"A dangerous doctor. Tell me what you really think!"

"I'll gladly tell you more. I think he's a pedophile! The last people he should be dealing with in his profession are babies and children. Dustin, I tell you, he manipulates their feelings so they trust him. I shudder to think of how far he would go to use a child."

Bob ignored the book and stared at her. No way did he want to work with Gillespie either.

"All right," Dustin said. "Keep your cool and do what you must for your rotation. Your information is important and we're going to act on it sooner than later. I must go, however."

Annabel felt a pang of sorrow. He had nothing to say about their relationship or why he hadn't been answering her calls.

"Oh, and by the way. You are correct. Dr. Gillespie's video recording without letting people know in the office is going to land him in trouble. Dr. Clark, her patients, and anyone else in those exam rooms should unequivocally expect a high level of privacy."

CHAPTER 27

Annabel closed the call and locked eyes with Bob.

"A pedophile?!" Bob exclaimed. "You think he's that wretched?"

Annabel nodded. "I did my duty and told someone who is in a position to do something about it."

"By 'someone,' you mean your boyfriend." Bob cocked his head. "I don't mean to pry, but has your dating with him slowed down?"

"Maybe. I don't know what's going on with him."

"After Oliver won last Saturday, I noticed he took off from the fair kind of abruptly."

"Hmm. You thought the same thing." She grimaced at her phone. "Just now, he didn't say hello to his partner Sean for me either, yet he didn't correct me that he wasn't there. Dustin was with some officer named Kendrick." Her mouth turned down and her chest heaved from a big breath.

"A police officer's job must be rough, Annabel. Lots of responsibility, like what we're going to face in the future. Perhaps he's going through a period when pulling back from his relationship is important."

"Guys always say that women are hard to figure out because they don't say what's on their mind. As if men are *supposed* to know what they're thinking. In my relationship now, the opposite is true."

"I'm sorry." From the side, Oliver planted his head on Bob's leg and looked up with his soulful eyes. "Oliver, go nuzzle Annabel instead. She could use your luvin'." Bob waved at the dog. "Go ahead."

Oliver pranced backwards. He rounded the corner and pressed his muzzle on her lap. "You just want my food." But Oliver licked her hand. "Oh, all right. You really are trying to lift my spirits."

"Dogs are windows to our hearts and souls. Even though it's my night with him, why don't you take him home when we finish studying and you leave? I had Oliver all day anyway."

"You're so sweet." A smile replaced her downtrodden expression. "I'll take that favor, if you don't pay me back for half of dinner."

"We've struck a deal. Now let's put the George Gillespie discussion to the side and dive into pediatric medical topics."

The police station was buzzing for a Thursday morning, as if on the brink of a Friday night with jammed downtown bars and backroom hustles. A cop walked in, clasping the arm of an armed robber of a fast food restaurant, and two other officers pushed two teenagers into chairs. They'd been feeding their van from the back door of a box store with wide screen TVs. "What were you thinking?" one of the officers asked. "Major retailers tape customers with video cameras."

"Not only big box stores," Dustin said to Kendrick, who leaned against his desk, "but certain doctors' offices too."

"We'll see about that. Come on. The captain gave us both the green light. Let's go down to the courthouse and get a search warrant on Gillespie."

"For which? His home or his office?"

"Both." Kendrick rose his arm and tossed a paper coffee cup across the aisle. He nailed the wastebasket.

Dustin followed Officer Kendrick outside. "Whose car?" Dustin asked.

"You ride around more than me. I vote for mine." He pointed further down the parallel-parked cars. When they arrived, Kendrick pointed. "Get in."

Dustin was impressed. In the courthouse, Kendrick voiced his plea in front of the judge like he was part cop, part Harvard law graduate, and part used car salesman.

"Judge Howell," Kendrick said, "wouldn't you be incensed to find out that your wife is taking your kids to a pediatrician who might be a pedophile? And you didn't know it all these years? And that he's practicing right here in the Cincinnati area?

"I've traced massive loads of child pornography to his home device and he's taping co-workers and patients in his office without their consent. I shudder at what we *don't* know yet about him. We're requesting search warrants for his home and office."

"What's his name?"

"George Gillespie. Can you imagine? Doctors are supposed to be the pillars of society."

"That's the way it goes with pedophiles who break the law, Officer Kendrick. They stand out in society like they are angels of God: sports coaches, school teachers, clergy, scout leaders, upstanding leaders in the community.

"I'll sign an order for your search warrant, but that was sexist of you. I bring my kids to the pediatrician sometimes too. But from now on, I'm not leaving one of my kids alone to be examined."

In several more minutes, after the judge reread what he was signing, Dustin and Kendrick trotted down the front steps of the courthouse. Kendrick's small frame beat Dustin to the car.

Marlene Gillespie stood at home in the downstairs bathroom. She applied lipstick in the mirror, outlining her lips like staying in the lines of some important paint-by-number canvas. She had a late lunch meeting at the hospital, so she was making sure she was dolled up ahead of time.

When she stepped outside the hallway powder room, she contemplated going inside George's office next door. Since the other night, she had not been brazen enough to pop onto his computer when he was not home. She was too afraid to.

What she had found the other night continued to rattle her nerves. She may have denied many aspects of her husband's behavior in the past, but this went way too far. Toddlers, children, and young teenagers were sacred beings and, all adults, not only their parents, carried a social responsibility for their welfare. To stalk or abuse them via photography, video content, or in real life was as good as committing a felony offense.

Marlene's curiosity was killing her because if she hadn't known about the content on his computer, what else didn't she know about? What she was worried about was if George had crossed the line of being an apparent pedophile. Being a pedophile amounted to having a psychiatric disorder, one in which his sexual attraction favored pre-pubescent children. But the serious moral wrong was if he'd had adult sexual contact with an underage minor.

She contemplated going into his room as the daylight beamed through the glass windows beside the front door. But as she made up her mind to keep out of his affairs, a display of blue light replaced the serenity of the previous sunshine.

As she sauntered over to the front door, she realized the new lights were from a police car. One which had parked in her driveway!

The brass door knocker sounded on the wood of the front door and Marlene froze with fear. Was George serving her with divorce papers? Then it struck her all at once. What harm would come from that? She'd be rid of living with his peculiarities, she could hire a lawyer sympathetic to the plight of physician spouses, and she would rake in hefty alimony. Everything would be split fifty-fifty or better than that in her favor. Their marriage was long overdue for a termination, she thought.

A louder thump sounded at the door and she turned the handle. A small officer and a second one with a mischievous dimple in his chin stood their ground on her porch.

"Ma'am, are you Mrs. Gillespie?" Dustin asked.

Here it comes, she thought. "Yes, is there a problem?"

"Is your husband at home?" Kendrick asked.

"No. He's at his office. He's a doctor."

"We have a search warrant, Ma'am." Dustin showed her the document.

Marlene automatically let the door swing open. They weren't here to let her off the hook from her husband. On the contrary, now she had something else to worry about. Her hands began to tremble as she thought about his hidden pornography.

With barely a few steps, Dustin stared into the first room on the right. "Is this your husband's study?"

Marlene bit her lip. "Yes, that's his personal computer, but I think he keeps all the information about his practice at the pediatric office location."

"Well, start in here. Thank you." Dustin gave her a look and she slinked towards the kitchen.

"I didn't say anything about his personal computer, did you?"

Kendrick smiled. "Not me. She knows something. What if she gets a kick out of his content as well? I've not had a spouse aware of their husband's dirty child porn before, but there's a first time for everything."

"Kendrick, women deliver babies and nurture them into children. The day I come across a woman who is 'into' child pornography is the day I give up on humanity."

The two men went through George's desk drawers and the top from either side and met in the middle at the computer.

"Well," Kendrick said, "like I said, I haven't come across a female pedophile acting out who I had to arrest. Apparently, there are no reliable estimates as to how rare they are."

Kendrick leaned over the computer keyboard and pressed a few keys. It took him less time to get into George's perverted material than Dustin took to access his draft emails. "Bingo. We're sending this computer to the crime lab."

Dustin shook his head. "Those pictures break my heart."

"Let's do a quick scan of other rooms, particularly the bedroom."

"Should we say something to her?"

"Be my guest."

Dustin stopped at the kitchen counter. "Do you ever use your husband's computer to watch the content he has on there?"

Marlene began spinning her wedding ring around her finger. "Uh, we don't keep the same pictures."

"What pictures does he keep?"

She shrugged her shoulders. "Vacation photos?"

"Some vacation photos," Kendrick said.

When the two men finished throwing electronic devices in plastic bags, they wished Marlene a nice day and slipped out the front door.

In the driveway, Dustin scowled. "Too bad she didn't come to us first with what she knew."

"Marriages are complicated. Maybe she's an enabler, an accomplice, or in denial of her husband's pet peeve."

"Now it's my turn. We're heading to Gillespie's office, where he practices. I drove my ex-girlfriend there one morning. I don't even have to pull up his address or let the GPS track him down."

Thursday morning in Dr. Gillespie's office, Annabel and

Stuart crouched down in the waiting room playing with a four-year-old. The boy's mother was in the bathroom and the two students engaged the boy with Legos. Both their doctors were filtering through business mail before seeing their first patients.

"I visited Bob last night," Annabel said, "and we studied until eleven o'clock, but I didn't get home and to bed until midnight. I could use a nap."

Stuart added five blocks to the building the little boy was making but spoke to Annabel. "You're ahead of me, and there will be less time to study once we hit the wards next week."

"I can't wait."

Stuart grimaced. "Hang in there, Annabel. Even though I like being here with Dr. Clark, I'm ready to see sicker patients on the wards. Only today and tomorrow are left."

Annabel dumped another box of classic Legos on the floor. "This building needs more height."

The boy beamed at both of them. "Then I'll fly off the top so my mom can't find me." He waved his arms in the air. ""Then I won't have to go in a room and Dr. Gillespie can't look in my throat!"

Annabel and Stuart weaved back to the hallway. "How about that?"

Stuart said. "Your patient doesn't even want your attending examining his throat."

Dr. Gillespie filed out of his back office and Annabel joined him. Their first patient came in because of a rash. After a thorough history and physical exam, George attributed it to a change in the family's fabric softener sheets for their dryer.

As the day wore on, and after the students came back from eating lunch, Annabel started clock watching more intently. The waiting room was fuller than the morning and nurses were filtering parents with babies and children to the back rooms.

She thought back to last night's call with Dustin. Secretly, she wished the police would do something with the information she provided. At least Dr. Gillespie deserved a slap on the wrist. However, she might never know. Her boyfriend, or ex-boyfriend, was not transparent with her anymore.

As the cases thinned, Becky sat at the desk with a child's chart and physician's orders. She logged in to the office schedule and picked out a date and time for a follow-up appointment. She turned her head to Annabel. "Ask them if next Tuesday would work at eleven o'clock."

Annabel nodded. She was trying to help Becky with the flow of patients and stuck her head back in the exam room, where the young patient was putting his T-shirt back on. "Next Tuesday at eleven o'clock work?"

"Sure," the mother said.

Annabel went back to Becky at the front desk. "That'll work."

"I think a police car just pulled into the parking lot," Becky said, narrowing her eyes towards the front window.

A parent in the waiting room stood. She walked to the window, put her hands on her hips, and swiveled around. "There are two cops and they're coming in!"

The door opened and the two officers appeared larger than life in the waiting room.

"Mommy, Mommy. They have guns!" A small boy jumped out of his chair.

"Settle down, son," Dustin said. He tipped his hand at the mother. "Nothing for patients to worry about." He flanked Kendrick, now at the reception counter.

Becky popped out of her chair and Annabel's jaw dropped.

"Is Dr. George Gillespie here?" Kendrick asked.

"Yes, sir," Becky responded and pointed to the back.

George was at the open door in a flash. "What's going on, officers?"

"We have a search warrant," Dustin said. "The rest of your afternoon is going to be disrupted. You should ask patients to reschedule." He re-shifted his gaze and gave Annabel an acknowledgement with his eyes.

"I love the police force, but you all have some nerve. Show me."

Dustin gladly thrust the warrant into his hand.

"I should probably call my lawyer to check this paperwork."

Dustin tried not to roll his eyes. "It's signed by a judge. You don't want to tick off the judge and impede this process. We are going to do our job right now."

Becky stopped trembling while George belabored his point. Like he had something to hide, she thought. She had no protocol for this unheard-of situation, so she slipped into the waiting room and made an announcement. "If it's imperative that your child sees a pediatrician today, see someone else or pop into the ER. If the appointment can wait, call us back and we'll reschedule."

The families picked up their things, gathered their children, and with open mouths and intense stares, they marched out of the waiting room.

"What on earth is going on here?" Heather Clark made a dead stop and scrutinized the officers like they were imposters on the planet. Stuart was beside her.

"Doctor, we have a search warrant," Kendrick said. "We'll be combing through this office. All rooms."

"Uhh," George mumbled. "I'm going back to my office for my computer. I'll put it in my car so I can work at home tonight."

"Show me where it is," Dustin said.

Kendrick nodded and stayed in place while Dustin and Gillespie trotted to his office.

"Here it is," George said. He laid his hands on both ends to pick it up, but Dustin stopped him. The screen lit up, revealing a room with a little boy swinging his legs off the side of an exam table and his mother reading a magazine.

"Interesting view," Dustin said.

"My next patient is waiting on me in the exam room. You can appreciate the need for extra security monitoring these days."

Dustin ignored him, unplugged the laptop, and clasped it with one hand. He started out the door and looked for closed exam doors. He came to the only one and knocked.

"Come in," a woman's voice sounded.

Dustin opened the door to a woman with a magazine and the young boy he just saw on George's computer. "Ma'am, who are you here to see?"

The woman bobbed her head in surprise. "Dr. Clark. Is there a problem? She's okay, isn't she?"

"Yes, but you will have to reschedule your appointment."

As Dustin arrived back up front, he called the station. "Kendrick and I have to search the pediatrician's office for more evidence. Send backup. An officer needs to take in George Gillespie."

CHAPTER 28

George Gillespie said nothing as Kendrick waited for two other officers to arrive.

"You're busted, you know," Kendrick said.

The doctor twirled his stubby fingers in front of his protruding abdomen and stared down, his bushy eyebrows camouflaging his eyes.

Upon Dustin's request, the office staff stayed in the front office. They were clueless over why the police came, except that the officers had permission to search the place. Some of them thought Dr. Gillespie acted a bit weird, but what were they physically looking for?

Backup police arrived. One of them stayed with Dustin and Kendrick and made sure staff hung around, out of the way, but available to answer questions.

Annabel and Stuart huddled by the front window and watched as the second officer ducked George Gillespie into the back of his patrol car. The doctor wore a scowl on his face and gave a last-minute stare at the front of his office.

"Adios," Annabel mumbled.

"This makes for a memorable rotation." Stuart grinned as he turned to her. "No surprise. You're on it."

As the patrol car took off, Dustin and Kendrick went back to Dr. Clark's empty exam rooms.

Dustin yanked Kendrick's sleeve. "In here. This is the room I viewed from his computer."

Closed cabinets with medical supplies stood above a counter and sink and ninety degrees from it were open shelves with medical props and books. Dustin combed the shelves, starting from the top. Next shelf down, he started on the end, where he found a plastic replica of four small back vertebrae.

"Damn," he said. "Will you take a look at these bones? They

sure are keeping an eye on things."

"Like Dr. Clark and her patients?"

"Oh yeah."

Kendrick looked closely. A round-eyed camera was planted between an intervertebral space. "I'll wrap up in this room, take pictures, and the evidence."

Dustin turned at the door. "I'll start on the next room," he said and chuckled. "I'll check out anatomy samples first."

A similar shelf was in the next room and Dustin went there first. A twelve inch plastic bone example of a child's forearm was mounted on a standing display. Dustin peeked closely and found the same camera model as the last room attached between the radius and ulna.

And so it went. Between the two officers combing both doctors' rooms and offices, they confiscated video camera equipment in every one of them.

But the last room turned Dustin's stomach upside down and, if he had the chance, he would sock George Gillespie right in the face. A camera, like an eyeball, peered out of a plastic ornament of a giraffe mounted in the children's bathroom.

"Thoughtful of him," Dustin said to Kendrick. "No camera is installed in the staff's bathroom, only the pediatric patients' commode."

"Dr. Clark," Kendrick said, "it's a second team's job to come in here and finish what we've started. Lots of evidence here. We're not at liberty to say much, but your office must close for a day or two."

"Evidence of what?"

Unaware of it, Heather held on to Becky's arm, as if for mental support. What was going on with her practice?

"Dr. Clark," Dustin said, "did you have any knowledge that

your rooms were being videotaped?"

Heather's eyes became moist. She let go of Becky and clasped her hands together. "No. Really? All this time? I was a new doctor fresh out of residency. I've been here for three years. He's been watching my rooms all along?" She wanted to sob.

"I'm sorry, ma'am. Why don't you come back to the police station and we'll get a statement. And let the rest of your employees go home for now."

Heather nodded. Drawers opened and Becky and the others grabbed their handbags and personal items. Kendrick kept an eye on the situation for anything unusual leaving the premises.

"Kendrick, I'll talk to the students," Dustin said. "Why don't I meet you outside with Dr. Clark?" He leaned in and spoke softly. "I'll be a few minutes."

Dr. Clark stopped at the door. "Annabel and Stuart, I'll make a call to the department chairman. Someone will inform you about what to do tomorrow."

Dustin waited for the activity to subside and for Heather to step outside. He walked over to Annabel and Stuart. "If we need to ask either of you questions, I can track you down. I have Annabel's number." Dustin focused on Stuart. "I need to talk to Annabel."

Glued to the floor all along, Stuart finally moved forward. He stepped to the door, looking back at Annabel, worried now about her relationship with the officer rather than what would happen to George Gillespie.

"Annabel, I'll text or call you later."

Annabel nodded and turned back to Dustin. Eye to eye, she melted over the features she loved about him.

"Good thing you told me about Dr. Gillespie spying on his partner's room," he said.

"Good thing you finally called me back to hear about it."

"Touché. I deserved that. Anyway, we found the camera and, in addition, many more. Including in the patients' bathroom. We also raided his home before coming here."

Annabel shuddered like ants were crawling up her leg. "The bathroom?"

Dustin didn't respond but nodded slowly.

"How come you went to his house?"

"Officer Kendrick hunted down your attending's secret stash of child pornography."

Annabel briefly closed her eyes. "How awful, how despicable." She shifted her weight from one foot to the other, and continued with passion in her voice. "Doctors take an oath when they become a physician and swear to uphold ethical standards. Dr. Gillespie did not hold up his side of the bargain when he took the Hippocratic Oath. He's a moral disgrace. It makes me sick to think I worked with him in the same room while he went overboard with physical exams. He's damn dangerous and seriously mentally ill."

"You're correct. Let's hope justice prevails and this is the beginning of his end in pediatric medicine."

An aching silence followed his words. Annabel felt the blow before it struck. Her next breath was difficult to inhale; her chest felt achy and her heart thumped with sadness.

"I won't be seeing you again, Annabel. Our relationship is over."

"I contemplated as much. I'm sorry to hear it."

She swallowed emphatically, trying to camouflage the emotion welling up in her eyes. It was a closed subject, she could tell. Whatever the problem was between them, he had no desire to tell her. She didn't dare ask him, either, and suffer an agonizing embarrassment.

He forced a slight laugh to break the uncomfortableness between them. "Unless, of course, I see you because of police work. You do have a knack for bringing problems to the attention of the sheriff's department."

She only gave him a slight nod. She wanted to tell him that

she wouldn't be bothering them anymore because, in less than one year, she would be out of Cincinnati and on to residency in another state. Hopefully, Tennessee.

But she didn't say it. And he didn't wish her any luck for her future in medicine. Everything with him was over.

The patrol car with George Gillespie in the back seat was gone when Annabel stepped outside. A buildup of summer clouds had materialized and, in the distance, they looked ominous.

She went to her car, her head low, not wanting to see or interact with anyone. She made it to her vehicle without any awareness if Stuart, Dr. Clark, or Officer Kendrick were still around. Dustin was then the last one to exit the office. He turned around and secured a special police lock on the door.

She wanted to drive away as inconspicuously as she'd walked to her car. After starting the ignition, she drove home, and when she opened her apartment door, she already didn't remember the details about driving home. She was a frazzled wreck.

Oliver jumped out of his dog bed, surprised to find her home. She leaned over and he swiped her mouth with his tongue, but she didn't mind. She spoke softly.

"I can't tell you how much I appreciate your kiss. You are such a love. It's you and me now, Oliver. No more Dustin." She grabbed his leash and continued talking out loud. "Let's go for a short spin. I'm too sad to take a long walk. Plus, I'm waiting for the medical school to determine what they're going to do with Stuart and me now that the dirtbag pediatrician has been hauled away."

Downstairs, Oliver balked. The sky was darkening more and more. She tugged him to the front tree and, in a minute, the dog reciprocated and walked her back the way they came.

"Who's walking whom?" Annabel commented. Upstairs, she unfolded the dog's thunder shirt. Most likely, she would wrap him in it before the end of the day.

She fluffed up her pillow and curled up on her bed as Oliver jumped up as well. It had been several years before Dustin that she had shared a serious relationship with a college student named David. In the end, they became close friends. It was only because of a basketball head injury and his prolonged recuperation that their romantic relationship dwindled away. He was no longer in college at the same time with her after his injury. Her father had even treated his secondary impact head injury, so David ended up beloved by the whole family.

As she stroked Oliver, her relationships with the opposite sex became crystal clear. It was as if sunlight slit through the ominous clouds and struck her with clarity, infallible self-reflection, and an understanding of herself. Between her relationships with David and Dustin, she actively used the dating app, Findar. The encounters from the site ended up being rash flings. They were diversions … sexual interludes fraught with risky behavior. How could she have done such a thing?

Being her first love, she had cared for David more than she realized. Witnessing his awful accident on the basketball court and his subsequent hospitalization was a tragic turn of events. No wonder she had experienced cold feet diving into another significant relationship. The social dating app and escapades had filled the void. But then her courage came back and she took a chance with Dustin.

With Dustin, their closeness and intimacy surpassed what she had shared with David. Her maturity grew as well as the depth of her feelings for a partner.

And now, it was over. Even worse, he had broken up with her.

She supposed she would never know the reason why,

because if she didn't have the answers now when the situation took place, then she couldn't fathom guessing the reason in the future.

She narrowed the space between her and Oliver and gave the dog a hug. The medical world in which she lived was difficult enough to maintain the responsibilities required of her, but the demise of her relationship on top of that was extreme. Her eyes moistened as she pictured Dustin in her mind. She allowed herself to cry.

The mattress was alive with movement as Oliver pranced straight over Annabel from her front to her back. As she opened her eyes, his head was above her and his body trembled.

She coaxed Oliver to the side while wondering how long she had slept. Although the storm was not above them, thunder rumbled close enough to render the dog a full-blown anxiety attack. She scooted off the bed, coaxed Oliver down, and secured his thunder shirt around his torso. Worried that she'd missed a call, she grabbed her iPhone.

A missed incoming call showed up and she scolded herself for having the volume off. Sometime during the hectic police invasion at Dr. Gillespie's office, she had muted it. The number was not familiar, but it was not Dr. Clark or Stuart. Someone had left a voicemail. She turned up the volume and pressed to play.

"I'm calling from the Pediatric Chairman's office. Dr. Fisher was informed of the temporary closure of the pediatrician's office on your rotation. Tomorrow morning, please report here at 9 a.m. The other student, Stuart Schneider, has been called as well."

Annabel mulled that over. At least she wouldn't have to wake up at the crack of dawn. Over the next hour, the storm ramped up and then ebbed off to the west. She took Oliver's shirt off and they both went to sleep.

On Friday morning at ten to nine, Annabel waited outside the Chairman's office. Stuart soon strolled into the outer office as well.

"What a disruption to our schedule," he said, "and I hate for Dr. Clark to suffer consequences as well."

"I suppose a lot will be up in the air for a while."

"Maybe your boyfriend can help in that regard. Boost the investigation along so she can get back to work."

Annabel twisted her mouth and glanced down.

"Uh-oh," Stuart said.

"I'll come right out with it. We're finished. I'm going to miss him, Stuart."

"I'm sorry. I'm always around in case you need someone to lean on besides Bob."

"I appreciate that, especially coming from you. You went through enough in an orphanage and with parents who adopted you when maybe they shouldn't have. As far as Bob, yes, I'm sure he'll be sympathetic. My news is hot off the press. I haven't even told him yet."

The door swung open and a stout man appeared wearing an attending's white coat. His mustache was the same length as his lips and closely-cropped directly above his lip. Dr. Fisher's smile still beamed on his lips and he stepped aside, letting the students enter his office.

"Annabel Tilson and Stuart Schneider, I heard about the drama at Gillespie's and Clark's office yesterday. We have issues to resolve." He waved both students into chairs and then focused on Stuart. "First, I understand you have taken a liking to pediatrics."

"Yes, sir. I plan on applying to pediatric residencies."

"I was told you are in the top of your class academically. I certainly hope you apply here."

"I must decide soon, but I will certainly opt for this region of the country."

"Annabel, you earned quite a reputation in your third year rotations, so whatever specialty you choose, I wish you much success. Now, as far as the dilemma we're faced with at present, there's a simple solution. You were switching to the wards next Monday, but chief residents are expecting you both today. There are four teams and you can choose which one you'd like.

"Bob Palmer is on a team, Annabel, and since you two are friends, it's not a problem if you join his."

"Thank you, but actually, I can't. We juggle around a dog we both own, so our call nights have to be different. He was going to Dr. Gillespie's office next Monday. Will that be cancelled?"

"Yes. We don't know how long Gillespie's office will be closed. Dr. Clark may be taking a little vacation in the interim.

"No point belaboring the point. When you report to the hospital ward, each of you choose a different team you want to be on. The chief residents will inform me."

Dr. Fisher sat down on the edge of his desk. "The health and safety of pediatric patients is the department's utmost concern. As far as Dr. Gillespie goes, the wheels of medicine and justice have been turning. Because of his arrest yesterday by the Cincinnati Police, the State Board of Medical Examiners has announced this morning that Dr. Gillespie's medical license is temporarily suspended."

CHAPTER 29

With Stuart beside her, Annabel rode the elevator to the ground floor after meeting with Dr. Fischer. "I'll text Bob," she said. "I wonder if the students at the hospital know that they're staying on rotation there."

"Lots of news to tell you! Stuart and I are heading over."

"The team will be in the doctors' lounge after we make rounds."

"We can meet them in the lounge," Annabel said as the doors slid open.

The pediatric hospital was nearby, so they decided to walk. They dodged big puddles but stayed on the sidewalk. Although they could take short cuts through grassy areas, the landscaped lawns were a soggy mess due to the overnight storm.

"This isn't a bad day," Stuart said as they approached the lounge in the hospital. "We slept in later than usual, I talked to the main doctor of perhaps my future residency, and now we're going for free food."

"Easy for you to say. I lost my boyfriend, the doctor I worked with for two weeks was arrested yesterday and is a pedophile, and a dog kept me up most of the night. But you're correct. I have to look for the bright side in all of that."

Stuart laughed as he opened the door. "You need to suck on a straw to extrapolate the bright side. But maybe there will be a break in the clouds for you, Annabel. Sometimes things work out for the best when you least expect them."

"You know, you would make a fine psychiatrist or pediatrician."

Stuart practically blushed as he looked away. In front of them, the room bustled with attendings, residents, and students.

"Grab something and come join us." Dr. Mares held a plate with a buttered bagel in one hand and a coffee in the other. With his long stride, he ended at a corner table by the window.

Annabel scooped scrambled eggs and sausage on a plate, poured coffee, and headed over. Stuart copied her breakfast and followed.

The four students and Rick Mares squeezed their chairs tighter together and added two more for Annabel and Stuart. Bob made sure an empty chair was next to him and remained standing. "Good morning." He waited for Annabel to sit.

"Likewise," she countered.

Rick cleared his throat and patted a spoon on the table. "Here ye, here ye!" He broke his seriousness and laughed. "I bring this team to order. All kidding aside, the chief residents were told about your fiasco yesterday and our team was just discussing Dr. Gillespie's poisonous behavior."

"Dr. Fisher said his license has been temporarily revoked," Annabel said.

"That status may change. It depends on the outcome of the charges. Fortunately, the Board has upheld its duty to safeguard patients as well as enforce the standards of the medical profession.

"Now, would one of you like to join our team for the last two weeks of your rotation?"

"I would love to." Annabel glanced at Bob despondently, but then smiled. "Bob and I are parents to a wonderful dog, however. We need to keep our schedules flexibly separate."

Bob nodded. "Bummer, but you're right."

"I would love to stay on," Stuart said.

"Wonderful." Rick eyed Annabel. "Join Dr. Overton's team. He teaches a lot. And by the way, your beloved patient Toby Owens went home this week. The orthopedic surgeon, Dr. Castle, was happy with how his leg fracture and PT was coming along. We were satisfied that he could continue recovering from his rat lung worm illness at home."

"Awesome. Maybe he won't even have to miss any school

work."

"All right, then." Rick rose with his plate and coffee. "I'm going to go talk shop with other residents. Y'all finish your food; there's work to do. Stuart, I'll assign you patients later."

Rick left and the students focused on their late breakfast.

"Wow," Bob said to Annabel. "Yesterday must have been exciting. Dustin must be a hero because of the information you fed him."

"There was an undercover cop who traced online pornography to Dr. Gillespie's home. Between the two of them, they made the arrest."

"You and Dustin are probably going to celebrate." He posed it as a question more than a statement and waited for her slow response.

She shook her head. "Not at all. Our relationship is officially over."

Bob sighed. He detected the sadness in her voice and he fully grasped, more than before, how much she cared about Dustin. "I'm truly sorry, Annabel. I don't know what to say."

"Thanks. It will take time to work him out of my system." She grimaced and then slowly nodded. "At least I have the rest of my senior year to divert my attention. And if I need more time, there's always at least four years of a grueling residency to look forward to."

At least Toby Owens felt a bit better and his energy was slowly returning, but he was downright bored. His mother was out shopping for him, purchasing the items left on his school list. She had made him stay home from the mall. Dragging him around, she had said, would make him tired and perhaps hamper his recovery. But, of course, most of the errand for him would allow her to accumulate "stuff" for herself.

He added more peanut butter to the crust of his sandwich and took a bite as the front doorbell rang. From the side bay window, he could see no car had pulled into the driveway, so he hoped it was Jonathon.

Toby stuck the last piece of bread into his mouth and opened the door. "Hey, am I ever glad to see you. I feel like a prisoner."

Jonathon stood on the wet front step, his sneakers toed-in, and his face with a silly grin. "At least you're out of the hospital."

The boys walked to the kitchen and Toby poured more chocolate milk. "Yeah, that was the pits. I hope I never go back to a hospital as long as I live."

"And you're damn lucky your mom changed you to Dr. Clark. My mom heard the biggest story today. Dr. Gillespie was arrested yesterday! Can you believe it? He's a criminal."

Toby's head bobbed back. "Like put in handcuffs and everything?"

"It beats me, but he's in jail."

"Didn't I tell you all that he was a weirdo? But what did they take him away for?"

Jonathon shrugged. "I don't think they can arrest people just for being weird." He took a clean glass from the dish rack and helped himself to the milk. "You should send him a get-well card wishing him to not be screwy anymore."

"That would be weird."

"Then send him a gift because you don't have him as your doctor anymore. Like a thank you for getting rid of him."

"Hell, I had rat lung worm when I first went to his office and he didn't figure it out."

"Maybe he couldn't have. You were just kind of getting sick. Before the hospital and all of that."

"Still. Yeah. I should send him a slug. Tell him how good they taste. He'll eat it and get rat lung worm like I did."

"You're the one who's crazy. A grownup wouldn't eat it.

They're not stupid like you or me."

"Grownups eat raw seafood all the time. Anyway, what a prank that would make."

"We can't go to Florida to get a slug."

"No, but we can look for one in the yard. It rained all night and the ground is soaking wet. I betcha I can find worms and maybe a slug or two."

Maneuvering his cast, Toby pushed away from the table. He went to the kitchen closet and started moving boxes from under the bottom shelf.

"What are you doing?" Jonathon asked.

"My mom recycles boxes she gets in the mail. I'm looking for a small one."

He backed out, being careful of his cast, and lined the bottom of a tiny box with a baggie. "Coming with me?" he asked as he opened the back door.

Toby picked the ground and grass behind his basketball hoop to begin his search. Jonathon was impressed. Toby knew when and where to find wormlike gastropods in his own backyard.

He put a slug, almost an inch long, on top of the plastic bag. After the boys went back inside, he wrote a note, inserted it, and closed the box.

Jonathon began laughing so hard, it was infectious. Toby joined in.

"You gotta wrap up the box," Jonathon managed to say.

"No way. We gotta get this to the police station before my mom comes home. We can take the bus."

"I'm in. Let's go."

Even though Toby fought off taking a nap during the bus ride, the two boys schemed the whole time. Either the box would end up in Gillespie's hands or not. In any case, it was diverting Toby's boredom and he wouldn't have it any other way.

They pulled the cord for their bus stop and walked a half block with Toby skillfully using his crutches. He held on to the box like it contained a diamond ring as they stepped to the front desk inside the police station.

"We heard our favorite doctor is here." Toby stared over the desk to the uniformed man. "We'd like to leave him a present."

Dustin passed in the hallway behind the front desk. He was still handling the aftermath of the Gillespie case with Kendrick and they were mostly bound to the office for the day. He popped his head in to see the two boys.

"I'll handle this," he said to the officer. "What can I do for you two boys?" He noticed the cast on Toby's leg.

"We heard," Toby said, "that Dr. Gillespie's in jail. He's my doctor and we want to give him a present. He must be down in the dumps."

"Like Monopoly," Jonathon said. "You can tell him it's a get-out-of-jail free pass. But you don't have to worry because it really won't break him out of jail."

Dustin narrowed his eyes. "I suppose so, boys. That's awfully kind of you, but he isn't going to be your doctor anymore, at least for a while. Sure you still want to give it to him?"

Both boys nodded.

"All right, then. Be on your way and I'll personally hand it to him."

Sitting on the bus stop bench, both boys again cackled. "It is a get-out-of-jail pass," Toby said. "If he gets rat lung worm, it'll be straight from jail to the hospital."

"Thanks for the fun afternoon, Toby, even though we didn't accomplish anything except for our own amusement."

"I needed it more than you. Who knows? I bet Dr. Gillespie is weird enough to eat it."

256

George Gillespie was never so aggravated in his whole life. He sat in a jail cell circling his stubby thumbs around each other. His stupid attorney was taking forever to take care of the bond money payment needed for his immediate release. In addition, the Board of Medical Licensure had put a temporary suspension on his license and his office was shut down.

Before he could fix the problem with his license or his office closure, he needed to get the hell out of jail. He suspected the cops had found his video cameras and maybe his pornography. However, lots of adults were into porn. In time, the whole mess might subside, and he could go back to doing what he loved. Taking care of kids.

Footsteps approached and he stood up. But it wasn't his attorney. It was the police officer named Dustin Lowe.

"There were two boys around twelve years old out front. They left this little box, a present, for you. One of them said you're his doctor. They sure are sweet kids to do that for the likes of you."

Dustin handed it through the bars and thought best to wait until he opened the package.

George half ignored Dustin and sat back down to savor the opening of a gift. He opened the lid and pulled out a little note.

"The food must be terrible in jail. This raw, delectable slug should provide additional protein until they let you out. We guarantee its freshness because we found it for you today. Enjoy."

Dr. Gillespie scrunched his face up as he peered down. Sure enough, a moist slug clung to a plastic bag like it was glued there with rubber cement.

"This must be some kind of joke," Gillespie said.

"I hope it's a good one." Dustin strutted away from the cell and went next door to finish his shift.

EPILOGUE

Nine Months Later

"This is the last major trip," Annabel said, "hauling my things out of here." A cardboard box and plastic container were stacked against the kitchen wall and she let out a big sigh.

Bob hoisted the box in his arms and disappeared down the flight of stairs to the rented U-Haul truck they had attached to her car. She followed him with the container and left Oliver in her apartment.

At the curb, Bob opened the back door and they slid their things in. "There will be plenty of space left over," he said. "I can't believe the smart deal you made with your landlord."

"Helped him and helped me." She was leaving her furniture to him, which wasn't much anyway, and he was going to now rent out her place as a furnished unit. In return, he granted her last month of rent free. All she had to move were her smaller personal belongings.

She sat on the edge of the truck. For a spring day in May, it already felt like summer. Annabel wore a cotton long-sleeved top, light capris, and summery footwear. She glanced up at her favorite tree.

"I'm going to miss the entertaining squirrel up this tree, Pete's Café, and the upstairs floor of this house where I've lived for four years."

"But you're going to a place that holds many more memories. And leaving Cincinnati may help you finally move forward after Dustin."

"It's been a challenge to get over him, but you're right."

She jumped off and Bob closed the doors.

"I'm a bit envious," Bob said, changing the subject. They single-filed up the staircase and opened the door. "Envious that you have nothing to do to set up a new residence in Nashville. That you can go straight to your parents and aunt's place for however long you want before getting your own place."

Inside, Oliver didn't bother to get up. Their coming in and out with boxes for the last hour had become a routine.

"You are not envious. You don't have an envious bone in your body. And I can't thank you enough for driving all the way up here to help me out."

"I packed and moved before graduation because I had an extra week off after my last elective. You weren't so fortunate."

"Graduation proved to be the best, most memorable, and hard-earned graduation and commencement ceremony I ever had. Plus, my sister and I started talking again that weekend."

"I agree about graduation. But, sadly, most students are going their separate ways."

"But at least we'll be in the same city."

"I'm going to like Nashville. I couldn't have been luckier to match there in an orthopedic residency. I still wonder if a recommendation from your dad was influential, especially when they were down to their last medical student candidates. Maybe his vote of confidence pushed me to the top of the list."

"We'll never know, but you earned it anyway. Your academic and clinical assessments were all stellar."

"So were yours."

"And Stuart. He made us proud finishing first in the class."

"I hope he's happy with the pediatric residency he snagged here in Cincinnati."

Annabel hooked Oliver to his leash and she and Bob each picked up a small suitcase. "Go ahead," she said. Bob stepped out the door and she stayed still, sweeping her eyes over the bedroom and kitchen. She would miss the place where she studied like a fiend late into the nights. The place she called home for four years.

Downstairs, they loaded the last items into the truck and Oliver took his last pee on the tree out front.

"How about we stop in two hours when we get to the outskirts of Louisville?" Annabel said. "Get a cup of coffee and gas somewhere?"

"Okay. I'll follow you. If we get separated, just give me a buzz."

With Oliver all the way in the back, Annabel started her SUV and pulled away from the curb. She glanced in the mirrors at the U-Haul and Bob's Honda behind her. It was time to go home to Tennessee.

They soon passed into Kentucky and Annabel set the music volume on low. Her graduation from medical school and becoming a doctor soared her spirits high during the drive. But before that day, she had passed another infamous day in her medical career ... Match Day.

Match Day in the fourth year of medical school always takes place on the same date - the third Friday in March. It had been a nail-biting experience for the students, the day in which residency candidates and residency programs "match" to fill the first and second year post-graduate training positions.

There had been lots of preparation for that day beforehand. For Annabel, it included making a decision. One that her friends had already made. What would she specialize in? What specialty would she apply for and where?

It never went away. The curiosity and interest she developed for anesthesiology during her first rotation of surgery never left. Most rotations were interesting, but she finally did more electives in anesthesia in her fourth year and she needed no convincing.

Anesthesiology was crazy, sometimes full of heart-throbbing crises and other times nice and easy. That is, if you knew tons of pharmacology, medicine, machinery, and hands-on skills like putting breathing tubes in tracheas when a patient's anatomy almost forbade it. She also liked the dynamics of being in the operating room.

She applied to Nashville's University residency program as her top choice and she was not the only one worried and restless over the outcome. Her family wanted her back in Nashville as much as she did.

Like her father would have done, she threw up a silent prayer to the heavens that Match Day morning, and also crossed her fingers. Perhaps none of the wishful thinking and methods helped, but she won her own lottery when she "matched" with Nashville's program on the third Friday in March.

Since Bob also "matched," she and Bob would both be in a "surgical" field and at the same University. They would certainly cross paths once in a while. Maybe even the same cases in the operating room. Their friendship would not die, at least for the next four years.

Annabel drove along with a smile on her face and a happy dog in the back when a hands-free call rang through. She pressed the plastic button on her steering wheel to answer. It must be Bob, she thought. His vehicle was two cars behind her.

"Hello?"

"Annabel, hey, I'm glad I caught you." Her heart squeezed in her chest. It was Dustin. Why was he calling? She could do without hearing his voice; the pain of their breakup was finally settling in and she was ready to move on.

"Dustin, I'm driving. Going back home to Tennessee. I graduated from medical school."

"How about that?! Congratulations."

"Thanks."

There was a pregnant pause and she held her breath.

"The reason I'm calling is because of a development. I called the Chairman of the Pediatric Department just now, Dr. Fisher, thinking many of the doctors might not know the big news yet. We both thought you would also like to be told."

"You have my attention."

"The total resolution of the criminal charges against Dr. Gillespie were still pending. If you remember, there was a temporary suspension of his license by the State Board of Medical Examiners, but he's now totally agreed to surrender his medical license. We were pulling up more dirt on him from before he started working here in Cincinnati, so his lawyer advised him to throw in the towel."

"Wow, no more Dr. Gillespie doing pediatric exams or getting his jollies by spying on children. His whole career is actually a real shame, Dustin. Every once in a while, I did watch him adequately treat a few kids." She thought back to some, like Stephanie Miller, the three-year-old he diagnosed with a neuroblastoma.

"However," she added, "this is the best possible outcome. Thanks for letting me know."

"You're welcome."

"Hey, give Solar a treat for me."

"Do the same with Oliver. Bye, then. Good luck."

"Bye," Annabel said and clicked off the call. Emotion welled up in her chest and she sighed heavily. She was glad he called to tell her the news, but also happy the call came before she arrived in Tennessee. She wanted a new start back home, including with men.

The sunshine was voluminous and the traffic light as Bob kept tabs on the U-Haul truck and Annabel's Nissan with a

"Dog on Board" bumper sticker. The five-hour drive was giving him plenty of opportunity to decide how he wanted to proceed with Annabel.

Based on his perception of her, he thought she was over the main hurdle of getting Dustin out of her system. He wanted to take the plunge and ask her out; change the nature of their relationship. Otherwise, he would never know if he had any kind of future with her.

From a guy's perspective, he had waited long enough. What if she got to Nashville and, boom, some new fellow asked her out, she accepted, and there he was again watching her date some other guy.

And what if she didn't want to date him? That would be embarrassing and hard to digest. Plus, it would make things uncomfortable when and if he bumped into her during residency.

But, it was now or never. He had to take the plunge.

His apartment was all set up in Nashville, and when they arrived, the day would be slipping away and he would need to get home after helping her unload at her parents' house.

But he needed to ask her. His mind was made up. No more excuses.

They stopped for coffee and food, gas, and an Oliver walk on the other side of Louisville, and then they both scurried to get back on the road. Their spirits were high and Oliver was as happy to jump back in the car as to take the stroll. The long car ride was amazing.

The next two hours, they polished off fast food sandwiches in their own vehicles, and directed their cars southeast when they hit the city. Annabel loved it when she finally turned on the street she knew so well ... her grandparents' street and to their house where her mom and dad, sister, and aunt and uncle now lived. The sprawling house accommodated everyone.

She parked in the driveway, stepped out, and stretched her

legs. The last of the sunshine beamed down on the walkway and the greenery that her grandmother, years ago, made sure encircled the house. She let Oliver jump out, but leashed him only because it was a permanent new place and she wanted him to get used to the boundaries.

Bob pulled into the double driveway and pushed open the driver's door. "I lost you for a bit back there. Luckily, I remembered the way from the trip we took when Dakota died."

"Yes, that was a sad trip after losing our family dog. But now my whole family will also have Oliver when he's with me. He's going to have so many people loving him and taking care of him."

"Ha, when he's with me, he'll need to catch up on his rest."

"I'm sorry. I hope that's not the case."

"I'm yanking your chain. His back and forth will be wonderful, just like in Cincinnati."

Annabel walked to the front step and sat down with Oliver. Bob lowered himself as well. *Perfect,* he thought.

"Dustin called me along the way," she said, which prompted a frown from Bob. "Only to give me an update on George Gillespie. He surrendered his medical license."

"Awesome. However, did Dustin try to open up old wounds with you?"

"No. It's okay. I'm glad he called."

The front door opened and they both turned.

"Welcome home, honey. Hi, Bob." Danny Tilson, her father, stepped forward and petted Oliver. He had met the dog when he was in Ohio for his daughter's medical school graduation. "You two have a decent drive?"

"We did." She stood up and hugged her father. "We'll be in after we take Oliver for a little spin."

"I'll tell everyone else you're here. By the way, which bedroom do you want?"

"Melissa's old room."

"You got it." Danny disappeared back inside and closed the door.

Bob stood. He signaled to take Oliver's leash, but he didn't want to start walking the dog yet. Annabel handed it over and looked at him.

Bob seized the opportunity to lock eyes with her. "Don't worry, we're super good friends in case you would rather not. Go out with me, that is."

"Go out? As in changing our relationship to more than a friendship?"

His eyes held. She couldn't resist his cheerful expression and those blue eyes.

He kept his mouth shut and nodded.

"I can't think of a nicer guy. Plus, you've been my dearest companion the whole time."

Bob's apprehension turned into a smile.

They narrowed the gap between them and had their first kiss in front of her family's home.

End

FROM THE AUTHOR

Barbara Ebel is a physician and an author. Since she practiced anesthesia, she brings credibility to the medical background of her plots. She lives with her husband and pets in a wildlife corridor in Tennessee but has lived up and down the East Coast.

Visit or contact her at her website:

http://barbaraebelmd.com

The following (two medical suspense series and other books) are also written by Dr. Barbara and are available as paperbacks and eBooks:

The Outlander Physician Series:

Corruption in the O.R.: A Medical Thriller (The Outlander Physician Series Book 1)

Wretched Results: A Medical Thriller (The Outlander Physician Series: Book 2)

Stand-alone Medical Fiction:

Outcome, A Novel

Her Flawless Disguise

EBook Box Sets:

The Dr. Danny Tilson Novels Box Set:
Books 1-4 (The Dr. Danny Tilson Series)

The Dr. Annabel Tilson Novels Box Set:

Books 1-3 (The Dr. Annabel Tilson Series)

The Dr. Annabel Tilson Novels Box Set:
Books 4-6 (The Dr. Annabel Tilson Series)

The Dr. Danny Tilson Series: (Individual paperbacks and ebooks):

Operation Neurosurgeon: You never know… who's in the OR (A Dr. Danny Tilson Novel: Book 1).

Silent Fear: a Medical Mystery (A Dr. Danny Tilson Novel: Book 2). Also an Audiobook.

Collateral Circulation: a Medical Mystery (A Dr. Danny Tilson Novel: Book 3). Also an Audiobook.

Secondary Impact (A Dr. Danny Tilson Novel: Book 4).

The Dr. Annabel Tilson Series: (Individual paperbacks and ebooks):

DEAD STILL: A Medical Thriller (Dr. Annabel Tilson Novels Book 1)

DEADLY DELUSIONS: A Medical Thriller (Dr. Annabel Tilson Novels Book 2)

DESPERATE TO DIE: A Medical Thriller (Dr. Annabel Tilson Novels Book 3)

DEATH GRIP: A Medical Thriller (Dr. Annabel Tilson Novels Book 4)

DOWNRIGHT DEAD: A Medical Thriller (Dr. Annabel Tilson Novels Book 5)

DANGEROUS DOCTOR: A Medical Thriller (Dr. Annabel Tilson Novels Book 6)

Also written and illustrated by Barbara Ebel: A children's book series about her loveable therapy dog; illustrated with real pictures:
Chester the Chesapeake Book One
Chester the Chesapeake Book Two: Summertime
Chester the Chesapeake Book Three: Wintertim
Chester the Chesapeake Book Four: My Brother Buck
Chester the Chesapeake Book Five: The Three Dogs of Christmas

Younger Next Decade: *After Fifty, the Transitional Decade, and What You Need to Know* (nonfiction health book).

Made in the USA
Middletown, DE
26 August 2022

72297144R10163